सफलतायै प्रयत्नः आवश्यकः
कस्यापि प्राप्यार्थम् तद् अन्वेषणीयम्

To succeed you must try, to find you must seek.

978-1-7395669-1-3

Formatting by Rae Davennor in collaboration with Stardust Book Services

Published by Sohum Books

To Mummy, Papa and my Kabir

This is for you, for teaching me patience and perseverance.

To all the seeds of karma that have been blown far away from the tree, who like me are reaching out to their roots in many creative ways.

Chapter 1

London

A metallic hand struck Joash's right temple and a blur spread across his eyes. A wet trickle of blood ran down from his nostril to his lip as his head recovered from the momentary giddiness. With his back leaning against the pole, he sank down to the floor of the ring and threw his head back. The ringing in his ear reminded him of the idiocy and absurdity of this situation. His opponent Rowan retreated and waited, a look of annoyance on his face.

The crowd roared and Joash's mouth curled in a half-smile as he lay there cherishing his pain for the last few moments before surrendering. He had been coming to these fights for a few years now. To win was never on his mind; all he wanted was to satisfy an inexplicable desire to feel pain.

He closed his eyes feeling content and suddenly a distant but clear scene replaced the blur. A flame-shape with a sparkling white centre and a red hue on the outside travelled from right to left and disappeared.

He opened his eyes wide and heard his sister Krupa's voice resound in his ears: *Do you really not believe in karma and reincarnation*? But she was thousands of miles away. Perhaps the knock had disturbed something inside his head.

Perplexed he sat up and looked at his opponent—a man with mechanically-enhanced limbs, curling his metal hands ready to strike again. Then he looked around; the raucous crowd was quietening down—they knew he was giving up. As Rowan got ready to charge again, Joash swiftly lay flat on the floor, spreading his arms and hands, accepting defeat.

***

"Please wait! Wait!" someone shouted behind him as he made his way out of the fighting ring and into the passage towards the changing rooms. Joash halted and turned around.

"Is it Joash, Joash Pundit?" The young man was out of breath.

"Yeah," he replied questioningly.

"Nice to meet you. I am Callum Bailey." The man extended his hand.

"Nice to meet you too, Callum Bailey." Joash was amused. "Such polite people generally don't come to a place like this."

"If a science journalist like you can come to fight in this club, a physics student like me can come at least to watch it." Callum grinned, showing his molar-to-molar smile.

Joash's forehead furrowed in a frown. "Student! Are you over sixteen?" He paused, then said, "Do I know you?"

"Ah, ah…" Callum fumbled as he visibly got nervous. "I am seventeen, actually. I am from the Physics Institute in London, just joined. You know Professor Rollings? She heads it, but I haven't seen her yet. Anyway, I like your blogs and your news channel. I think your analysis of climate change is unlike anyone else's. I am here with a friend who is researching limb movement in cyborgs. He couldn't recognize you because of the headgear, of course. We were here last Thursday too. I was almost sure it was you and now I know."

After a moment of awkward silence, Joash smiled and said, "Seventeen? I'm more than ten years older than you; you're making me feel ancient! Well, thank you, Callum, and you have good eyes. Professor Rollings … ah, interesting. Now if you'll excuse me, I have somewhere to be."

"Just one more thing, I'll be quick." There was an obvious desperation in Callum's voice.

Joash leaned his head to one side, accepting that he would have to hear this kid out.

"I know you sometimes write about new automobiles too," Callum said hurriedly. "I have developed a new flycycle. It ascends very smoothly and has the potential to be an alternative to the clunky hoplings for short trips. It can be invaluable to environmental research at a time when we are trying to figure out chemical interactions at various heights in the atmosphere and their link to the lightning storms. I will be very grateful if you would write about it. I can do a demo for you. I promise you will not be disappointed. Please, please, please…"

By the time he finished, Callum was breathless, and Joash was staring at him in puzzled amazement. This was the first time someone had approached him to write about something with such passion. Moreover, there was something quite likeable about this fast-speaking, skinny teenager.

"Okay, I would like to see your flycycle and then we will decide. But the only time I have got is six o'clock tomorrow morning," said Joash.

"I don't mind. You don't know how helpful your words can be for my project work."

"I will meet you at my aunt's place. Come with your flycycle tomorrow. Here's the address." Joash waved his hand and a set of bright numbers jumped from his wrist-pad to Callum's.

Joash turned around and opened his palm. His wrist-pad buzzed, and a message appeared in bright green words on his palm—seven missed calls from Aunt Sue. Joash sighed; he had forgotten to call Krupa.

***

Back on the street, the water level was just above Joash's ankles. He looked through the mizzle—the gloom in the city was deepening. The bars and restaurants had shut early, most buildings were just dark, and the streetlights had been dimmed. Occasional streaks of lightning zigzagged the sky. The air felt still and stagnant.

Joash strode through the water with a certain nonchalance, hands inside the deep pockets of his yellow rain jacket and his head covered with its hood. Now and again, he bent his head towards one shoulder and then the other. He did this quite often—it was his way to align his thoughts.

He had not walked far when there was a sudden roar from the sky and a loud blast shook the street, sending debris flying everywhere. The shock made him squat and cover his head with his arms. He turned and squinted towards a Level Two road. A red hopling was teetering dangerously along the broken edge of the road; its propellers were bent but still moving slowly, sending small sparks erratically. With a loud clang, the hopling leaned further downwards. The rider was waving one hand.

Loud sirens could be heard blaring as Joash straightened up to go towards the crash site.

"Do not interfere." A police robot was standing right in front of him. It blinked scanning Joash's face and said, "Joash Pundit. This is an authority matter."

***

Joash stood quietly staring out of the large glass window of his bedroom. The lights of the sprawling city of London were like an entire galaxy spread out beneath him, but the scene was fuzzy, partly because of the rain and partly because of his eye. He touched his pulsating head and made a futile effort to open his right eyelids fully; they were distinctly swollen now. Shaking his head, he said loudly, "Home?"

The wall behind Joash glowed and a cheery voice said, "Yes, Joash, I am here."

"Please call Krupa," said Joash not looking away from the glimmering scene.

The response was instant. "The number cannot be reached and is likely to have been discontinued."

Joash glanced sideways looking thoughtful. "Call Subba then."

Soon a life-sized, three-dimensional image of a man appeared on the wall. Joash turned to face him. The man was burly, with black hair, a beard and a moustache. He took a few seconds to observe Joash and then burst out laughing.

"Look at you, man," said Subba trying to catch his breath. "Is it a regular thing now or what?"

Joash pursed his lips. "I am all human and they are enhanced. You won't get it, Subba—leave it. Tell me, anything new?"

"Hmm. We are getting close, I think." Subba had sobered up at once. "There seems to be a relation between the old plastic waste piles and lightning. It is pretty weird. Once I am able to get the right video, I will send it to you. By the way, your Professor Rollings won't share her research with us. What's she up to?"

Joash nodded, "I can't say. She doesn't seem to be the typical scientist, yet she is the chief scientific advisor. I am going to her conference tomorrow." He paused and continued, "There's one more thing. I can't reach Krupa. How are things in the Himalayas?"

Subba folded his arms across his bulky chest. "Oh, your little sister, right—Krupa? Storms are getting worse all over. You should know better than me. We have had some very strange earthquakes near Mumbai. Last I saw, the Himalayas were in the news for snowstorms. Yes, that could easily affect the comms. But where exactly in the Himalayas is she?"

"There is a monastery in a small village called Jispa. Higher than Shimla, I think. She has a teacher there, Swami Poorvananda."

Chapter 2

Jispa, Himalayas

A gust of wind pushed Krupa forward jolting her out of her thoughts. She placed her hand on the door and a sudden chill ran through her body. At that moment, she had a foreboding -*Something is coming*. She took a deep breath in. The familiar morning aromas of the valley were comforting. Steadying her mind and feet, she looked ahead. It was a heavy, rusty brown wooden door with rough-hewn carvings of leaves and flowers running along the withered borders. An ancient-looking thick iron chain, which was the latch, hung vertically from the upper border. She tapped it twice and then pushed the door slowly.

The door opened with a squeak revealing an austere room.

At the far end of this empty-looking space was a slightly raised platform on which sat Swamiji. His legs were crossed in the lotus position and his eyes were closed. Soft orange rays of the morning sun filtered through the window mesh, bouncing off his shiny head. He was only a small man, four feet something, but one would say his presence was enormous.

As Krupa stepped inside, she was struck by an otherworldly calmness. Something felt different about the room today. She walked across the cold stone floor and sat down in front of him.

It was rare for Swamiji to ask for Krupa other than at their weekly lessons. As she waited for the reason for this meeting to be revealed, her fingers started to fidget restlessly with the long chain of yellow beads that hung freely from her neck and her clear blue eyes started to blink furiously.

"Krupa, my child!" said Swamiji slowly as he opened his eyes, "How is it going? Any progress?"

"I am afraid not, Swamiji!" replied Krupa almost feeling guilty. "I cannot sit still for more than five minutes."

Swamiji's eyes peering through the folds of his drooping eyelids looked thoughtful. He gently smiled - kindness shining through his radiant countenance. "Hmm. Meditation is like everything else in life—the more you try, the more likely you are to succeed. But I can feel your intuition is getting stronger." He smiled softly.

Krupa noticed that his head was shaking slightly today, also his shoulders were drooping more, or maybe his back was somewhat hunched. *Is he tired?* she thought but did not dare ask.

Swamiji's perfectly round face lit up and numerous concentric lines filled his cheeks as he let out a chortle, "Even monks and yogis get old, Krupa! Although the process is much slower. Worry not, I am not yet tired." Krupa was embarrassed but not surprised.

"You spoke well this morning during the interview," he continued. "Now, there are a few things I need to speak to you about."

She raised her gaze.

A hint of seriousness rang through Swamiji's words, "I know you do not want to face the thought of losing this place, but the ashram building will not be able to stand the storm that is coming, Krupa. I hope we are all prepared. We need to leave soon—the storm is going to reach here a bit earlier than I had expected."

"Yes, Swamiji, we are ready." There was a sudden spurt of confidence in Krupa. She was the best at organizing things after all.

"Good!" He paused and changed the subject swiftly. "Now pick up the scroll next to the Jyot."

She quickly turned around and looked at the left rear corner of the room. On the floor was a small earthen lamp burning steadily with the most soothing glow. The flame was like a wavering leaf in shape, five to six inches tall, its body was made of sparkling white dots moving downwards and its red border disappeared seamlessly into the surroundings. In her astonishment, she understood the reason for the room feeling different. She had never thought she would ever witness the eternal flame of the Sheersha Yoga Gurus. She folded her hands in reverence towards the flame, picked up the scroll, and returned to her seat.

Before she could ask her question, Swamiji spoke. "I too have never seen the Jyot before. Do you know what this means?"

"The first sign—the Sangam—a period when different realms cross over." Krupa could feel her heart thumping. Of course, she believed in it like every other teaching of Sheersha yoga, but she had never dreamt it would happen in her lifetime.

"Yes, Krupa. The world as we know it, is about to change. The unseen will become seen. What lies in store for humanity, no one can say." Swamiji paused and closed his eyes. A few moments later, he smiled. "There should be no despair with the Sheersha yogis by our side. They gave us the answers long before the question even came into existence. This can be a wondrous magical time." Opening his eyes, he raised his fine white eyebrows and pointed towards the scroll. "Now, what do you see?"

"This is in Sanskrit. I have seen parchment like this in my

father's library. It could easily be a thousand years old." Krupa's heart was racing with excitement as she went through the text. "It is a poem," she said slowly. "Maybe a riddle."

"Can you solve it?"

Her eyes narrowed as she concentrated. "It is about the state of the world. In order to correct the imbalance, the five elements will have to be brought together by the…" Her voice faded into a whisper as she said, "The Tirtha Rakshaks."

"That is right."

"But Tirtha—"

"Is not a mythical imaginary place as you would have heard in your childhood. It is a real place, here in the Himalayas. And you always knew your ancestors were also known as the Rakshaks. This text makes it clear. They were the Rakshaks of the Tirtha, the guardians of the sacred spot. And so are you."

Quietly, Krupa let the words sink in. "So, the five elements need to be brought to this place?"

"Yes."

"Where is the Tirtha, Swamiji?"

"We do not know. Maybe it is up to you to find it. But I do know that it holds the answer to the present turmoil in nature—a turmoil brought on by the Sangam, made worse by humankind. To get those answers you must find the remaining part of this text. It was looked after by your grandfather."

"But my ancestral home…" Krupa looked puzzled.

"Is mostly under water," said Swamiji. "I understand. Your father was very accomplished and wise. I cannot imagine him not planning to save the things he valued so much."

Silence ensued as Krupa tried to gauge the seriousness of the matter in her mind. She turned her gaze back towards the top of the parchment. The words in black still stood out on the yellowing parchment—Prakruti Saram. Immediately, she recognized the picture drawn below it—a circle with rays, a sign of the sun, and a seven-petalled lotus which was drawn partly inside the circle. She had seen this symbol before, engraved on the side of her father's desk, painted on the wall behind his chair, and on a special wooden box, she was not allowed to touch.

Dark clouds started to gather in the Himalayan valley and sunlight vanished from the room, but Swamiji in his saffron-coloured robe shone like the sun itself. He stood up and spoke in an authoritative tone this time, "You are not the only Tirtha Rakshak, Krupa. It is as much Joash's karma as it is yours. He has spent enough time wandering. If he chooses the path that was laid for him by your father, he can do the extraordinary and so can you, Krupa."

Swamiji took a few firm steps and opened the old wooden

door wide. Feeling perturbed, Krupa rose to her feet and followed him. She was beginning to realize that he was probably the only person in the world who could make her feel nervous.

"Joash has abandoned the spiritual path, Swamiji. He has a different life. He might not understand…" Krupa's voice trailed off.

The squall from outside entered the room, making Swamiji's robe swell and pushing Krupa. Although the sky was greying, the light was blinding. A fine spray of rain mixed with snow on her face washed off any doubt in her mind about the urgency of the matter. A shiver ran through her as she tried to keep her stance.

Swamiji looked sideways and this time he gave a clear instruction, "Krupa, my child, both you and Joash have a role in reducing the suffering of countless beings. You have the soul of the mountains. The Tirtha will find you. But Joash must find the elements. This is what all his education with the greatest guru of our times will amount to. Tell him Tirtha is calling him. A journey like no other awaits him."

Chapter 3

London

"This is Joash Pundit." He looked at a robot's face on a screen on the wall and tilted his head to one side, moving his bright yellow hood off his head to show his face fully. He shrugged his shoulders. "Are you going to open or what, Mary?"

But the robot's image was stuck.

"Slow network again!" Joash sighed knowing very well how different his own face was looking today.

"Joash! Good morning," the robot replied finally. "Your aunt is still sleeping. Would you like me to wake her up?"

"Yes please."

The robot disappeared but the building door still did not

open. Thunder rumbled in the grey sky. Joash looked up, soaking his face in the rain. Around him, the empty streets seemed full of an eerie dreariness.

The building door buzzed loudly and opened. "Enter, Joash Pundit."

On the fortieth floor, he was received by a bright and colourful robot. "Welcome, Joash, you may go to the dining room. I shall get you some strong coffee, just as you like it," said Mary, then she rolled away.

"Thank you, Mary." As Joash stepped inside Aunt Sue's apartment, he realized he had not been here for a few months now. He knew what was coming.

In the front room, he stopped to look at the wall where the paintings displayed changed every few seconds—some were virtual illusory designs that seemed to come out of the screen and float in the room. Soon, his favourite one appeared—a classical painting, *The Waterfall*—an enthralling waterfall of vivid yet earthy colours with big snow-capped mountains in the background. It was just a play of paint and brush strokes, yet the sparkling water and the foamy froth looked so realistic that one could almost hear the burble. This was not the first time Joash had got lost in this painting, but today he longed to step inside it, into this world where the sharp sunrays pierced the fast-flowing water, turning it into countless diamonds, where the sight of snow was soothing, where the silence was expectant yet complete.

"You do like this one, don't you?" said Aunt Sue as she came and stood behind Joash.

Joash turned around and greeted his aunt with a smile—the left corner of his mouth lifted, sending gentle waves on his cheek up to the depression that created an unusually wide dimple.

Aunt Sue looked horrified. "Just look at yourself, Joash. A black eye again and you are going to a press conference like this? Is this why you did not return my calls?"

Joash remained quiet and waited for more to come. Moving his long, wet hair behind his ears, he looked down.

Aunt Sue took a deep breath in and closed her eyes, trying to calm herself. "So, you don't call me. You don't see me. And now this is the only time you have for me, five-thirty in the morning? I am an old woman you know," she said managing a smile.

"No, you are not." Joash embraced her in a hug.

"Don't try to flatter me. You live a few streets away and yet I have to leave twenty messages to get you to visit me." Her long neck seemed to grow longer as she elegantly moved her head from side to side trying to sound stern, but it did not last long. She wrapped her arm around Joash's, and they began to walk together. As they entered the grand dining room, she stopped, turned around, and looked up at him—he stood more than a foot taller than her. "Tell me, have you been able to get through to Krupa?"

"No, Aunty. There seems to be a network problem in that area." Joash quietly walked away to the far end of the room.

Aunt Sue was not smiling anymore as she sat at the other end of the long white marble table. "How is your girlfriend?" she asked, looking unsure.

"Alicia? She's my ex-girlfriend. We haven't spoken for months now. She has gone back to America." Joash placed his forearms on the table and crossed his hands.

Aunt Sue frowned. "I should think girls would queue up for a handsome and intelligent man like you, but they seem to run away as soon as they come."

"You should say *weird and intelligent*, Aunty," Joash said trying to lighten her mood.

Aunt Sue knew that he was never one for vague conversations. She got up and stood next to the window. The lines on her forehead were curled into a frown as she gazed out. "So, tell me when did you speak to your sister last?" she asked.

"I did try to call her yesterday but…" Joash paused and then said slowly, "I spoke to her on her birthday."

"Which was three months ago! And when did you see her last?"

"Same as you, last summer when she came over."

"What is it with you two? I don't understand!" Aunt Sue could barely contain her exasperation. "She thinks she is some yogini or hippie and can wander around without us having a clue and you have distanced yourself from anything to do with India. What are you punishing yourself for by going to these fight clubs? You know perfectly well how that is going to end." She turned to face Joash and looked him in the eyes. "Can you tell me that Krupa is safe and sound?"

Joash looked clueless as he gazed back at his aunt from the table. The question had hit him exactly the way she had wanted.

"It has been eleven years since you moved here and still you won't talk about what happened. You are twenty-eight, Joash, not a child. She is your little sister." Aunt Sue leaned over the table and said softly, "Your only immediate family!"

"She is, Aunty, but she would not want me tracing her steps. You know her." Joash was beginning to get frustrated at being treated like a child.

Aunt Sue toned down as she straightened up and took slow steps towards him. "I understand that there have been some snowstorms and landslides in the Himalayan regions of India." Clouds of worry darkened her bright face as she stood holding the back of a chair, staring at the wall.

Joash knew he should have checked what was going on with

the storms in the Himalayas; it was his domain and yet he knew nothing. After a minute's silence, he said, "She is a smart girl. She would have kept track of the forecast in times like these. I am sure she is okay." It was a vague effort to reassure himself.

"You know very well how much we can rely on forecasts." Panic was clear in Aunt Sue's voice. "You either find out where she is, or I am packing my bags and going there myself." She got up and left the room.

Joash walked up to the large window overlooking Level Four road. Far away, the silhouette of Tower Bridge was lurking behind the rain. He opened the window slightly and let the cold air rush in to chill his face. Perhaps he should have thought of Krupa but then he was sure she was made of steel and even bad weather could not dent her.

As he was immersed in his thoughts, his gaze went upwards to the sky where he spotted some unusual activity. Someone was pedalling a flycyle. Immediately, Joash checked the time and knew who this was. He didn't know if he was amused or annoyed by Callum's stunt, but he continued to watch anyway.

The two tyres with fluorescent green spokes were moving fast and the red balloon just above Callum's head was growing bigger as the flycycle rose steadily in a straight line. The brightly coloured air suit made him look like a green giant, but he was at a far greater height than was allowed for flycycles. Suddenly, the flycycle lurched sideways. It stopped, about fifty feet above where Joash was. Callum then started fiddling with something.

Just then, there was a loud rumble and lightning lit up the sky. Callum was thrown off his precarious seat with a jerk, but he managed to grab one end of the flycycle. A strap around his waist seemed to be attached to the crossbar and his hands were holding the handlebars, but his body was dangling dangerously.

"Wah…!" Joash was watching with his eyes wide open, his hands squeezing the window frame. The next moment, the balloon started to deflate and the flycycle started to descend haphazardly. Joash turned around and sprinted towards the front door just as Aunt Sue walked in with Mary.

"What's the matter?" she shouted behind him.

"Someone has fallen off a flycycle." Joash jumped into the lift.

In the elevator, he strapped himself in and spoke loudly and clearly. "Take me to ground level, maximum speed."

The elevator, which was a metal cylinder with a thin column of glass looking to the outside, lit up with a blue glow. A red laser beam scanned him from head to toe, then a voice resounded, "Adult male, scan approved. Put your seat belt on. Warning, this might be unpleasant. The air is to help prevent nausea."

A loud bell rang, and a blast of air blew onto his face. He

held the straps tightly and scrunched up his face as the lift descended, almost in freefall.

Within a few seconds, he was at ground level. As he hurried towards the heap of red and green, he could hear the soft painful moans. *Callum is alive*, he thought.

"You were supposed to meet me inside my aunt's apartment not outside," shouted Joash as he leaned over Callum. He did not look badly injured.

"I think I am okay. It came down slowly, but I might have twisted my ankle. Could you please help me?"

***

"Oh dear!" exclaimed Aunt Sue as Joash came out of the lift, holding Callum who was limping and smiling.

"You must be Joash's aunt. Nice to meet you. Sorry to arrive like this," said Callum.

Aunt Sue stared at her nephew, looking puzzled.

"He is a new friend. I had called him here for a meeting," said Joash. "Sorry, I should have asked your permission first."

"Oh, never mind now." Aunt Sue turned towards Callum again, "I like your Scottish accent. Are you okay? Whatever were you doing up in the sky in this weather on that thing?"

Callum smiled looking awkward.

Aunt Sue sat down next to him while Joash made him lay

down in a large couch and asked Mary to scan his ankle.

"No fracture that I can detect," announced Mary.

"Good." Joash was sipping his coffee.

Callum said suddenly, "Oh, I forgot to introduce myself properly. I am Callum, Callum Bailey uh…"

"Susan Anderson, call me Sue," said Aunt Sue.

"Of course, Ma'am. I looked you up when Joash said I could meet him at yours today. Your paintings are amazing indeed. In fact, we have one in our physics institute somewhere on the fourth floor. I will check it out when I am there next. And you are absolutely right, I am from Glasgow, been in London for just over three months."

Joash stood up. "So, Callum, I am not sure if your flycycle is ready yet. Maybe you can work a bit more on the safety features before showcasing it—"

"Oh no, no," Callum said urgently. "It is safe, and I know I was at a greater height than allowed for flycycles but that's the whole point of my work. It works by manual power, so no need for solar chips like hoplings."

"Sounds interesting. We can talk about it some other time. I am afraid I need to leave now for a press conference. Are you able to walk?"

"Callum Bailey should not walk just yet." Mary placed a

cold pack around Callum's foot.

"She is very good, isn't she?" said Callum, admiring the domestic robot.

"At my age, you need your robot to be medically up to date, dear." Aunt Sue shifted and spoke to Joash. "I know the conference is important for you, Joash. Why don't you carry on? Let Callum rest here for a bit. I don't mind a bit of company. He seems like a nice boy."

"Oh, thank you so much Ma'am," said Callum delightedly.

"Sorry about all this, Aunty. And I *will* find Krupa," said Joash and left.

Chapter 4

London

The thunderstorm had come out of nowhere. The cool wind was a welcome change; it soothed Joash's sore body. Ahead of him, he could see the network of roads at different altitudes stretched like a web between the tall buildings. The road levels were numbered, and the higher-level roads had byways connecting to higher levels of buildings. The sky, which would have been dotted with different coloured hoplings, was just a featureless grey background today. The streets looked empty; the air smelled of burnt tar.

After an hour of wading through the waterlogged streets, Joash reached his destination—The London Communications Centre. As he entered the main hall, he was struck by the number of people who had come. On the stage, there were two robots and two men. The hubbub suddenly stopped when a lady dressed in a turquoise suit walked on the stage and took a seat right in the centre of the stage. Professor Rollings looked exactly the same as her online profile—in her late thirties, she had a long face marked by a sharp chin and wore thick, black-rimmed cat-eye-shaped glasses, had very short hair and an expression that said there was no time for nonsense.

"Everyone, please settle down," said a robot, its head scanning the crowd of mechanical note-takers and human journalists. "The authority wishes to inform you of further measures we are taking to keep the population safe. In addition to the advice of not using flying automobiles, all international flights have been cancelled from tonight till further notice."

A loud murmur started in the room—this was unexpected.

"We have every reason to believe that the two airline crashes last week were due to lightning storms. In London, tube services have been suspended due to rising water levels; this is expected to be sorted out within days. We advise only essential travel by hovercars, trains or on foot and check all routes for damage to roads. At present, mostly Level Three and Four roads are affected."

A husky-looking, elderly man with curly grey hair spoke next. "Now, as you all know, Professor Stella Rollings, Chief Scientific

Advisor, and honourable authority cabinet member has called this conference to discuss current climate-related matters and answer any questions. Professor Rollings—over to you."

The professor cleared her throat loudly. "Thank you, Patrick. Good morning, everybody. Thank you to all of you who have taken the trouble to come here and also to all of you listening from your devices. Let me update you on the current scenario first— even after thirty days of relentless rainfall on our mainland, we have not yet understood this weather phenomenon. Lightning strikes are becoming a major source of disruption as they are increasing in frequency and causing more damage. That is the reason why we have advised people not to use flying automobiles. This pattern of sudden climate change is not confined just to the UK but is global, with all types of severe weather events happening everywhere. We are still trying to work out if science can find a way to solve any of this."

A man sitting in the front row asked, "For several decades humans have changed their ways to help climate stabilise and yet we face these extremities. Do you have any idea what the problem is this time?"

"Well, we have worked out that there is a new element in nature, something to add to the periodic table. It seems to be very high in concentration in all problem areas. I have provisionally named it Elusium."

"How is it related to adverse weather phenomena?" came another voice from one of the screens in the air.

"We do not know yet; it is early days."

"And what about the old plastic waste piles?" asked Joash from the back of the room.

"What about them?" Professor Rollings raised an eyebrow. She glanced at the small air screen on her table and saw 'Joash Pundit, climate journalist' under his photo.

"Have you not seen any evidence connecting the plastic waste piles and the storms?" Joash stared at her intently. He knew her opinion on plastics.

"I have always maintained that plastics have got more bad press than they deserve." Professor Rollings spoke coolly, unfazed by his stare. "The waste piles have been lying all over the world for the past fifty or what, sixty years?" She shrugged her shoulders. "They continue to degrade and will vanish in the next few hundred years. I have not come across any verifiable evidence of their role in the current scenario."

"Or have you just shoved it under the carpet?" Joash trusted his sources and he could not believe that the professor had less information than him.

Professor Rollings' eyes widened, and she shifted

uncomfortably in her chair. She looked at the small crowd in front of her hoping that someone else would ask a question. When no one spoke she said, "I am not a politician. I am a scientist. I follow good-quality evidence and disregard poor-quality evidence. It really is as simple as that." This time she stared back at Joash trying to measure him up.

"Are you really a scientist?" Joash asked.

At this statement, all heads in the room turned towards him. Professor Rollings moved her head back and frowned deeply, waiting for what was to come next.

The attention only boosted Joash's confidence as he carried on, "According to *Scientist Daily*, you have a keener interest in the paranormal than modern science. You even believe in E.T."

Everyone in the room laughed.

"What has that got to do with climate change?" Professor Rollings looked infuriated.

"It poses a question on your credibility as a scientist. A person who believes in anecdotes cannot lead scientific investigations. We are not talking about movies here; it's a real-life crisis, which only science can solve."

"I do not need a lesson from anyone on the credentials of a scientist. You look like you enjoy messing with people or maybe you just took a wrong step and hurt yourself," said the professor, stopping a smirk before it was too obvious on her face. Suddenly, she sat back looking thoughtful. When she spoke again it was with a new brightness. "You see it is not about me or you. I am doing my job to the best of my ability. You cannot know the nature of reality just by doing a science degree. And belief in one thing does not necessarily invalidate belief in another. The universe is full of secrets; you too should explore other ideas. But perhaps this is not the time and place for this debate." She smiled at Joash icily.

"Is it true that in your hometown, Edinburgh, you were labelled a misanthrope? You moved to London and within two years you have acquired the power to influence the authority. How did you do that? Secondly, is it true that you have requested access to the latest Air Force Stealth Aircraft for so-called research purposes?"

Professor Rollings's mouth opened as she looked at Joash in disbelief.

"So, I was right," he said. "Why would you keep it a secret? It is the country's resources after all. And where do you want to go to, when you are telling others not to travel? Should your research not be more transparent?"

"I am not going to answer any of this," came Professor Rolling's sharp reply. Before he could say anything more, she swiftly added, "Now please let us not waste time. I can assure all of you that my team is coordinating with teams in eight other countries and the number keeps growing. Our investigations are based on robust scientific methods and common sense, of course." Then looking at Joash she quietly added, "That can be so hard to find."

For a second, Joash felt an inexplicable sense of pity towards her. He thought he had overdone it. He could not stop staring at her, even when she looked away. And then, he could not place his feelings—anger, annoyance, longing to speak to her. A missed opportunity.

Someone nudged Joash. "Don't be so creepy, man. She will call the police. You should know she is best friends with the Chief Authority Manager."

The man's voice faded as Joash looked away.

***

Joash had wasted no time in posting his analysis of the conference on his news channel. What irked him most was the fact that the professor had advised him to explore other ideas. She had no idea how baseless other ideas were. But what could he say when his own sister was deep into these things? That reminded him of Krupa—where could she be?

As he walked past the gates of the Natural History Museum, the rain started hitting hard. He turned left and presently a humungous black shiny structure came into view. Perhaps the Global Live TV Centre could give him some answers.

The place was buzzing with people. The roof of the building had two large separate domes, each for one-half of the globe. Every country was a different colour and screens corresponding to different areas were floating beneath. Joash spotted India and climbed up three levels to reach the screen for northern India.

Soon he was enlarging the satellite image of Himachal Pradesh. He kept tapping, moving closer and closer to land. Before long, the scene opened up—mountain after mountain was laden with snow and shining white in the afternoon sun. Further down, he could see the village of Jispa. In the quiet valley hung a curtain of fog through which the roaring river Bagha was easy to spot. The fog cleared revealing a splendid view of the serene valley. As his gaze moved down along the great slopes, white turned into green and then bubbling blue.

He kept moving down along the river and the scene changed dramatically. There were houses with broken, half-collapsed walls and piles of rubble on what possibly could have been the streets. Everything looked wet and muddy. He tapped the icon for his virtual self to be allowed on the street, but a message flashed, *'Virtual descent and speech not supported—no local network.'*

There were no people to be seen as Joash moved from street

to street. Eventually, he saw an orange-coloured building with lots of windows and small balconies. On taking a closer look, he saw that this place was quite damaged too. The next moment, he saw two men appear from the half-broken entrance gate, carrying bricks and debris in wheelbarrows. His heart sank. One of them was wearing maroon overalls. If only he could speak to them… Growing restless, he clicked on the screen to get a news update on Jispa. Nothing on the day. He went back one day and saw 'ten lives lost in the storm'. On a few days' old page, he saw 'Jispa to be evacuated … as urged by Swami Poorvananda from the local ashram. However, weather forecasters don't say the same.'

Just then, his wrist-pad buzzed and a message from Subba appeared on his palm. 'Check out this video.'

Chapter 5

London

Back in his apartment, Joash was getting ready to watch the video related to Jispa when the door buzzed.

"Visitor identified as Callum Bailey," said Home.

"Thank you, thank you so much Joash," Callum said gratefully. Limping slightly, he entered the living room. "My place is so far from here. Everything seems to have stopped. I am sure my foot will be better by tomorrow morning, and I will be off."

Sitting on a couch next to a large window Joash smiled, "I don't mind, make yourself comfortable. You can take the room to the left and the kitchen is here right behind me."

As Callum disappeared, Joash moved his head from one

shoulder to the other stretching his neck. One thing at a time, he told himself, putting aside his concern for Krupa and brought up the video.

"Yes, you heard it right. I have interviewed the elusive yogi, Shri Poorvananda," came a high-pitched voice from the air-screen. Joash was both surprised and curious. He moved to the kitchen and the small screen moved with him.

"So, Swami Poorvananda ji! You were born in Indonesia and moved to the Himalayas over fifty years ago to pursue your spiritual practices. Most of us have never heard of you but you have suddenly become quite famous since some of your predictions about climate upheaval came true—the hurricane in New Orleans, the snowstorms of the Alps, and just this morning the tsunami on the South African shore. How are you beating the meteorologists?"

Joash placed a cup under the coffee machine.

"It is the *Dhi*—meditation," came a calm reply.

Like pebbles falling on the surface of still water, those words created ripples and stirred something inside Joash. The muscles of his face tensed up and he shot a hard gaze towards the screen.

"Hmm, interesting! What is *Dhi*? Are you another school of yoga philosophy or a Buddhist monastery? Or are you a cult? Or maybe you practice some kind of occult magic? And what is this place?" The female voice paused and then as if realizing how she might have sounded, she added with some hesitation, "If I may, Swami Poorvananda ji."

"Maya, this is Krupa—one of my students. She can answer your questions very well."

Joash was struck with surprise to see Krupa's face on the screen. Eagerly he waited for her next words.

Krupa, who was standing right next to Swamiji, poised herself as she began. "*Dhi* is simply the energy of the universe—it is in empty spaces; it is in every electron, and it is in the mighty Mount Everest. It is what escapes the body when one dies, it is what burns the sun, and makes flowers bloom. It cannot be sensed by any senses, yet it is possible for the mind to tap into it. And that is what Sheersha yoga teaches us—how to connect with the energy of this cosmos. Where you stand today was a one-room house by the river Bagha forty years ago. Now, there is a whole monastery built around it. We call it the ashram. We follow the ancient philosophy of *Sheersha Dhi*, which are Sanskrit words for highest mind or best meditation." She stopped and looked at Swamiji.

He nodded.

"We live a simple life here, looking after each other and the nature around us." Her words flowed as her face shone with a quiet assurance. "You will find people from different parts of the world who have made this place their home. We meditate upon *Dhi*. Anyone who lives like this could be called a yogi or even a hermit. There are many parallels with Buddhist and Yoga philosophies, hence some people call this the Sheersha Yoga School, but it has never been compared with occult magic or called a cult." Krupa had made her point.

Maya said quickly, "Oh, I did not mean any offence when I said that. As you will remember, Swamiji, we had the great floods eleven years ago. Did your *Dhi* tell you anything then?"

"Yes, it did tell me something," he said. "My visions were not as clear then."

"And have you had any recent foreboding?"

"A storm is going to be in our valley in the next six to eight hours." Swamiji's expression was that of a stoic.

"Uh, yes of course. I was informed before we started. You need to leave soon. When do you think, things are going to go back to normal?"

"Do you think there has been a single year in the history of this world when there were no storms?"

When no one spoke for a few seconds, Swamiji's face lit up with a smile once again. "No one can predict the future precisely," he said. "Let us be kind to each other and to nature. I am sure we will receive kindness in return." He brought his hands together and bent his head, indicating politely that the interview was over.

Joash sat in silence, clasping his hands together close to his chin. He was not sure what to make of this. *Was it a planned evacuation then?* he wondered.

The next moment, Home announced, "Unidentified caller from India."

Joash was alert again as he watched a highly blurred image of a person appear about a foot away from him. He said, "Yes?"

First came a few unintelligible words and then, "Joash…" Finally, he could hear—it was Krupa. As her voice became decipherable, the image disappeared.

"Krupa?" His heart was racing. He wanted to ask how she was, where she was but words refused to come out of his mouth. Till now, he had not realised how worried he had been. He would have liked to sigh with relief but not yet.

"I guess you want to ask how I am. I am fine," she uttered hesitantly and then continued, "We had to vacate the ashram due to bad weather. We are all taking shelter in our second ashram higher up in the Himalayas. It is quite remote, I had to travel down to this village to contact you. But things are bad here too and I might get disconnected. Now, can you hear me still?" She always spoke to her brother in a firm tone.

Joash gulped trying to orient himself. "Uh… yes," he said.

"Things are settled where we are, but we can't be there forever. We will run short of supplies soon. Swamiji believes with some effort from us the balance in nature can be restored. Do you remember Papa talking about the Rakshaks?"

He was just listening to her voice, trying to understand if she was okay. Her sudden question jolted him out of his confused state. He blinked. "What?"

Krupa went silent for a moment as if deciding her words. "I am going to send you the picture of an original text. Read it."

"Okay." He was still puzzled. "We have been trying to reach you, Krupa. Aunty is really worried."

"I just told you that Jispa is destroyed. There has been no connection for weeks and my number stopped working ages ago. I have spoken to Aunty just now. Now there are more urgent matters at hand than you and me. Tell me, what do you know of Rakshaks?"

"Rakshaks? That's a designation given to our family. I don't think it has any relevance."

"Well, it is more relevant than ever. Sure, you have been taught about seven lives, fourteen dimensions." There was a sudden excitement in Krupa's voice. "What about the various realms and their crossing—The Sangam?"

"Krupa, stop." Joash was serious. "Are you a child still? Have you called me after so many months to discuss fantasy stories?"

"I know you would rather forget your education in Sheersha *Dhi*, but Swamiji says it is time that you come here and do your part."

He was irked by these words. "What is my part? I am doing my duties, living as I should."

"That is what you tell yourself," Krupa's words were piercing. "But the truth is you have duties much bigger than you can imagine. Do you think you are strong? I think you are weak; weak to turn away from your reality, from *Dhi*. No one knows why your guru disappeared, but mine is here. I have seen miracles and I have every reason to trust him. The question is, can you trust me?"

Joash was standing up facing a blank wall; his entire body was shaking. He shut his eyes hard, trying not to scream. What would he even say? He was weak, weak to be unable to bear the loss of his parents, weak to run away from everything he had known and come to London, weak to leave his thirteen-year-old sister in a yoga school without any family.

Finally, he spoke. "What do you want from me?"

"Believe me. We can help solve the climate crisis; we are still the Rakshaks. Look at the text I am going to send you, you can solve it. You can get the elements together. The remaining pages of this book were with Papa. All the locks in the house recognize you, not me. Help me get it. Help me do my karma and do yours."

"This sounds crazy. How can I even get there with all that is going on?" said Joash, looking around vexed.

"What if I die? Will you come to do my last rites? What if I said I don't know if I am going to survive this, Joash—will you see me before I go away forever?" Krupa challenged her brother.

He was too stunned to respond.

"You have to find a way," she said. "Here, the tunnel is blocked, and snow is increasing each day, but I will find a way too." Seriously, she added, "I will wait for you in Jaipur. And if you disappoint me, I will never forgive you."

With that, the call got disconnected. Joash tried to beep the ID a few times but had no luck.

As he stood frozen to the spot, his eyes stared ahead blankly, and his mind grappled with questions. *Did she mean what she said? How can I even travel at this time?*

He turned around and saw Callum standing right behind him. Callum moved his glasses up his nose and said slowly, "I am sorry. Was I not supposed to hear all this?"

"It's … it's okay." Joash did not know what else to say.

"Was it your sister?" Unable to hide his curiosity he continued hesitantly, "She must be very brave. A solution to climate crisis!

Wow. Where is this blocked tunnel and snow? Maybe I could help you in some way?"

Joash looked at him. "I doubt if anyone can help me right now. She is somewhere in the Himalayas, and I don't know how hard things are for her."

Chapter 6

The Himalayas

Krupa was keeping a good pace despite the craggy terrain. The path was foggy, but in her mind, she was clear that she did not want to depend on Joash. She had never depended on him for anything. Every time she thought of her brother, a certain sadness began to engulf her, so she shook the thought off. She would go back to the base and set off for Jaipur as soon as she could. But how to find the Tirtha? She looked up into the curtain of fog and sighed.

She had been trekking for over three hours taking frequent breaks—the plains were behind her now, the path was uphill—on she went with a rucksack on her back. She was alone in the middle of a dense Himalayan forest this afternoon but that did not bother her. When she had insisted that she must go alone to make the call, Swamiji had not objected—that was enough for her to know that it was going to be all right.

The next village with internet had been only a two-hour walk from Jispa but everyone had left for the base a day before she began her journey. She had to let the worst of the storm pass and then start in the morning. And now, as she trekked with two sticks in her hands, covered from head to toe in a white snowsuit, battling the wet weather, she realised time was not on her side. But she was hopeful that she would be close to the base before sunset.

She stopped to catch her breath and looked around taking in the surroundings. The snow had melted away in these mountains, leaving the ground slushy. The conifers were looming tall, standing still like giants. Here and there, shafts of sunlight danced through the canopy as the clouds above drifted across the sky. The intermittent fine drizzle felt cold on her face which looked perfectly oval with the dark border of her hood sealing it well. Everything felt unusually still—*was it the calm before another storm?* Krupa could hear her own breath ringing loud in her ears with every puff of white vapour her mouth sent out. *Where are the birds, the animals?* she wondered. She placed the right stick forward and continued her climb. This was not the route she would have taken from Jispa, but as she had gone further away from the base, going through these forests should save her time.

Soon the ground was more even and forgiving. The fog started to lift. There were groups of birch trees interspersed among oak trees, indicating the forest was changing. Krupa felt a sense of ease as the drizzle stopped too. But that did not last long—suddenly, she heard a low grunt and then a long sniff. She stopped dead on the spot, then turning slowly she leaned in the direction of the noise. The grunting continued and moved as did the beast that was making it. Before long, a large black bear appeared some thirty feet away from her, snorting and jerking its head. Just then, there was a rustling noise right behind her. Instantly she turned and to her alarm, she saw the cubs. There were two of them. She was standing glued to the ground right in between the bear and her cubs. She was thinking fast but no answers came to her. All she could do was rely on her instincts.

She turned slowly to face the bear again—it was still in the same place with its gaze fixed on her. It was a big one, maybe three times Krupa's size and suddenly it looked furious. It stood on its hind legs, growled loudly, and then, pounding its paws on the ground, charged towards her. Krupa dropped the sticks and darted straight ahead; the bear followed her making loud gruff noises. She was running blind, her feet were running nearly as fast as her heart, jumping over bushes and rocks, pushing the tree branches aside. Getting away from the bear was the only thought on her mind; it didn't matter where she was going. Suddenly the wind picked up speed, so much so that she could feel the forward push. Clouds cracked loudly above the forest—a fresh storm was brewing.

Krupa glanced up with exasperation and then back towards her path.

A birch tree was leaning low in her way. Instinctively she held the bough and jumped over it. As she made it to the other side there was a loud thud. She looked back—the wind had torn the tree to the ground and behind it, the disgruntled bear shook its head and roared. Krupa's chest heaved as she held the trunk of another tree and watched the bear turn and retreat. She put the rucksack to one side, closed her eyes with relief, leaned against the tree, and slid down to the ground.

Raindrops started to wet her sweaty face as she sat waiting for her agitation to pass. She was not scared—no, that was not in her. She just did not think she could run this fast. As she thought of her little victory, her face split into a wide smile. The wind started to settle, and the earthy aromas of the forest refreshed her senses. She got up, covered her head with the hood again, and zipped up her suit.

"One last thing," she said to herself. She walked up to the tree that had saved her life, leaned over to hug the trunk, and touched her forehead to it as if it were a human. She thought of Swamiji's words—*Everything in nature has the same Dhi as you and me. When you connect to it, the wonders unfold.*

But now Krupa had lost all sense of direction. She turned her wrist and tapped her wristpad several times—no, it was not going to come on suddenly now. It had stopped working a week ago. She decided to carry on straight, nonetheless. It was uphill again and more arduous than she had anticipated. She clambered up while little streams of water ran down the slopes of the mountain as the rain continued. The sound of babbling and trickling brooks soothed her ears. Suddenly the ground felt soft—her foot slipped as the mud beneath disappeared. Down she went tumbling and screaming, landing at the same spot where she was half an hour ago.

By now, her face was full of shiny red scratches, her legs felt sore, and her white suit was torn and muddy brown in colour. She felt a burning pain in her right knee. Sitting on the ground, she brought her knee up slowly and examined it through the hole in her suit and the clothes underneath—the skin on her knee had stripped off and the bare flesh was shining red. Quickly, she took out a clean scarf from her bag and tied it around tightly.

Never mind, she thought, picking herself up, ignoring the aches and pains. *If this is my test, I'm not going to fail.* She found a clear stream and splashed her muddy face with more water.

Then the rain started to quieten down and suddenly there was a beautiful fragrance in the air. Krupa slowly looked around searching for the source, her steps following the smell. Something was moving in the bush—as Krupa approached, it came out, as if it wanted her to know it was there. A shiny dark brown deer, it had no tail, its eyes were glistening with a strange intelligence, and it stood there majestic and proud—a musk deer. *Is it?* mused a bewildered Krupa. *How can this be? Musk deer were declared extinct a few years ago. But it has this unmistakable scent around it, it can be nothing else. Also, they don't like to be near humans and this one is standing here, just a few feet away from me. What—*

The deer moved its ears, then its head sideways. For a second, Krupa thought it was gesturing to her to follow. She stayed still, baffled by what she was looking at. The deer bleated loudly and repeated the action. This time it leapt eastwards and ran away.

Without a second thought, she followed the deer. She soon understood her path was going around the mountain slope from here. As the scene opened, she saw there was a valley below with the river rushing at its base. She was on the slope of a mountain and the deer was waiting at a cliff edge, higher up and further along a wide path on this slope. She had never been here, and she wondered how many others had. As it wound around the mountain, the wide path was replaced by narrow jagged rocks. Soon she found herself taking careful steps, holding the rocky ledges on the mountain slope on one side while the gorge lay with its mouth open beneath her. The deer was nowhere to be seen now. But forward was the only way to go. One slip and it would be the end of her journey.

The rain lashed down, making her fully wet inside her torn suit. She shivered with cold. The wind that had started to howl in this narrow valley pierced her skin, reaching her very bones. With each precarious step she took, she rose a bit higher. Finally, Krupa reached the top. She was now on a wide, flat area on the side of this gigantic mountain. The deer was waiting for her at the far end. There was an old oak tree not far from the deer and next to it a ledge projecting from the sheer rocky face of the mountain had formed a shallow cave. The deer stood by the tree, glanced at Krupa, and then looked away. She plodded wearily towards it.

The rain stopped and the light in the sky got dim as afternoon turned into evening. Yet the clouds parted, the view got clearer, and Krupa saw a new ray of light when she realised where she was. Beyond the oak tree, another rocky path led down to a small platform. This path was not as steep. From the platform, a rickety bridge spanned across another gorge and held onto the next mountain. This mountain had a yellow flag, a small yellow wavering dot on its summit. On the other side of this giant was the base; this mountain was the Moksha Parvat.

Krupa's heart leapt with delight. She turned to thank her guide, but it was not to be seen anymore. Her hand was now resting on the tree trunk. As she moved it, the surface felt strange. Curiously, she examined it—there were deep engravings—a circular shape of the sun with rays emanating from it and a lotus partly inside it; above it was what looked like phases of the moon starting from a thin crescent to a full circle. Her eyes were wide with surprise.

She looked around, there was nothing else growing in this space by the rocky mountainside. She went to the shallow cave and sat down. Realising there were similar engravings on the cave wall too, she moved her hand gently on the markings—it was a quaint, calm feeling. Her heart leapt with joy as she realised what had just happened—she had found the sacred spot: the Tirtha.

The storm was behind her now, her weariness was gone. She took a few sips of water from her canteen and munched on some large raisins. Soon she rose to her feet again shining with a new energy and in no time, she was scaling the bridge.

It was nothing more than a few ropes and pieces of rotting wood, but Krupa felt a strong sense of safety. The swaying reminded her of the swings in the garden at her parents' house. She always had

Joash to push her, at least till the time he got too busy with Guruji. That instant, her foot went through a hollow piece of wood, and she found herself hanging mid-air with the other foot still stuck on the last rung. She held the ropes tightly and pulled herself up with all the strength she had. Carefully, she found her footing again. This time, she was not going to let any thoughts sway her attention. And she did just that. She had reached Moksha Parvat—the liberation mountain, a name given by the villagers.

Soon she disappeared into the thickets looking for paths to go to the other side of the mountain.

"Krupa! Krupa!" The calls came loud and clear.

"Meera?" shouted back Krupa.

The friends rushed to hug each other.

"How did you find me? This is not the usual way," asked Krupa astonished.

"Swamiji. He asked Alok and me to come here and look for you. He said you were tired and hurt," replied Meera looking relieved and amazed at the same time. "Oh, look at you. It is okay. You are home now. Let us go."

"Yes. Let us go," said Krupa with a quiver in her voice as she finally gave in to the cold and allowed herself to shiver.

Meera wrapped her in a warm blanket. "Did you speak to him?" she asked in a whisper.

Krupa nodded.

Alok joined them too. "How did you know about this way, Krupa?"

"I had heard Uboyo speak about the path through that forest," she replied as the three of them made their way to the base.

"But that path would have led you to the foot of Moksha Parvat. I have never seen that bridge before. The way it looks, you are lucky you could cross it."

"Yes," said Krupa feeling a quiet elation. "I guess I was supposed to come this way."

"I am glad you are back. We are expecting guests. We cannot take instructions from Bheema anymore," said Meera and the three of them laughed.

As they emerged from the coppice, the sun had set behind them and in front of them was a large clearing. A small wooden house, elevated on four wooden poles that were like giant tree trunks, stood at the far end of the clearing. People had gathered around a gently dancing bonfire, swaying and humming a peaceful melody.

Krupa let out a big sigh feeling warm inside, "Ah, the base."

Meera placed her hand on Krupa's shoulder. "Do you think he will come?"

The look of relief vanished instantly from Krupa's face. How she wished she had an answer to this question.

Chapter 7

London

Joash and Callum stood at the gigantic entrance gate of King's Cross station. The place was bustling with people scurrying in all directions.

"Oh no!" exclaimed Callum above the clamour of the crowd. "We have missed the train by five seconds."

Joash sighed. "Remind me again, Callum, what am I doing here with you?"

"Going to Scotland," replied Callum meekly.

Joash looked away as if disappointed with himself and started walking aimlessly. He had not quite figured out what he really wanted to do.

Callum started jogging after him, "Look, let me explain again. It is not a bad idea. Trust me." He looked at Joash pleadingly, confusing him even more.

"You want to go to India because your sister needs you. Right?"

Joash shrugged his shoulders.

"There are no commercial flights, no ships, no trains to go there. So, if you take my dad's prototype long-distance kropter and offer to give it a test run, you have a chance to go to India. Because flying is technically not banned."

"But why would your dad give it to me?"

"Valid question! We can figure all that out once we get there. Hey, I just thought, that underground tunnel travel is quite cool too. They strap you to a seat in a tube, sedate you and literally throw you at supersonic speed from one end of the tunnel to the other. Aren't these places antipodes? Perhaps you can find one in India."

Joash rolled his eyes. "No. There are none in India. You have to be super-rich and super-crazy to actually use them."

"So again, my idea is the best. And think about the fight clubs in Edinburgh. I thought if you were so much into these things you would have tried them by now. Plus, you have a better chance of winning there. We Scots are all about equality."

"That is a promising proposition. But what's in it for you?"

"Valid question yet again! I like to help people." He grinned his full-fledged grin while Joash raised an eyebrow of doubt. He was enjoying his company, nonetheless.

"Okay," said Callum. "You haven't had the time to discuss my flycycle yet. I understand there's a lot going on, but I can give you access to all my little inventions that I have worked on since childhood. You will have a fantastic story."

Joash laughed, his eyes searching for a coffee shop.

As he walked towards one, he took in the strangeness of the station; he rarely travelled by train. The roof of the station seemed to touch the sky as it had been moved up with every new level of train. Just like the roads, the train tracks ran at various heights, supported by lofty colourful columns. For some people, the higher-level trains were like joyrides of theme parks, while some could never dare to look out of the windows.

"As I had told you, there are no trains to Glasgow. Once we reach Edinburgh, we can figure out what to do." Callum's glasses turned dark as he projected the screen in front of them and said, "The next train is only at six in the evening. I wish we could walk it."

"It's only just gone three o'clock now," said Joash, adjusting his neck and sipping his black coffee. "I just hope the time passes quickly."

And six o'clock did arrive but after much waiting and wandering. Callum had not stopped talking about physics, the climate, or new automobiles and even asked lots of questions about Joash's family, but he had forgotten to give Joash any chance to answer. As bemused as Joash was with Callum's chatter, he was glad to see the train when they arrived at platform nine on Level Two.

The platform floor was glass, giving an illusion of people levitating. The train tracks emanating from platforms at lower levels could be seen going in different directions. Their shiny grey train with a very sharp bullet nose was ready to shoot like an arrow.

"I love train journeys, but I think they should go a bit slower," said Callum as Joash settled in the seat opposite him. "You said you could use this trip for work?"

"Yes. My contact has told me about a storm forecast in western Edinburgh tomorrow early morning. It is supposed to move further north. I would like to see if I can chase this one."

"Hmm, interesting. Can I come with you?" There was a cautious eagerness in Callum's voice.

"At your own risk." Joash smiled and nodded.

Half an hour later, the train suddenly halted. Callum got up to look outside. "Whoa!" The scene was as spectacular as it was shocking. The sky outside was an orange-grey colour, reminiscent of the evening sun. Way below was the vast stretch of dark water as far as the eye could see, the train and the bridge stood lonely as if in the middle of an ocean. A fine spray of rain created countless ephemeral dimples on the surface of murky water.

"Looking at the countryside, lads?" said a joyful man passing down the centre of the train carriage.

"Where will all this water go?" Callum looked troubled.

Joash peered out in silence.

∗

"A hundred-and-twenty searches on modes of travel to India in one hour." Patrick Zuma stared at Professor Rollings; his head was bent down but his eyes were raised up.

The professor got up from her green velvet armchair. "What is his background?"

Patrick shook his head, looked at the screen again and mumbled, "You should let go, Stella. He is just another journalist. Everyone will forget his article in a few days, no matter how malicious it sounds to you today. He does not know how things are actually done."

"He has a lot of followers, and he has questioned my integrity."

"Oh, come on," Patrick raised his hands high. "What do you want to do? Avenge yourself?"

At this, she turned sharply towards Patrick, then looked away, clasping her hands together. "I want to do what I want to do. First, I want to check the claims of this yogi about a place that is not going to be affected by storms. All of his storm predictions have come true. He knows something I don't. And I want to go there myself, without anyone having a clue." As she spoke these words, Professor Rollings thought about how restless she had felt since she had seen Joash Pundit. It was true that she despised him but why it had led to a burning fury inside her she did not know. She needed a strong distraction.

"We can get the call any moment now. As far as I am aware, just the authority manager and Air Force Chief are aware of your trip," said Patrick.

"Are you sure you don't mind coming with me, Patrick?"

"You know I have faith in you. More importantly, I am an old man. Even if I die, no harm done," Patrick chuckled softly.

But Professor Rollings was in no mood to smile today. "I hope Joash Pundit does not get to find whatever he is looking for." A touch of anger gleamed in her dark eyes.

***

With the train halting frequently, by the time they reached Edinburgh, it was 9.30 pm and the last of the daylight had receded.

"Have you informed your dad that we are here?" asked Joash getting off the train.

"Nope!" replied Callum casually, almost skipping alongside Joash who noticed that Callum's limp was gone.

"I can see that reaching Scotland has added a spring to your feet," said Joash with a smile.

Callum beamed. "I am not going to deny that!"

"So, what are we doing now?"

"What about finding a place to stay?"

"I am going to check out the fight club in the city centre," said Joash as he took firm strides towards the exit of the station.

"But there is one problem." Both the men stopped as Callum continued, "You have to be over eighteen to enter the club."

"So, you can't go. They do things differently in Scotland, don't they?"

They ambled through the high street. Unlike London, the roads were dry, but the air carried a message of approaching rain. Joash had a strange feeling that it was not his first time in Edinburgh. He looked around; his eyes surveyed the buildings and his mind tried to figure out if it felt like some other place he had been to. The high street was a wide cobbled road with five-storey buildings on both sides. The road gradually sloped down as they walked on. Suddenly, Joash stopped and found himself staring intently at a medieval building. As he gazed towards it, his mind went into a momentary trance—he could almost feel the thud of hooves and clattering of cartwheels on the ground— as if time had not moved on.

"This is St Giles' Cathedral," said Callum, jerking Joash back to the present. "Have you been here before?" he asked curiously.

"No," said Joash still staring at the imposing building with keen eyes.

"I would not have imagined you to be interested in architecture and history," said Callum.

"You are right. I have surprised myself today." Joash was still taking in his surroundings as they walked past more historical statues and sandstone buildings that must have stood there for several centuries. The more he gazed at them, the more peculiar he felt to be there.

The crowd was notably sparse; people seemed to have retreated early for the night. The lights from several restaurants glittered and some random beats of music escaped their front doors, spilling onto the high street.

Soon they found the hostel they were looking for. The two friends stood facing an old grumpy-looking man who sat behind a counter. He had agreed to give them a room for the night. Though his scanner had scanned their faces, the man continued to stare at the duo suspiciously.

"You! Scottish fellow," said the man looking at Callum, "I want no funny business here. This place is for decent men only. If you come back drunk, sleep on the road. Tell your Londoner friend. I have no robots here, only me. And there will be a power cut later tonight so don't be roaming around after ten."

Callum shot a quick look towards Joash and then spoke to the man in his most polite voice, "Oh yes, sir! We are not here to party. We are well-behaved boys."

Chapter 8

Edinburgh

Bruised and sore from the fight club, Joash trudged on the dark streets of Edinburgh city centre. His head pulsated with the dilemma he faced. More than twice during the fight tonight, he had heard Krupa's voice as if she was there inside his head, asking him to come. Could she not see, that if yoga was so powerful why did it not protect their parents during the great floods? And what could this book be about? Could he go back to the ancestral building again? Could he bear to see it in that state, with all the love he had known, all the joy he had known, submerged in water after the big floods? He wasn't sure.

Fine rain started to sprinkle the roads as the city quietly

slept. It was an unusually silent rain. The mellow haloes of the streetlights grew dim, not a shape stirred in the stillness around. Joash's jaw tightened with nervous tension as an eerie air started to envelop the street.

The next moment, his eyes fell upon a building with an archway at its entrance. As he was staring at it, a small flame shape appeared in the air right outside it. It was not a torch nor a laser but more like a lamp floating in the air. It just did not make sense. It disappeared as quickly as it had appeared. Joash blinked and blinked and there it was again, really floating. It travelled from the dark inside, hung around near the road, and went back in.

Trying to find the flame, he reached an open yard. In front of him was a tall statue—a man trying to control a horse. The horse was made of stone and still as a mountain with its forelegs raised high in the air; it seemed like it was going to gallop forward any moment. As Joash looked on with wide eyes and a thumping heart, a loud whine pierced through the silent night and all the lights went out.

Startled and dizzy, Joash stepped back, his eyes groping in the dark. Before his perplexed mind could work out anything, the flame appeared again. It was there, just a few yards from him, a few feet above the glistening wet pavement. It had a strange red hue about it and it felt like it was looking directly at him. It stayed waiting as Joash took slow steps towards it. He had seen this before, yes, in the fighting ring the other day. And it struck him: he had learned about a flame like this—a sparkling white body with a red halo—from his guru. A part of him said he was hallucinating, another part wanted to find out more. As he came closer the flame started to move again. Joash followed. Soon he found himself in front of the dark passage, where the flame had retreated. He put his wrist-light on. There was a big sign above the passage: 'Mary King's Close—closed for repair work'.

With every step now, Joash's mind became quieter, the questions disappeared, and he simply walked as if drawn by an invisible string. Following the flame, he entered the building and was soon descending on wide stone steps in a tunnel-like dark passage. A sudden draught of wind blew his hood and brought a painfully familiar smell with it. A slow pounding started in his head, but no thought of turning back occurred to him. He carried on in this damp dungeon with a strange anticipation.

Presently, he stopped. He felt someone was there right next to him. Slowly, he turned to see—it was a lady in tattered clothes with wrinkly sagging skin, staring towards the ground and standing very still. He stepped closer and realised it was just a life-like statue.

The flame maintained a uniform distance from him. Joash understood he was in the basement of the building, there were several interconnected rooms with more human statues in them. The place was some sort of a museum or a horror walk. Streams of water were running away on the floor. The alleyways were narrow with lofty side walls; he could not see the end. He turned another corner and entered a small room. The flame flickered steadily in one corner of this room.

Joash looked around and all of a sudden, his headache became unbearably sharp. His face distorted in pain, and he went down on his knees. He held his head with his hands; his eyes were red and watering. In a trembling voice, he screamed, "Ma!"

A few moments later, the pain started to ease off. Breathing heavily and shaking slightly he looked up with rheumy eyes, his face covered in numerous droplets of sweat. He glanced at the flame again and then looked around the room. It was a small room, dark and dismal, bare and broken, waiting for centuries to tell its story. There were broken bricks in one corner and the mud-coloured walls had cracks running through them. A crippled chair right next to him looked like it had been thrown into the room not so long ago. Feeling a sudden surge of agitation, Joash picked up the chair and flung it towards the flame. It hit the wall and crashed to the floor in several pieces.

"Who is trying to trick me?" he screamed. "The eternal flame of the gurus. Huh! It is not going to work. I have no guru and I am not going to fall for this."

"Joash." A voice resounded in his head. There was no one else there. He held his head with his hands and sat down on the floor. His mind started to race trying to explain the situation he was in. Possibly a head injury, he told himself. He just needed to rest. Shaking back and forth, he shut his eyes and then heard a sound he had not heard for eleven years. "Hmm…" It is the first sound to start meditation, a sound to invite *Dhi*—the great energy. Before he could react, a feeling of profound calmness swept through him.

Every cell of his body began to vibrate rhythmically with the sound as he sat with his eyes closed. Then, scenes from his childhood came rushing to him. He saw the large beautifully symmetric Sacred Fig tree—the Peepal tree, he could even hear the heart-shaped leaves rustling in the gentle breeze just like the chinking of a dancer's bangles. He now visualised the circular cemented area around the trunk that was painted white. And there he was, Guruji, sitting under the Peepal looking at him with a kind of love that was indescribable. The memories that he had managed to shut off successfully were being paraded in front of his eyes and it felt like he had no power to resist.

He had been sure he was abandoned by his teacher, he was certain he never was a good enough disciple and yet today, after so many years, it was Guruji's face smiling at him.

There was a burst of bright light. He opened his eyes and a different scene started to play. This time he saw a little girl, a very pale and weak-looking child with an angelic smile. She had rough ginger hair, fair skin, and greenish eyes. She was playing with a tiny wooden horse in a dingy, poorly kept room with mud-coloured walls and a low ceiling. There were no windows, no furniture. It felt so real that he could smell the dampness in the squalid room, touch the rough walls and feel the dirt on the floor.

Someone walked in through the door. Joash knew this person was him. He looked nothing like himself but still, he had no doubt. He looked thin, had a long face and a sharp nose. He too had rough ginger hair, green eyes and was wearing dirty clothes.

He shouted, "Rhona!"

A loud cough and a moan came back from the far corner of the room. Someone was covered in a tattered blanket and shivering.

The little girl came running to the man, hugged his stick-like legs, and said, "Dada, I am hungry."

"Rhona, give Miria something to eat." He put his hand on Miria's head for a second, then moved away rather callously. Joash who was watching the scene wanted to help the girl, but the one in the scene was frantically looking for something.

"Mama can't. Look at her," begged Miria.

"She will. She is not too bad." He did not even look at his wife. He just needed some money; if he won tonight, somehow everything would be fine.

The little girl stared innocently at her father, hoping he would make her mother better. She had been waiting for him to come back all day Now he was busy turning vessels upside down, looking annoyed as he usually did. A little lamp flickered somewhere in the room, but it seemed like no light could change the dark sadness of that place.

With a sudden burst of anger, the man threw a metal utensil on the floor. Breathing heavily, he ran his fingers through his dirty hair. His eyes were fiery with an inferno burning inside him which he was not trying to conceal from his daughter. With his clenched jaws, he kicked the vessel. Miria got scared and huddled close to her moaning mother. He walked out slamming the door behind him and the little girl watched her father disappear into the darkness again.

As the man passed through the crowded narrow alleyways full of people shouting, grumbling, and coughing, the only thought going through his mind was, *I will borrow more and play, but this time I will win.*

The scene changed. He was now walking back through the same rank alleyways, but it was daytime. The cold was biting, and he did not have enough clothes to keep warm, but he had won some money finally with his gambling. He thought he could buy some food and some medicine for Rhona.

Suddenly, a big older woman came charging right at him. She looked furious and shouted as loud as she could showing all her brown-black teeth, "Where were you, Fingal? Do you have any sense? You are a monster to leave a child like that. I tried to help her, but I don't know how long she's been suffering alone. You monster!" She screamed her final insult.

Fingal, yes, that was his name then.

"Miria!" he shouted, running towards his home.

Some people were huddled outside his door. Inside, there were a few women who moved aside to reveal Miria. She was lying on the floor with her small body shivering miserably. He looked up and saw Rhona was still in the same place but not shivering anymore. Her face was now fully covered.

"Rhona died last night," said someone from behind him.

Shocked, as if hit by an invisible hammer, he looked at his dead wife and then turned to his daughter. He wrapped Miria in his arms; the pain was unbearable. "I am here, I will get you some medicine now." He was desperate, but Miria could not hear him. He held her tender body, trying to cover her with a blanket that was full of holes. And then she stopped shivering.

He looked at her face which looked white like frost. He wailed, "Miria!" Floods of tears blinded him. He had done this. How could he? He had failed his wife and his child. He had gone blind to their needs; all he wanted to do was gamble. His heart was sinking, falling into a deep hollow pit with no end.

***

Joash blinked and opened his eyes wide to the present. Just like that, the scene was gone. A scream was stuck in his throat, stifling him. He got up and looked around in despair; his head throbbed, and tears streamed down his face. He was in the wretched room he had just seen. It was not a dream; he was not even asleep. Breathing heavily, he wiped his tears and walked around the room looking for answers, but a great sadness had taken hold of him, and he just could not think. He sat down on the floor, put his face between his knees, and sobbed like a child. The tears eventually stopped, but the feelings of guilt, remorse, and hopelessness stayed.

Then he felt something warm, like a ray of morning sunshine falling on him. He looked up and it was the same flame glowing softly in one corner of the room. Wearily, Joash walked up close to the flame. Sitting down on his knees he peered at the flame with tired eyes. He felt its warmth on his face and a familiar smell surrounded him once again. He looked even harder and could not believe what he saw. It was the face of Guruji in the minutest form with eyes gazing softly at him and a gentle smile on his lips. Joash rubbed his eyes and looked again. He could make no mistake in recognizing this face—the radiant white beard, the curly tresses tied up with a string of brown beads.

"Guruji!" he begged. "What is all this?"

He received no reply.

"Where were you all this time?" bellowed Joash. "And why have you come now?" His voice reverberated through the empty rooms and passages and then all was still again.

He moved restlessly about the room. His world had been turned upside down. He could not deny anything; he could not turn away from anything. He knew everything that he had seen had happened once upon a time, in a different life in this place. He had been Fingal and Miria was none other than Krupa. Like the truth of day and night, life and death, this knowledge needed no proof.

He sharply turned towards the flame again. It rose higher. Words resounded in his head, "To succeed you must try, to find you must seek."

And then the flame went out.

Chapter 9

Edinburgh

Joash collapsed onto the floor. The glow from his wrist-light was still sending unearthly shadows to the walls. He sat up and rested his arms on his bent knees. A battle was starting within him. Staring hard towards the floor, he tried to ebb his emotional turmoil and make sense of it all.

Drip, drip, drip. The sound of water dripping somewhere far away trickled through the still air and finally reverberated in Joash's ears. Something started to wake in the dark alleyways of his memory—a slow thumping of drums began. He lifted his gaze and the memory of the day of his initiation came back to him.

***

The sun had not yet broken the horizon, but the sky looked expectant with a tinge of red. Joash was walking next to his mother on this crisp morning, climbing up the open steps to the terrace. His mother had looked like a picture of a goddess that day—golden hair tied back, blue eyes full of clarity, a soft smile that never left her lips, a red Bindi between her eyebrows, and a green sari that flowed gently behind her as she walked. She looked at her son with adoration.

Joash smiled back nervously. He was only eight years old then. Something was different about that day. His head had just been shaven clean, he was wearing new bright yellow clothes—a loose shirt and pants so wide someone thrice his size could fit in. It was not his look that bothered him but the ceremony that was about to happen. The number of people in the garden gave him a sinking feeling in the pit of his stomach. He did not want to be the centre of attraction, and neither did he want to be sent away from home to be a monk.

Sensing her son's anxiety, Erin said, "It is so exciting. I don't know about you, but I cannot wait for the ceremony to begin. Papa has already arranged all sorts of musical instruments in the main garden. It is going to be fun."

They crossed the full length of the stone terrace to reach the study—his father's most treasured room. As Erin opened the door, certain trepidation had started to make Joash shake a bit. Erin looked at him and pursed her lips, then with a worried frown she said, "Kartik, come here please. You need to speak to him now." She took her son by his hand and settled him in a chair as Kartik emerged from the second room.

Joash's father was a tall, lean man with a dusky complexion and short black hair. His big eyes shone with patience and wisdom. Usually dressed in a crisp white shirt and dark trousers, today he too was wearing a bright yellow wraparound *dhoti*, a garment worn for prayers, and a very loose yellow shirt. Joash looked curiously at his father's outfit and then stared at his face, forgetting his own predicament for a second.

"What's the matter?" said Kartik in his lilting voice, knowing perfectly well what the matter was.

Erin's eyes did not leave her son.

Kartik looked at his wife and shook his head. She was a bit too soft when it came to her children. "He is fine," He patted Joash's shoulder with great enthusiasm.

Next to them was a rather large desk made of dark shisham, a smooth rosewood, scratched with overuse and certainly a lot older than anyone in the room. But even older were the books that lay open on it. A piece of withered parchment paper, which looked like a hand-drawn diagram of some kind, was spread out next to the books. Joash looked at the desk and then towards his father.

"Nervous?" asked Kartik.

Joash nodded quietly.

"I know, I should have explained things a bit more to my little man. But I will try my best now," said Kartik settling in a chair behind the desk.

"I am not little," Joash protested.

Kartik smiled and winked at Joash. "Oh, of course, my fault again."

Joash smiled, showing his new front teeth, while Erin sat down in the chair next to him.

"Look at this," Kartik leaned forward on the table and moved the parchment paper in front of Joash. The word 'Ahwaan' was at the top; next to it was the familiar symbol with a bright pink lotus half-inside a sun.

"This was drawn by your grandfather, my father when you were born. Ahwaan is the real name of the ceremony that is about to begin. I have told you that it is the beginning of your spiritual education. But what is the one most important thing you need for education?" Kartik looked at Joash who was listening intently now.

Joash shrugged his shoulders. "Computers? Books?"

Karthik laughed and stood straight again, "No. A teacher!

Today we are going to call upon a teacher to come and accept you as a student."

"Call upon?" Joash was still bewildered.

"I am not doing very well." Kartik sighed and looked at Erin who nodded asking him to carry on.

"Okay let us revise what I have taught you. What is *Dhi*?"

"It is the great energy that flows through the whole universe."

"How do we start meditation?"

"With this sound—hmm."

"Why?"

"To concentrate on the *Dhi*."

"Correct. Just as when we tap the right point on a screen or say the right words, we choose the right channel we want to watch on TV, by making the right sound and thinking the right things we tune into the great energy. What if I told you that in this world there still are some people with extraordinary powers, people who are experts in tuning in to the *Dhi*? Would that be exciting?"

"Yes." Joash nodded vigorously, his interest peaking.

"These people are called Sheersha yogis," continued Kartik. "And today if we do the right thing, we think one will accept you as a student."

"The right thing?"

"Your grandfather was told by a great yogi that you, his

grandson, could be a Sheersha yogi one day."

Joash's eyes opened wide with astonishment.

"On the tenth day after your eighth birthday, if we generate the correct vibrations around you and you ask for a teacher with full concentration, a teacher will certainly reply. Just like when we select the right channel, we can watch what we want. And how do we make the right vibrations? Music." Kartik pointed to the chart with a pen as Joash leaned over with his forearms on the table. "This shows all the musical instruments that are being placed around the Peepal tree and the notes to be played. It is going to be fantastic!"

"And if nothing happens?" asked Joash.

"Then at least we tried," said Erin holding her son's hand. "Think of this as a musical festival, a prayer for your eighth birthday! Enjoy it Joash, it is not a test. Your Papa and Ma are with you, it will be all right."

Joash sat back in his chair feeling relieved but wondering at the same time, if this meant he was going be a superhero one day.

"And let me tell you a very interesting fact." Kartik had the look of a magician who had one last trick left in his bag.

Joash gazed at his father who was looking more joyful by the moment. "The only time an Ahwaan has been known to occur was several hundred years ago, for a prince." Kartik raised his eyebrows, looking triumphant at last. "It's an ancient ceremony; it only happens in special circumstances."

Joash beamed; this was enough to make him feel special.

***

Down in the garden, the drums began to beat, sending a slow thumping sound straight to the study.

Soon Joash was walking towards the Peepal tree through the garden path lined with fragrant jasmine bushes, flanked by his parents and little Krupa holding his hand.

Wow! he thought, as his heart started to beat with the same rhythm as the drums. He had never seen these people before and he had never seen so many of these beautiful instruments before, though he knew some of them—the tabla, the djembe, the tambourine, and of course the large drums which were being played by a very tall muscular man as though he was in a king's court. There was nothing gentle about this music; it felt like slowly the atmosphere was being built up to something, like laying bricks carefully to make a grand palace. Then came the haunting sound of a didgeridoo from somewhere. Joash turned around, trying to find it. On one side of the path, behind the bushes stood a woman engrossed with the long wooden instrument. She moved around with her eyes closed, blowing air into the mouthpiece. The earthy soulful drone felt like the sounds of nature from a deep dark forest.

The garden was full of fragrant flowers at this time of the year but never had Joash smelled the sweet, the bitter, the woody, the minty all together. Mesmerising as it was, the suspense was making his heart race with anticipation. Krupa pulled her hand away from his and asked her mum to pick her up.

He reached the tree; it had a new circular sitting area that hugged its trunk all around. As he sat down, all the music stopped. He gulped and looked around; his mother, father and sister were sitting in chairs placed ten feet away to the right; just in front of them on the ground sat a man with a pair of tabla. He looked content with a gentle smile crossing his lips, his palms resting on the tabla and fingers ready to start tapping any moment. Next to him was a young boy, a teenager, with a silver flute. The boy gave Joash a knowing look, Joash had probably seen him in his music school, though he had stopped going there a few months ago as he had found the flute very tough to learn. On the chairs to the left, there was another boy with a violin and a cheerful-looking girl with a guitar. Joash could not think what a violin sounded like, but the guitar was his absolute favourite. He could play a bit himself. For a moment, he felt a desire to play the strings and let a punchy happy tune flow that would make him forget where he was.

A little behind the boy and girl sat an old man Joash had often seen in the temple; if he had an instrument, it was not visible. Further away almost in a semicircle were more musicians with drums and some instruments Joash didn't recognise.

Joash's chest was visibly heaving now. His eyes met his mother's, and her quick look of reassurance calmed him down. The minute of silence ended as the sound of the flute filled the air. It was a soothing melody, like birdsong in the morning or a mother's warm embrace. Then came the sound of large metal bells, shrill yet pious. And slowly the other musicians joined in, making it a tune of joy and hope. A long, sustained call of a conch shell, blown by the old man from the temple, reminded Joash of what he was supposed to do. He closed his eyes gently and started humming, "Hmm." The music went on and without realising Joash was being transferred into a trance of beatitude.

When fifteen minutes had passed, not even Kartik and Erin could believe that Joash had sat still for so long. Then again, all the music stopped, and a wafting sound of violin began, with a quirk of a string it quickly changed from calm to sombre and then the drums took over. Joash frowned getting tense but sat still, a boy of grit determination as he was. The beats were coming fast now, louder, stronger, harder; rising into a crescendo the music penetrated the ground and possibly the souls of those around.

Suddenly, in front of his closed eyes appeared the bright red hue of a burning fire. His forehead broke into beads of sweat as he opened his eyes wide. And there in the middle of everything stood a man, inspiring awe and exuding a supernatural sort of power like he had never seen before.

The music stopped and maybe time did too, as every eye was fixed on this man who seemed to have appeared out of thin air. He had silvery-white hair, which would be long and flowing if it hadn't been tied up at the top of his head, held by a string of brown beads. His long snow-like beard, though, was free to flow with his ochre robe in the gentle breeze that had just started to pick up. In his right hand was the strangest staff one could imagine; it had three sharp claw-like projections at the top and at the bottom where it touched the earth. It was made of light-coloured wood that twisted and intertwined like an old creeper. His silvery eyebrows and eyelashes added to the shine of his glittering eyes that fixed on Joash with a piercing gaze.

As for Joash, he returned the gaze unblinkingly without fear or doubt in his eyes, only wonder and amazement and a longing to know this person.

The man took firm steps with his bare feet towards Joash; even with the fierce power he carried, a vapour of calm floated about him. When he reached him, he placed his left hand gently on his head and said in a deep voice, "Rise, my son! Let us begin!"

**

Joash rose from what must have been a deep sleep. Looking about, he saw there was no sign of Guruji, only the damp walls of a drab room and the hard, wet floor where he had been lying. It felt like he was holding something in one hand. Slowly he sat up and directed the wrist-light to his other palm. It unfolded to reveal a clear vial, a small bottle that was the clearest form of glass he had ever set his eyes upon. It was empty with a narrow neck and a stop. The top was tied with a thick white string with two open ends that trailed long enough for the bottle to be a pendant around someone's neck. Bringing the bottle closer to him, he saw the engraving on the base of the vial—a circular ring shape with rays and the form of a lotus half-inside the circle. The proof that he had not been hallucinating or dreaming had just been presented to him. He wrapped the string around the vial and placed it in his pocket.

His heart, his head, and his ears seemed to be thumping in harmony as he pulled his body up. With every inch of his being aching and his head swimming, he plodded in the dark passages to find the exit.

He emerged on the road, back into the relentless rain. Through eyes half-covered by his dishevelled hair, he saw two shapes at the other end of the road. One of them turned his head quickly and ran towards him.

"Joash! It's three a.m.! What were you doing in there? What has…" Callum sounded frantic.

Joash could hear the words but neither his mouth nor his mind allowed him to answer. As he trudged towards the hotel, he felt the sharp stare of the caretaker who stood close to the main door. Joash glanced back at him from the corner of his eye and the man jumped back as if a fireball had been thrown at him.

The two men stood watching, befuddled, but Joash quietly carried on to his room. In his bed, he pulled out the vial again. *The symbol of Rakshaks—my family.* He wondered where Krupa was and if she knew what this meant. With these thoughts, Joash soon sank into the deepest, dreamless sleep he would ever know.

Chapter 10

Edinburgh

Joash sat up in his bed with a start, his almond-shaped eyes wide open and staring ahead intensely. His eyes fell upon Callum and instantly his breathing eased as he came back to the present.

Callum was sitting right across him slouching in a chair with his feet resting on the bed and looking at him with great curiosity. He moved his glasses up the bridge of his nose, straightened up, and then came closer to Joash with a quizzical look on his face.

Protruding his neck forward like an ostrich, he brought his face close to Joash's and said, "Are you okay?"

Joash wanted to say he was not. "I am," he uttered instead.

"Okay!" Callum's neck wound back like he had a spring in it. "You do sound fine, but you look a bit different. What were you doing in that creepy place, if you don't mind me asking?"

The muscles of Joash's face visibly tightened as he tried to detangle the recent and the more distant memories. Under the blanket, his hand fell upon the small glass vial and the reality of it all hit him once again.

When he did not speak for a few seconds, Callum went back to the chair and started flicking through some content on his air-screen. "Hey! Do you remember anything from last night? Do you sleepwalk or something?" he asked casually without looking back.

But Joash could not answer any of the questions. He was fighting a sensation of drowning. Callum's voice was muffled except for a few words which hit Joash's ears loud and clear.

"REMEMBER when I spent a few hours with YOUR aunt? She spoke so much about you as a kid—your horse-riding LESSONS, you were a swimming champion too. She even told me you have always had trouble sleeping. Interestingly, she believes in star SIGNS. And here you ARE, running after storms EVERYWHERE that don't even happen. Maybe about time, the weather forecast is made by people who can read stars." Callum laughed and turned to look at him.

Joash had his eyes closed tightly; he was sweating profusely. Suddenly, as if he had understood something, he shook his head and opened his eyes.

"You are starting to freak me out a bit, mate," said Callum. "Are you really okay or do you need a doctor?"

"Sorry," said Joash and took a deep breath in. "I am fine, it is just too warm today. I am going to open the windows."

"Hey, it is okay. You don't have to worry about explaining last night to me if you don't want to. We all have weird sides. Frankly, I would not have even known if Mr Williamson had not woken me up."

Joash, who was now standing next to the window, said nothing.

"Uh, he is the caretaker you know," Callum continued with some hesitation. And then he laughed loudly which made Joash look at him. "Do you know what he said?" After a second's silence, when he was sure he had his attention, Callum spoke again, "He thinks that either you had seen a ghost, or you are one." With that, he burst out laughing again.

A wry smile crossed Joash's pursed lips and his face turned towards the window again. He placed the glass vial back in his pocket.

Joash checked the time. "The storm forecast was for five a.m."

"That is what I was trying to tell you. It did not happen.

Are you still okay to come with me? Who knows you might find a storm in Glasgow." Callum shrugged and then continued brightly, "I spoke to my dad! He suggests we take the eleven-thirty train. If we miss it, we'll have to walk. I don't fancy that."

All Joash knew was that he had to keep moving, keep following Callum till his own path was clear.

***

The duo stepped outside again to start their trek towards the Edinburgh Waverly station. The smell of bread baking somewhere made the morning feel fresh. It was a bit brighter than mornings in London—even the clouds looked less forbidding. Joash spotted the sign across the road. At least this street was more familiar now. It did not take long to reach the station and find the levitating train.

"Hey, let me tell you some interesting facts about this train," Callum began sprightly. "It is a Maglev. My dad was a part of the group that worked on making it more energy efficient and many more are coming to Scotland." He beamed with pride and bowed slightly. Most of all, he managed to put a smile on Joash's face.

Presently, Callum fell into a slumber. Sitting across him Joash turned his gaze to the outside. But just like his mind, the train was racing too fast, and the scenes were a blur of green and grey. The sound of a little girl giggling caught his attention.

At the other window, a girl was holding a daisy and counting the petals. "Five, six, seven. Oops!" She jumped as a small flying insect came out of the flower. Soon a tiny ladybird was sitting on the back of Joash's hand. As he looked at it, a peculiar feeling came over him. It was years ago…

***

"Look hard, Joash! Try!" those were Guruji's words. "*Remember your lessons!*"

Joash was just a young boy mesmerised by a marigold that had magically appeared on his lap. "I see colours, yellow, orange, maroon. I see soft petals."

"The past, the present, the future, everything is right here in this moment. Look deeper!" said the deep firm voice.

Joash knew instinctively that he was not meant to tear the flower apart; he was just meant to concentrate more and so he did. As he held the flower closer, a minute red-black bee emerged slowly from the depths of the layers of velvety petals and a drop of moisture closely followed, getting flatter and finally settling at the edge of the petal. Just then, like flashes of lightning, several scenes crossed his eyes—a small bush full of flowers, the young tendrils, the bright green wavy leaves, the morning dew, the hovering bees, a garland of marigold flowers. And then came the sounds, the buzzing of bees, the clanging of bells. When a sweet smell of hundreds of marigolds enveloped him, his innocent eyes blinked in astonishment and found Guruji's hand gently resting on his shoulder.

"What if I don't like what I see, Guruji?" he asked.

"Then do something about it. The past is done. Learn your lessons, do the right karma in your present and you can change the future to a better one. The soul that does not correct the mistakes of the past has to go through the same misery over and over again. Joash, always do the right karma, no matter how hard it is, because the future is never fixed." Guruji's eyes, as clear as the air and as deep as the universe, smiled down at him as if telling him—the magic of *Dhi* will flow through him again.

***

With his eyes closed, Joash sat back, only one thought running through him—past, present, future, past, present, future. He thought of Miria, how could he see her face so clearly, he did not know. He looked hard into her eyes; he could hear her giggles. Then, her face changed to young Krupa—a strong, determined child. Next was the face of Krupa at present but she was crying as if in enormous pain. Half-buried in the snow, her body was shivering. Her face turned pale and the next moment she was falling from a great height.

Joash's mind was jolted back to the present. He looked around, then interlacing his fingers bent his head down. To change the future to a better one, he had to do the right karma in the present.

Was Krupa in danger? he wondered, then dismissed the thought immediately. Her words came back to him—*if you cannot believe me; if you don't want to find the elements, don't bother coming.*

***

The train came to a halt.

"We are here!" Callum exclaimed.

Just outside the station, several names were shining brightly in the air. The vibrant-coloured words and numbers—indicating passengers' names and the parking bay numbers their vehicles were waiting in—were enclosed in all sorts of shapes giving the place the vibe of a funfair. The sign for *Callum Bailey* was easy to spot; it hung above the rest inside the shape of a fluorescent green balloon.

They walked up to a squarish car with tyres that spanned the entire base of the car. It started with a clanking sound of several metal plates banging together. Soon, the windscreen turned into a map.

"Ready to go to the NARD Plant or Mr Bailey's residence, sir?" the car spoke.

"Let us go to the NARD building."

"Sure, sir!"

As they rode on the deserted fourth-level road, Callum shouted in astonishment, "Look!" Half of the road was missing on one side as if a bomb had dropped. Some roads were blocked, others functioned despite the damage. "Life has to go on," he mused.

The car soon took a side road, which led to a dome-shaped structure. The seamless gates moved, and they drove into a grand enclosed space. Callum stepped out. With his arms stretched wide, he walked backwards in the fulgently lit hall and took on the role of an animated guide again. "Welcome Joash! This is the National Automobile Research and Development Building. Originally known as Ca'D'Oro, the building was made in 1870. Many more floors have been added since. A lot of work goes on in here."

The sprawling building had a glass roof with a crisscross pattern of grey beams almost like Scottish plaid. As they walked on, it was easier to see that they were on the top floor. It was like a museum with all the latest models of hoplings, sleek cars, hoverbikes, and even flycycles in glass cases. In one large area was the kropter, the latest flying machine that Callum was talking about. Joash walked up to the object of interest.

Standing close to the display glass Joash stared quietly at the alluring flying machine which glistened and revolved in the all-white display area.

"The only long-distance hopling. Looks super cool, doesn't

it?" Callum came and stood behind Joash. "We will figure something out. Let's go!"

They crossed the black railings which encircled the common space where railings of other floors were visible as they spiralled downward along the enormous milky-white staircase. Right at the bottom was the hub of activity, the ground floor. Train tracks could be seen crossing the floor and a few robots and some men in white overalls were busy with what looked like an engine carriage. The air was warm with a hint of spark of metal on metal.

Joash looked down towards the ground floor and a sudden tension ran up his spine. Gripping the railing tight with his hands, he looked towards Callum. "Remove all men from there," he said.

Callum simply stared at him bewildered.

"I said remove these people," repeated Joash firmly.

"And what would be the reason for that?" That was Adam Bailey. "See me in my office, both of you."

Soon Joash and Callum found themselves in front of the boss of the building, a man with long dishevelled grey hair, an overgrown beard, a thin face, tired eyes, and a soft, confused expression. His office was a bare room with shining white square-shaped tiles on the floor and walls and no furniture. Adam Bailey was standing in one corner with hands crossed behind his back. His small, lean frame seemed to be burdened with his weariness. He forced a smile and looked at his son, then towards Joash.

"So, you were saying?" he asked.

"Forgive me, sir; I don't know what I was saying," Joash replied, looking embarrassed.

"Ah, Dad, my ankle is all better now," Callum jumped in. "Thanks to Joash. Um … this is Joash. Remember? The thing is, Dad, he needs our help. He has to go to India as soon as possible and there is no means of travel." Callum spoke quickly, knowing well that his father never had time for pleasantries.

Adam gave a quiet nod of acknowledgement. Then he began in an almost inaudible soft voice, "Well you just need to wait, young man. The authorities know what they are doing. Flights will start at some point."

Joash slowly nodded, quietly contemplating what to say next. He was not going to beg, and he could not remember the last time he had convinced someone with a speech.

"When do you think flights will start, Dad?" Callum twitched uncomfortably.

"I don't have a definite answer to that question. What does your professor say?" Adam now seemed willing to play along till his son came to the point.

"I haven't seen her at all." Callum had the look of a child

who could not solve a maths problem.

Adam Bailey replied, "Hmm, if you think I have any inside information, Callum, you're mistaken. I don't."

Callum quickly followed, "Dad, Joash's sister is in trouble—he needs to go. I told him that you might be able to lend him the new kropter." He bit his tongue.

"What? Do you think he is the only man who cannot reach his family?" Adam Bailey was exasperated at this outrageous suggestion. "And what do you even know about the kropter, Callum? It hasn't been tested on a long flight. And no one, *no one* is flying these days. We don't even know what's going on."

Callum moved in his seat and spoke as intelligently as he could, "That's what I meant, Dad. It can be the test run. We are not flying here but things might be better around other parts of the world."

Joash was quietly staring at the floor trying to understand his experience next to the railing.

"You don't understand, boys! It is not ready yet. It needs lots of tweaking. I want it to be as good as any long-distance flight, but I have had no time to work on it." Adam sighed and looked at the wall screen where the image of a train was glowing. "The authority has given us the task of developing the Maglev in Scotland." He looked at Callum directly. "Some of them have to be up and running within the next week, but we are struggling. I have had to abandon the kropter project, at least for the time being. I cannot help, sorry."

Joash looked at Adam Bailey, a troubled guileless overworked man who had just been given a new dilemma. He discerned a need to hold himself and speak assertively. "Mr Bailey, I am ready to take any risk; you would not be responsible for my actions."

Adam was shocked and puzzled. To get into an argument was uncharacteristic of him, yet he asked with bubbling impatience, "Why is your need above everything else that is going on? Why should I help you?"

"What if you knew that if you reach a certain place, you can avert all other storms? It is true that I need to reach my sister, but more depends on my journey. What if you were asked to trade an aircraft in return for calm in nature? Would you not just do it?" For a moment Joash could not believe his own words. His left hand reached the vial, which he had now tied around his neck. Then came the welcome realization that all the veils of doubt had lifted from his mind. The *Dhi* was real, and his path was clear; he had a purpose, a journey to make.

And then he remembered, he had not looked at Krupa's message yet.

Adam was left dumbfounded. Joash did not look insane to his wise eyes and yet he had given this bizarre explanation for a preposterous request.

As for Callum, he was just staring at Joash with a new sense of wonder. *Is this the grand adventure I've been waiting for?* he thought.

"Some rest will be good for you, young man," said Adam Bailey. "Go home with Callum. I will see you both soon."

Chapter 11

Glasgow

"What are you up to Joash?" asked Callum as he rummaged through some drawers.

Joash was sitting on a couch, looking at his screen with serious thoughtfulness.

"Here, try this!" He threw a small packet towards Joash.

Joash shot a quick glance towards his host.

"Oops, sorry. That is my favourite muffin! It looks like my dad had the time to fill the kitchen before we came—muffins, sandwiches, and even chocolate cake." Callum grinned. He took a seat next to Joash as he munched. "You look troubled. Anything I can help with?"

"I am trying to work out a riddle," replied Joash.

"May I? Uh, what language is this?"

"Sanskrit. I am not sure if this is your kind of stuff."

"Try me. Do you mind translating for me?" Callum waited with earnest keenness.

"Okay, this is the first part. It refers to a place. *Underneath the red skies, the oldest grave will crumble. Underneath the burning sand, hidden paths will open. No one has been to those old alleyways, where even air is not allowed. Through the dark passages full of restless souls lies a path to the chasm of old. Its depths are an abyss for the weak, a cradle for the fearless. There shines the sacred soil.*"

"Wow! It sounds so cool. Red skies and oldest grave… sounds like I know this…" Callum tried hard to think. "Do you remember covering something like this?"

Joash's eyes widened. "Yes. I went to Egypt last year, just before all this started. A strange weather phenomenon was leading to red skies in the afternoons. It still is…" Joash continued after a pause, "The oldest tomb would be the oldest grave—it refers to the step pyramid. A storm had caused a lot of damage to it. That is why I was there. I have been told that more recently, an earthquake has caused even more damage—"

Callum felt a fiery excitement. "What would be the hidden path then?"

"I have a contact in Cairo, I will have to speak to him." Joash looked at Callum. "You are a physics student, right? Do you like geography too?"

"I love solving mysteries, puzzles, and riddles. I would have loved to be a detective, but Dad won't have it." Callum shrugged his shoulders. "Never mind that. You said you need to speak to someone. What kind of a riddle is this then? Does it serve a purpose I mean?"

"Sort of," Joash tried to dismiss Callum's question. "Let's see if you can help me with the other bits then," he said, rubbing his hands together.

"Sarita means a brook or stream. So, where the higher beings will go, a cloudless rain will follow them. A glimpse of distant stars, an ethereal bliss…" Joash scrunched up his nose trying to work out the correct words. "Bliss or maybe blessing from far. The water from a stream touched by this rain is what you need to heal, to grow."

"Higher beings … what does that mean?"

"I think it means beings from a higher dimension. That is what Sheersha yoga says. But I don't get it. Where will they go? Who has ever seen higher beings?"

"What if you cannot see them? I mean, what if they are invisible? And this special rain is their sign."

Joash glanced at Callum, astonished at the clarity of his thinking. "I am sure you have seen the videos of so-called 'silver rain' that have been circulating."

"None of my sources has reported that. And it looked like animation to me. I have not been able to verify those."

"But what else can cloudless rain be? A spray from a hosepipe?"

Joash shook his head. "I am going to move on. This is a tough one. I know it is about fire. Find the eyes that burn in the night. Fierce is their power. Deep in the jungle, when real thunder strikes, there you will find the gift of fire."

"This one is a bit vague, isn't it? Which jungle? Any jungle? But if this is in Sanskrit, it might just refer to an Indian jungle." Callum was lost in thought with his mouth protruding and one hand scratching his chin.

Joash stood up without speaking a word. It was odd that he shared this with Callum, but he could not deny that it had been helpful. He would have to figure it all out somehow.

"This is all related to your chat with your sister, isn't it?" asked Callum.

Joash simply pursed his lips together. "You are quite clever, Callum. I wish I could discuss your flycycle in detail, but I must leave. If your dad can't help, I will try and arrange any aircraft I can find."

"Can I ask you something?"

Joash nodded.

"You know, you and your sister were talking about all this mystic stuff the other day? Have you ever experienced anything to make you believe there is something more out there?"

Joash was intrigued by the unlikely ponderous statement from Callum. He understood his friend had more to say.

"Some things happened when my mum was dying," said Callum. "I was thirteen. She had been very ill and it was clear she was not going to live. On her last day, I woke up in the morning and went to her room. It was unusually calm. I remember it was a sunny morning and her window was open. Lying down in her bed, she held my hand and said look your nana has come to take me. For a second, I felt like someone was right behind me. I was really scared. But then, there was nobody. I looked at her and she looked so relieved and happy. The next minute she was gone. I buried my face in the blanket next to her and suddenly I heard something. I turned around and saw a robin, my mum's favourite bird. It was right there on the windowsill. It flew straight down, sat on my mum's feet, looked at me for a few seconds, and flew back out."

Joash was quiet, listening to his friend. "Was your dad there?" he asked.

"No, he wasn't there that morning. He had buried himself in

work because he could not bear to see her like that. He dismissed everything I told him as nothing. He doesn't believe me when I tell him that I still see that robin whenever I miss Mum badly; it has a round black mark right in the centre of its orange chest." Callum suddenly went quiet and gulped, holding back his tears.

Joash gently placed his hand on Callum's shoulder. "I would have been like your dad a few days ago but now I totally get you. I guess I didn't want to believe that my parents were gone. I lost them in the great floods. We had a big mansion in Jaipur, built by my grandfather. *Pundit ji ki Haveli* it was called. It was eleven years ago. The rain… I had never seen anything like it. I looked down from the first-floor window and the street was like a river. The entrance gate to our home, even that was half-submerged in muddy water."

"Were you on your own?"

"No, I ran through the hallway looking for my mum. I still remember how cold the marble floor felt under my bare feet. Ma looked very tense. She was sorting some books in her bedroom. My father had not returned, and we were supposed to leave the house soon. She asked me to take some books to the study on the second floor. Those books looked special, very old. They had maroon covers and intricate golden designs on the side. I guessed it was important to keep them safe. The staircase was in the open and water was coming down on it with great force. As

I was climbing the steps hurriedly, I heard some people scream. Next thing, I slipped, and my head hit the edge of a step. What happened next is something I have refused to recall or believe."

Joash was quiet for a few moments Callum held his breath. With a great effort, Joash spoke again. "There was a sudden sharp pain in my head. The next moment, I felt as light as a feather. I was floating higher and higher while my body lay on the top of the staircase. There was no pain, just a feeling of lightness and an awareness of rising. And then, I saw a bright, soft white light. It was far away, and I could feel a sense of longing for it. It was still and tranquil. But it did not last. Something crossed the space between me and the white light—a kind of flame. Suddenly, I could feel my body getting heavy and the same sharp pain returned to my head. But I was not at home. I woke up only to find out that my Ma and Papa were gone. A kind man told me that they had found me dead. But at some point, when they were transporting me, I took a loud sharp breath and came back to life. A miracle, he had said. I know I had died that day, but something intervened and I came back. But what was the point of it? I had no right to be alive if the ones I loved were not. I should have stayed with Ma, and I could have saved her—"

"Where was your sister?" asked Callum.

"She was in a residential yoga school, a few hundred miles

from Jaipur. She was safe."

"You were sent back for her then, don't you think?"

Joash stared at Callum, a look of shock on his face, realising how he had disregarded Krupa's presence in his life.

Realising he might have touched a nerve, Callum swiftly changed the subject. "My dad is a real softy. If I were you, I would wait until the morning." He got up and walked to the window. "On a clear day, you can see the NARD building from here, you know. If Dad does not come by morning, we will go there again and beg him."

***

Joash fell asleep after midnight but soon woke up to a deafening boom as if the sky had cracked open. At the same instant, a faint quiver ran from the bed to his body. He jumped out of bed and darted towards the window to look outside. The wind and the rain were slapping the glass ferociously, nothing else was visible.

Callum came running into his room. "Did you hear that?"

"Yes! Is your dad home?" Joash knew what had just happened; a sense of urgency was starting to grip him. Another storm, another call for him to act. He had to go.

"No, he's not."

"I need to see him, Callum. I will need to use that car," said

Joash as he flung his backpack onto his shoulder.

"Of course." Callum paused and blinked. "I am coming with you." He had the expression of a stubborn child and Joash had no idea how to deal with him.

Soon they stepped out of the car in the NARD building. Strident sirens and the stir of commotion filled the place.

"You shouldn't be here, Callum," said Adam Bailey who looked panic-stricken.

The office lights started blinking, the wall behind went blank and Adam started to tap his wrist frantically. The whole place reverberated with his voice as he spoke. "All human operators down to the basement shelter right now. All mechanical operators straight to your resting stations."

Callum was watching the screen with his eyes wide open, a message appeared: *Systems going into emergency mode.* A bright yellow robot rolled into the room at super-fast speed and part of a wall opened up to reveal a cabinet where the robot quickly positioned itself. It looked at Adam Bailey and nodded and the door closed again.

"We have five minutes before the place goes dark. We need to be in the basement. Quick now, let's go," said Adam.

Callum turned towards the corner of the room where the lift was.

"No, the steps!" Adam shook his head with exasperation.

"Of course, Dad."

The three men emerged out of Adam's office into the grand hall with all the displays. They were the last ones on the top floor. People in white lab coats were running down the steps.

Joash's eyes found the case with the kropter in. Standing still, he stared at it. His gaze grew deeper, and he found himself in a sort of trance. It was only a fraction of a moment, but he could feel something connecting him to the machine—he could see the minutest cracks appearing in the glass case. A hand on his shoulder broke the trance.

"We need to go to the basement," said Callum.

And then, it happened. Like a precise blow of an axe a bolt of lightning streaked down through the roof, shattering it, then travelled down through the central space wrapped by the staircase and cracked the floor open. With a blast, the engine on the floor went up in flames. Everyone was pushed back towards the wall as the intense wind from outside found its way inside along with the big pieces of debris from the roof. The screams and cries of people ebbed by the din of destruction.

Callum ran after his father, while all Joash could see was the kropter. He walked around the debris towards it.

With its casing shattered, it stood there in the open—ten

feet high, multiple wings on each side—a large insect waiting to start fluttering. Suddenly, the lights went out and all was dark except for the light from Joash's wrist-pad. He was sitting inside the kropter, working its controls, giving all possible commands. He tried to think of the video Callum had shown him. He tapped the control screen again and again, clenching his teeth, expecting some magic to light it up. The wind howled in his ears as if mocking him. With a nervous surge of restlessness, he jumped out of the cockpit and stepped on one of the wings. Walking over the front part of the aircraft, which was a sharp cone, he stood at its very end and looked around for clues to start it. Just then, the kropter lights came on and Joash felt it lift from the floor. He looked back—Callum was at the controls, waving him to come back in.

Within minutes the kropter had flown out of the gaping hole in the roof.

Chapter 12

Glasgow

Joash's heart was racing as the gravity of what he had done started to sink in, but there was no looking back now.

"Are you okay?" asked Callum.

"Yes." Joash was still looking ahead at the fluff of clouds in the dark sky. "Why did you do this? Why did you help me?"

"Um … let me think. My dad got busy dealing with the commotion. I came back to check on you and hey, I figured out your cool plan. Anyway, the point is that I think I know what you might be up to. I cannot miss the chance of such a great adventure. It is so crazy, right? Solve the climate crisis by finding some…" Callum fumbled for words and then said, "I bet you're wishing I had never heard your conversation with your sister."

"This is dangerous, Callum. You just saw what lightning can do. And we have just broken the law."

"Relax, Joash. No law has been broken. Technically, everything in that building belongs to me as much as it belongs to my father. I have a flying licence and I decided to take the kropter for a test flight. I only needed to work out the password to start this. And I can take you straight to the mega-charging hub. Get you ready for the long journey. Now will you let me come please?" Callum was folding his hands facing Joash. "Or I will never tell you the password."

Joash shook his head, "Not till you and your dad have understood what you are getting into."

"Yes!" Callum punched the air.

***

The kropter shuddered through the thick clouds, whipping wind and rain. After a brief rocky ride, suddenly everything became calm. Callum drifted into sleep. Twenty minutes had passed when Joash woke up with a start to find that the kropter's navigation system was beeping and a voice said, "Attention, rough weather. Additional manual steering is advised. Time to destination—five minutes."

The beep turned into a loud siren as the kropter swayed

and Callum opened his eyes. Joash quickly took control of the aircraft. As they rolled right and left, Callum screamed in delight as if he was on a joyride. Soon it all settled, and balloons emerged from three sides to hold them both as they landed.

"Arrived! The Mushroom, energy station no. 134456."

The Mushroom was a gigantic mushroom-shaped structure; the old BT tower right next to it was completely dwarfed by it and along with it most of the other buildings in the area. The dome of the mushroom, which was like a large mass of wire-mesh, faced skywards and had more than a hundred gates, all of which individually opened to allow different size aircrafts to enter and get charged. However, the most unique thing about it was that every inch of its surface was laden with living plants—creepers, shrubs and their flowers—and countless birds' nests. During the day, this enormous plant-based energy generator was like something out of a wonderland with all shades of green, purple and red, but at night it was a dark breathing giant with numerous white eyes; the white rectangles being the gates. The inside of the cubicle they were in was just as green as the outside.

A voice spoke. "Hello! The aircraft has been identified as a new type, kropter, property of NARD. Access to charge has been blocked."

The next voice came from the kropter screen. "Joash Pundit,

how dare you?" Adam looked furious.

Callum spoke loudly. "I did it, Dad, not him."

"Do you think this is funny, Callum? You could have died. What were you thinking?"

"Of getting noticed by you?" Callum replied meekly.

"What!" Adam threw his hands up.

"No, really Dad. I might not be as good as you, but I can do stuff… I can make incredible things." Callum paused and twisted his lips. "I am sorry for all this. But I think Mom would have understood me—she would have understood Joash."

Just then, there was a flutter. A bird came and perched on the edge of a seat handle. Dumbfounded, Adam stared at it, the grey and orange creature moved its head this way and that.

The black mark on it was unmissable as Joash looked at it in amazement. Before they knew, the robin flew back out.

"Joash, you knew something about the lightning, didn't you?" Adam's voice was barely a whisper now. "How did you know?"

Joash remained silent; a frown of deep thought sat on his forehead.

Adam's face was grim. "Two of my engineers have died on the floor."

Joash and Callum looked at each other.

"I have no explanation for what I said, Adam," said Joash.

"I remember everything you had told me, young man, and I don't understand a thing. I have more important things to deal with than this robbery. Take it if you must but I don't think you know Callum. His thirst for adventure is dangerous. He must not go anywhere with you."

With that, the screen went blank. A voice resounded again in the chamber, "Charging in progress. Please complete the checks for international travel. Your travel overseas in an individual aircraft is your responsibility. In case of emergency, assistance will be provided based on the result of the 'balance of resources and risks equation', the details of which can be found on the authority website."

The gate opened and rain splashed their faces once again.

"Didn't I say he is a softy?" said Callum as they took their seats. He smiled, looking victorious.

Joash narrowed his eyes trying to gauge Callum. "You are not coming with me, right?"

"Who me? To the Himalayas? Oh no. You just heard my dad. My professor should be back in action soon. I will be busy with work. In fact, I had no idea how tall those mountains were. It must be hard to breathe in those areas. Your sister … sister, right? She must be so brave; I hope she's okay…" Callum was in no mood to stop talking as the kropter ejected out of the Mushroom.

Chapter 13

Moksha Parvat, Himalayas

Krupa was making her way upwards on the slopes right next to the ashram. This place was at an altitude greater than Jispa with breathtakingly beautiful views. The ashram building here was barely a hut, situated on flat ground with rocky slopes going up to the west and down towards the east. Surprisingly, snow was not a big problem here, just a thin layer, already melting away in places. Towards the east, the side of the mountain gradually sloped down to another vast flat area, where some of the villagers who had chosen to stay with Swamiji were camping. Nature had been a bit forgiving towards them here. Some of them had even started their attempts at planting the small plants and seeds they had brought with them. Others were busy making more solid homes in case the weather got worse.

Today was a particularly calm morning with songs of bulbuls and cuckoos adding heartening notes to the air. Krupa was doing her best to climb but the slope was getting steeper. Her boots started to slip on the scree when someone shouted from behind, "What are you doing, Krupa? Where are you going?"

She knew that annoying voice. Breathless, she did not look back or answer. Bheema was catching up with her. *Not you again!* she thought.

A stout young man, Bheema was one of the villagers who stayed with Swamiji quite a lot. Although he had moved to Jispa only a few years ago, he had quickly earned people's favour by being overly helpful. He frequently used to say, "My only mission in life is to serve Swamiji." Swamiji never reacted to this, but Bheema thought he was one of his favourites. He certainly was not Krupa's favourite. He was a bit too inquisitive about where she was going or what she was doing. His wide toothy smile did not bring out the best emotions in her. Krupa was quite disappointed with herself for not being able to be kind to him, but it was a natural reaction she was struggling to change.

She managed to scamper the last few steps and reached the top. Bheema followed soon after. Catching her breath she asked,

"What is it, Bheema?"

"Nothing! I just saw you going up and thought you might need help."

"Thank you. I am fine, you can carry on with anything else you might have to do," said Krupa and looked away.

"I am free. I heard Swamiji saying some people are coming here soon. We need to prepare the ground."

"That's right, Bheema. I am doing just that. I need to check the area where the plane will land." With that Krupa started walking towards a wooded area.

Just behind the dense row of elm trees, there was a vast clearing. Two young men were busy levelling the glade with some basic hand tools. As Krupa approached, they stopped and walked up to her.

Suddenly the wind picked up, bringing in some dark clouds. Bheema shouted, "I think we should go back, Krupa."

But Krupa was trying to listen to the two men over the noise of the wind. Her long orange scarf and dark hair were now blowing in all directions.

"It's almost done, Krupa," one of them shouted. "Should be okay on this side but pretty rocky on that side." He pointed to the far side of the glade.

"Thank you very much, Alok and Migel. We don't really

know what type of plane it will be. This is all we can do. Just pray for the best," said Krupa holding her hair back.

"Who is coming, Krupa? Will they be arriving by plane?" enquired Bheema.

"There is no other way to reach this place now, Bheema. As you might know, all roads are either blocked or damaged. And it will be better if you ask Swamiji who they are because I don't really know."

Bheema smiled in response to Krupa's answers. To her his expression was plainly fake—how could one not react to constant rejection?

"What time is it expected, Krupa?" asked Migel.

"Anytime now. We can camp near the trees and wait."

The sun turned into a slither of orange behind the clouds and the air grew bitterly cold. Krupa, Migel and Alok lit up a small fire outside the camp they had set, while Bheema ambled, aimlessly kicking pebbles.

Soon Meera arrived with a box and a smile of accomplishment at making it up the slope. "I've got something for you hard-working people to eat," she said sitting down next to the fire. "Swamiji is sitting out today. He has asked everyone to get their musical instruments."

"Oh, I think I must go then," Bheema said suddenly and

quickly made his way back towards the ashram.

Meera and Alok suppressed their giggles while Migel said, "Does he even like music?"

Krupa shook her head. With her head fully wrapped in her scarf and hands spread out to catch the warmth of the fire she looked towards the horizon. In the company of these teenagers, she felt like a leader. However, with Swamiji she was no more than a child, and with Joash … she did not know. The book—she wondered if Joash was going to do this. Maybe it was for her to get it. What point is there in relying on anyone else to do something that must be done?

As the four of them laughed and giggled around the flames that seemed to be pulled in different directions by the cold wind, a dark grey and blue blanket seemed to be stretching across the sky.

"I wonder where these people are?" said Krupa seriously.

"Do you know them?" asked Meera.

"No, but they are coming for some important work related to the weather."

"Do you hear that?" said Meera.

They all looked up towards the west and a strange-looking aircraft appeared in the sky.

"Look!" shouted Meera.

It was blue-grey in colour, difficult to make out against

the sky, but part of one wing was broken and hanging down, hitting loudly against the side of the aircraft and inadvertently announcing its approach.

Krupa stood on the spot with her arms spread out, indicating to the others to stay back behind her. They looked on, trying to gauge whether the unsteady aircraft was going to land or crash.

Within a minute the aircraft jittered to the ground but did not stop. As the four of them watched in horror, it skidded towards the edge of the mountain, sending mud and pebbles flying, finally stopping only a few feet short of the cliff edge.

Krupa gasped and ran towards the aircraft.

Patiently they waited as a wide tongue-like extension appeared from the side of the aircraft and uncurled to touch the ground. With a click, steps appeared on it and the door at its other end opened. A tall woman appeared at the door.

Inspecting her surroundings she said, "Good evening! My friend is a little stuck inside, we have had quite a ride. Would you mind helping the captain to get him on his feet?"

"Of course, they would not." The four youngsters turned and found Swamiji standing right behind them.

While Alok and Migel rushed inside the aircraft, Swamiji walked closer to an astounded Krupa and Meera, "Did you not trust my old legs to climb up here?" he laughed softly.

"I am Stella Rollings." The professor bowed slightly in front of Swamiji. "Great to see you in person. Um …what do they call you here?"

"Swamiji," said Krupa.

The professor's eyes met Krupa's and she smiled warmly.

"Welcome Stella." Swamiji turned to face the girls. "Meera and Krupa, meet Professor Stella Rollings. She is the chief scientific advisor in the UK and a well-known physicist."

Professor Rollings beamed. "And keen to learn the ways of Sheersha yoga."

As Krupa looked towards the aircraft, another figure appeared at the door. He was in a uniform and had a vibrancy about him. His jet-black eyes shone with the light of youth and intelligence. When Meera nudged her, Krupa realised she had been staring.

"That is Captain Durgesh," said Professor Rollings.

Swamiji nodded and looked at the professor enquiringly.

"Ah yes, we don't need human captains, but our authority manager insisted that he came along. I guess he did not trust me with his latest stealth aircraft." The professor laughed again. "He is of Indian heritage and proved invaluable in rough skies. Ah…" She stopped and waved as another older man climbed down the steps waving his hands. "And that is my fellow scientist and dear friend, Patrick Zuma. He is a lovely man."

"Any others?" asked Swamiji as the professor turned to face him again.

"For now, it is just the two of us and Captain Durgesh," the professor replied.

The group assembled together and Swamiji said, "Welcome to Moksha Parvat."

***

The night was mild, and the bonfire seemed mellow as Professor Rollings settled herself on a large log of wood next to Swamiji. Most of the villagers had gone to their tents and Patrick Zuma was slowly hobbling towards them from his tent. The professor crossed one of her legs over the other, her long fingers rhythmically tapping the wood and her gaze obliquely fixed on the gracefully dancing flames.

"You look thoughtful, Stella." Swamiji's eyes twinkled in the glow of the fire.

"Oh, excuse me. I have not spent much time outdoors of late, but this is wonderful indeed."

"You have a lot on your mind."

"Hmm…" nodded the professor quietly. Her train of thought halted when Patrick Zuma joined the two. She looked at Swamiji and said, "Do you know we have a robot member of the authority cabinet?"

Patrick scoffed at the mention of the robot and shook his head.

"He has a personality, a shrewd one and he is developing rather fast picking up on the emotions of those around him. I say it is a recipe for disaster," said the professor.

"That is true," started Patrick. "The authority manager had no problem granting permission for this trip, but the robot created a scene in a cabinet meeting calling it a waste of resources."

Swamiji looked amused. He said in his slow voice, "But you managed to get here okay."

"The head of our country is a good man," said the professor. "He manages to find his way around algorithms, but there are many who are more than willing to let science take over fully and let robots run the country."

"That is not the only thing on your mind," said Swamiji.

"Yes. There are a few other things," continued the professor. "When I spoke to you about the discovery of this new element in our atmosphere, you know Elusium, you said something about your chemistry lessons and how you thought this was a step in the right direction. I wondered, what does a yogi know about the periodic table? But then I took some hints from that communication and carried on. I can now confirm that Elusium is randomly reacting with oxygen and causing the extreme lightning events. Of course, there are other factors like water vapour and air pressure, but how ... how did you know?"

Swamiji gazed stoically at the professor with his head moving slowly. "It was you who discovered it. I merely shared my thoughts."

Professor Rollings looked at Patrick with her eyebrows raised and then shook her head. "Okay, there is more to it. I think the concentration of Elusium is more in areas that were historically more polluted. This research is still ongoing. Do you have any thoughts on that?"

"I think you are right," replied Swamiji. "My science knowledge is very basic."

"And yet you were happy for us to come and study the composition of air in this place. And you reckon it is a very important step." The professor was puzzled.

"That knowledge is from *Dhi*."

She knew what that meant but did not understand it. She could not deny that the discoveries of the last few days had kindled a desire in her heart to understand *Dhi*.

"Tell me more about Elusium. Is there anything that you haven't discussed at the cabinet meeting?" Patrick looked at the professor, goggling at her with a child-like eagerness.

She spoke again. "I have received reports from different sources of some underground activity. They claim it is a creature causing very localised disturbances rather than the tectonic plates and that is leading to earthquakes, even in areas not prone to them."

Patrick looked at the professor. "I don't understand."

"Neither do I." She shifted forward and looked at Swamiji.

"If this is a creature, I do not yet know anything about it," said Swamiji.

The professor sat back, pondering in silence once again. Finding answers and solving problems fuelled her brain but this time the stakes were high and the path she had chosen was unconventional.

"If we forget about the underground puzzle for now, I reckon the most important question then would be whether anything can neutralise Elusium." A sense of urgency was clear in Patrick's voice.

"Swami, if you believe that the base is going to be unaffected by the extreme weather events, it is quite possible that there is no Elusium here and if we can create similar conditions all over the planet, we might just solve this crisis."

The professor's eyes followed Krupa who had just joined a group of young people sitting by the fire. "Are all these people from your monastery?"

"Some are. Some are regular villagers and others have come from far and wide." Swamiji was observing the professor, but it was like trying to look through a thick curtain. He wondered what her real karma was.

"You have just arrived, Stella. Keep an open mind and give nature a chance. You might find the answers in the most unexpected ways."

Chapter 14

London

Lassitude had not touched Joash yet. He had been busy all morning. He had met and reassured Aunt Sue, looked up information on Saqqara, and spoken to his contact, Hamza, in Cairo.

As he hurriedly threw things in his backpack, he recapped all that Hamza had told him. There was an abandoned excavation site near the Djoser pyramid, hailed to be an extensive underground city by archaeologists, but no real excavation had been done because of several unexplained deaths and the area was rumoured to be infested with grave robbers. Hamza was ready to meet and help Joash, but he did not like the idea of going anywhere near this place.

"I was thinking about your riddles. You know two brains will be better than one. You might need my help," said Callum who was standing at the door of Joash's bedroom.

"I can always call you," said Joash.

"This is such an important quest. You cannot rely on technology like networks. I should be there to help you when you need it."

Joash stopped and turned around. "So, your dad does know you well. Don't you remember what he said? And why would you want to risk your life when you don't have to?"

"Because I know it will be fine. I just know it." Callum leaned on the door frame with his hands in his pockets and looked up. "Even when I was falling down with my flycycle the other day I knew someone would come and help me."

Joash gave him a sideways glance.

"What?" said Callum pulling his shoulders up. "I mean it! Besides, it might be my best chance of real-life adventure."

"Look you can stay in this apartment as long as you like, but coming with me? Sorry, Callum! There is absolutely no chance," Joash said firmly. Turning his back towards his friend, he brought up the air-screen.

The aeronautical chart of Cairo was up in front of Joash while next to it was a detailed map of Saqqara.

"What is that for?" enquired Callum looking curiously over Joash's shoulder.

"My first stop," he answered as he kept looking for points on one map and then relating it to the other.

"Oh, I get it."

"I must leave now while things look settled outside." Joash patted Callum's shoulder and said, "Thank you for everything."

Callum pursed his lips and stared at the floor looking glum. Then, as if he had suddenly remembered something important, he spoke hurriedly, "Okay mate! Good luck with your journey!" He quickly turned and walked off trying to avoid eye contact.

Joash's heart sank a little with the realization that he might never see Callum again, he might never reach his destination, he might never come back to this city again.

***

When Joash reached the roof parking, the sombreness of the day had not changed but the weather seemed kinder. The clocks struck twelve as he rose above the concrete jungle in the black-and-orange flying machine and zoomed east.

"Three hours to Saqqara and five and half hours to Jispa if you don't stop, not taking into account any unfavourable weather conditions," the kropter said in a deep manly voice.

Joash sat up straight, moved his head towards one shoulder

and then the other. This was his time to contemplate. He was going back, back to where his life had started. The more he thought about it, the more his belief in the relevance of the book grew. *But how will it ease the burden of my past karma? Can I defy lightning, tide over storms, and call upon the Dhi?* Joash did not know, but he did know that he had not nurtured what he had learned. In fact, he had callously tried to forget it all—the thought pierced his soul like a sharp knife. His eyes were fixed on the endless dark clouds that the kropter penetrated as his mind began to dive into the memories of brighter days, hoping to find what he had lost.

***

Guruji was sitting under the tree with eyes closed. Nine-year-old Joash came running and stood in front of him, breathing heavily and waiting patiently for his teacher to open his eyes. As Joash's breath settled, Guruji opened his eyes, "Ah Joash!" he said with a big smile. "I was waiting for you. So?"

Joash sat down on the ground. "Today's question is—what are extraordinary powers, Guruji?"

Guruji raised an eyebrow and asked, "Is this to do with some of your superheroes?"

Joash giggled. "No, Guruji, I heard Papa talk about a yogi who can walk on water. Is it real? Is it possible?"

"Yes, it is possible. Anything is possible."

"Can I get such powers?"

Guruji laughed lightly. "Don't aim for power, my child. Aim for wisdom and powers will follow. Concentration, absorption and integration—in other words, deep meditation until you feel one with everything."

Joash looked a bit confused.

Guruji rose to his feet; strength and power were the two horses he commanded, and wisdom was the chariot he rode. He walked to the rose bush nearby and Joash followed him.

"Look at this rose, or even this thorn. By focusing with perfect discipline on a rose, one can get the qualities of a rose; by focusing with perfect discipline on a thorn, one can be like a thorn. By mastering the flow of energy in the body one can walk on water, one can move a mountain." Guruji now looked directly at Joash again and smiled with a glint of playfulness in his eyes. "There is a lot that you too can do but it's a journey and everything will come to you when you are ready. Remember I told you about rebirth?"

Joash nodded.

"We are all on our own journeys." Guruji put his arm around Joash as they walked on the grass.

"But you also said karma is important. Can I meditate and

do my karma too?" asked Joash.

"When you do your karma with concentration without worrying about the end result, it is nothing but meditation."

"What is my karma right now, Guruji?"

"The sacred soil!"

***

Joash's eyes widened as he heard the last three words aloud in his ears; that was not from his memory.

The next moment, sirens started to blare and the kropter started to judder.

"Emergency landing advised—bad weather ahead. Clear field approaching in two minutes—Saqqara will be three miles on foot due east. Are you ready to land, Joash Pundit?"

"Yes!" said Joash loudly as he braced himself, gripping the armrest and stiffening his body.

The kropter swayed in different directions and a bitter nausea started in Joash's gut as dust and wind bashed the aircraft. The balloons were out again to cushion him as they landed with a thud. Quickly he removed his belt, grabbed his backpack, and jumped out of the side door.

As soon as his feet touched the ground, Joash threw up. Every bit of his exposed skin smarted with lashings of sand. He could barely keep to his feet on the ground when another violent whip of the wind threw him back towards the kropter. He held on to the kropter for a few minutes until the dust storm started to settle, and then he began his trek towards his destination.

**

The afternoon sun was hazy, still, the heat was sweltering beyond imagination. The sky was not red like he remembered it from his last visit, but still had a tinge of strange colours. There was a sea of sand with rippled, rolling dunes in every direction that Joash could see. He trudged on, falling and getting up, getting a battering from every direction. For a moment he wondered if he was heading in the right direction. Soon his doubts were cleared when he saw the shape of a man standing on top of a mound that was higher than the dunes of sand.

The man disappeared behind the mound. Within minutes a small truck with large tyres, that seemed to be made specially to trundle on sand came and parked in front of him. The window of the truck rolled down to reveal a big sinewy man in the front seat. He had beady eyes and a peculiarly pointy nose with a heavy-set jawline.

"Still in one piece?" said the man in his squeaky voice and laughed. It felt like the voice did not belong to him.

"Yes, Hamza, still in one piece. Glad to see you." And so, he really was as he climbed inside the truck. "This is a beast," he said.

"Yes, it is. Very sturdy in sandstorms unlike my last one." Hamza had a thick Arabic accent and kind mannerisms, quite opposite to his looks, Joash always thought.

"So, tell me what kind of storm are you investigating underground," continued Hamza.

"It is difficult to explain but I need to look for something in the underground city."

Hamza glanced seriously towards Joash. "I don't think you took me seriously. It is a dangerous place."

"Is there any other underground city in this area? I don't mean single pyramids—"

"No, this is the only place. The authority here has tried to suppress all news about this place."

"Could you just drop me somewhere close? I think I will manage… I am sure I will be fine."

Hamza shook his head. "Do you have any weapons?"

"No." The question did not surprise Joash. This was not going to be easy; he had a feeling the real test had started.

"Look Joash, if I was you, I wouldn't go there. But of course, you are you and that is what you do—you jump into danger. But this is different. In fact, I don't have any proper information about this place. I can tell you that there is nothing for miles around the entrance to the site. I have heard that technology is of no use there, but I could be wrong. Keep this knife and take this lighter in case your wrist-light does not work. Sorry, I could not find a gun." Hamza passed a small cloth bag to Joash. "I feel horrible to leave you but…"

"It's fine," said Joash. "Don't worry."

The truck came to a halt and the two men looked to their right.

"That is the rubble of Djoser," Hamza had a sadness in his voice as he gazed towards the heap of debris that once was the step pyramid. "Keep going west behind this, you will see it at some point."

Joash thanked Hamza and got out of the truck. Tightening the straps of his backpack he said, "Can I call you when I am done?"

Hamza nodded without a word and left.

***

After a long trek, Joash was standing at the top edge of a deep hollow, certainly dug up by people. He slid down along the slope and found himself standing a hundred feet away from a sheer sandy cliff face. As he walked closer, he could see there was an entrance at its base. Several tools were scattered about the place, hammers, chisels and the like. At the centre of the entrance, two rail tracks appeared to emerge side by side from the depths of a dark tunnel. Two wagons—large wooden platforms on four metal wheels—were lined up on the tracks just outside. But there was no sign of any people until Joash heard something.

He quickly turned around. A thin figure of a man stood at the same spot where he had stood a few minutes ago. The person started to run down the sandy slope. Joash's hands went to grip the knife he now had along his waist.

His stomach churned with horror when he realised who the person was.

Chapter 15

Saqqara

Callum ran towards Joash and hugged him. "Thank god, Joash!" He leaned closer and said, "By the way, your friend was very kind to drop me close to this place and give me directions."

Shocked and outraged, Joash could not say a word.

Callum gulped and looked at his friend, waiting for a response.

The sky started to fill with the strangest colours—purple and red streaks in a quickly greying sky. In the desert, the shine of the unending waves of golden brown began to be dulled by the outlandish sky. A dry heat was building up that would burn the skin in minutes. Joash knew they could not stay outside for long—a sandstorm was coming.

Callum looked at the sky in wonder and then towards the entrance at the bottom of the cliff face. "What's your plan?" he said.

Joash pursed his lips in annoyance and walked away to the wagon with the rope he had just picked up from the ground.

"Please speak to me," shouted Callum following Joash. "I am sorry, okay? But I am here now, so talk to me," he pleaded. "Please—"

"What do you expect me to say—welcome?" Joash did not try to hide his frustration. "I do pity your dad. You don't know a thing about what I am doing, and you have followed me here. I don't know if I am going to survive this, what am I supposed to do with you?"

Callum blinked looking thoughtful and then replied, "Let us go in order. I don't expect you to say welcome. This isn't exactly a welcoming kind of place." He smiled with tight closed lips and then continued, "Please do not pity my dad. He is used to it. He knows whenever I disappear eventually, I do go back to him. Thirdly, I do know a thing or two about what you are up to and now that I am in it with you, I would love to know more. By the way, I did not follow you, I was sleeping comfortably in the back compartment of the kropter, which I suppose you do not know exists." Callum pointed a finger towards Joash. "That landing was catastrophic, knocked me out for God knows how long. And lastly, don't despair. You will survive this because you have me, the adventure mastermind. I can be pretty useful you know."

By the time he had finished speaking, Joash had made a small pile of tools on the wagon. He let out a loud sigh and turned to face Callum. "Look, do you see this track sloping down? I am going down there. As soon as I find the signs of an underground city, I am going to collect some mud and come back up. I don't know what's down there but staying out in the open is almost certain death." Joash looked around and said seriously, "I see all the signs of a dangerous sandstorm."

"Wait, wait, wait," said Callum. "Let me show you something."

He tapped his wrist-pad a few times to bring up his screen, but nothing happened. Puzzled he looked at Joash. "Is yours working?"

Joash tapped his wrist-pad and again there was no response. "Possibly the weather," he said.

"Right, when I was looking for you, I surveyed the area. I could see parts of this tunnel and maybe the tops of some underground structures. This is east, towards the west there was something closer to the surface, possibly another path. They must have done a lot of digging—"

"Okay Callum, thank you for your research. Now you either get on this wagon or find your way back to the kropter," said an irritated Joash.

Presently, Joash removed the large boulder that was holding the wheel of the wagon and jumped up to the platform to join

Callum as the wagon started to roll down. The wind started to pick up as they disappeared into the mouth of the tunnel. It was a wide space, progressively getting darker. Joash put on the torch from the packet that Hamza had given. The roof of the tunnel had been reinforced with metal rods and wire mesh. Ropes were running along the roof and the sides of the tunnel. The track went like a serpent, winding and descending slowly towards the depths of the earth, towards an unknown gloom.

Suddenly, the track dipped sharply. Callum yelled with excitement. Soon after, came a wide flat area, and the wagon came to a halt. The track however continued to run as it turned and disappeared behind the tunnel wall to the right.

Joash and Callum got out of their vehicle, examining their surroundings. The tunnel roof was lower here. The air had a stagnant feel to it, the cone of their light revealed thick dust floating in it. Joash felt stifled and his vision started to go hazy. Callum coughed loudly behind him.

"I am okay, I am okay," he said quickly as Joash turned back to look at him.

Handing over the small torch to Callum, Joash bent down to pick up something from the ground. Soon a flame torch was alight, and they could see much better around them.

The place was much wider than Joash had perceived. Some

ten to twelve feet away from them was a tall pile of rocks and boulders blocking a door, just the top of which was visible. The tunnel wall around the door seemed to be stony. Behind the wall on their right, the wagon track was ascending. Ropes and pulleys, all sorts of contraptions were there to pull wagons up manually. It did seem like technology had been jilted here.

"I will move the boulders and open that door. You don't have to come inside with me," said Joash.

"I am fine. It's cool, I can come." Callum was undeterred now.

Joash shook his head. Planting his flaming torch in the wall, he began to move the boulders aside. The job was harder than it looked. Hammer, chisel, spade and bare hands—he tried everything he could to move or break the stones. Callum was efficiently moving any debris out of the way.

"Aren't you glad I am here to help?" said Callum.

Just as Joash moved a large boulder at the base, the top pile of stones rolled down. He stood staring at the door—it was made of stone, the inscriptions and drawings were all scratched, but there was a hole in the middle part going to the other side. He moved closer and placed his right eye against it. It was a peculiar feeling, like looking at a starless, moonless sky with a telescope. And he remembered the moment he had felt like this last.

***

"What can you see?" asked Guruji and placed his hand on young Joash's shoulder.

He moved away from the telescope, disappointed. "Nothing, Guruji."

"That is because you are using only your eyes. What do you expect to see?"

"Stars, planets. Aliens."

Guruji laughed heartily, "You are right, my son. But remember, there are many more things around us that we cannot see, than those that we can see. The universe is full of wonders beyond our imagination. Respect all creation and don't just try to see—feel, listen, imagine."

***

A tap on his back jolted Joash out of his memory.

"What can you see?" asked Callum.

"Nothing," Joash replied, "but I can feel there is a lot to see behind this door."

"Ooh, spooky."

With that, they were back at their job. Soon, the door was clear. Joash pushed it slightly and to his surprise, it moved with ease. A new smell entered the area and with it came a sinking feeling. For a fleeting second, he had a strong desire to run away. Looking back, he saw a tinge of fear in Callum's eyes for the first time.

Chapter 16

Saqqara

The door opened fully. There was a faint noise, like something was running towards them. Holding the flaming torch aloft, Joash and Callum waited with bated breath for something wild to leap from the dark. With a piercing cry, a man came into their vision. Reflexively, they jumped aside as the man bolted towards the door, past them, and along the wagon track in the tunnel. He looked dishevelled, with long knotted hair standing up, tattered clothes, dusty skin, and hands waving frantically in the air. Their eyes followed the man; he did not stop, did not turn back as he disappeared in the tunnel.

"Huh?" Callum broke the silence, "What was he doing in there?"

"Looks like this door wasn't blocked that long ago. People must have left in a hurry, and he got locked in."

Joash tore his eyes off from the far end of the tunnel and looked towards the darkness in front of him. A part of him wanted to go after the man and see if he was okay, so he turned around again. "He will need food and water. Let's go find him," he said.

Just around the next bend in the path Joash and Callum found the man cowering against the wall. He was shaking, his face buried between his knees.

"Hello," said Joash slowly as Callum went closer with a bottle of water. "Are you okay?"

The man looked up and accepted the water with trembling hands. He murmured something in Arabic, which was lost on them.

"English? Little English?" said Callum. "Devices not working to translate." He pointed towards his wrist-pad and made a gesture with his hand.

"How many days were you there?" Joash asked, hoping for some helpful information.

The man simply shook his head, he had no idea, but Joash's guess was at least a few days.

"No go, no go," said the man suddenly looking terrified. "Woo, woo, shh, shh." He made some noises and moved around indicating what he had heard inside.

"But he is alive all right. Guess just unlucky to get trapped in there," said Callum.

"And lucky that we found him," Joash replied seriously. "Stay here. There's a storm outside." He tried to explain himself with actions as best as he could.

They left some energy food and drink tubes next to the man and headed back towards their predicament.

***

Joash slowly moved his light around. It was an empty hall, bare as far as he could see. The walls looked muddy, some glass-like pieces shone here and there. The ceiling was flat, made of big stones, possibly the same as the floor they were walking on. But there was no mud, no soil. All was silent except the faint rustling of the flame.

At the far end, they found themselves standing against another door. The pulsating light revealed several rectangles on the door face, carved one inside the other with the smallest one closer to the ground. Inside the smallest rectangle was the shape of a cat-like creature painted in white and red.

Callum marvelled at how easily the heavy stone door moved with one push.

Beyond the second door was more darkness and a strong stench, like nothing that they could compare with. They stepped on the ramp on the other side of the door. It was a narrow alleyway, and the floor was yet again rough stone. They moved forward slowly and cautiously. The flickering light revealed the neatly lined rows of doors on either side. Each door was flanked by carved pillars with colourful hieroglyphics and cracks that could suck one's soul if one stared long enough. Some doors were closed, some were slightly open—inside was an eerie darkness. Yet, Joash could sense his curiosity peaking.

He looked up, there was no roof, no sky, just deep blackness that could drown anything. The air was still and stale, the darkness seemed to be whispering—this was no place for a creature of flesh and blood. He felt like a robber, a thief, but knew he did not want to be one.

The pillars and doors seemed endless, and the alleyway seemed to stretch to infinity. It was hard to tell how far away they had come from the first door.

Suddenly, two doors on either side of the path flung open and deafening screeches filled the air. As if darkness itself had been stirred, a sudden strong wind gushed and hit Joash, dust rose from the ground to blind him. The flaming torch was thrown away as he struggled to stay on his feet. He felt something push him from side to side. He tried to fight it, moving his hands and legs desperately but all he was doing was kicking in thin air. After a few minutes of struggle, his back hit one of the pillars and he fell to the ground. He looked back towards the path—Callum was trying to get back to his feet; he had been thrown backwards.

A mass of dust particles moved away from him, pulsating slowly as if watching him. Joash was dizzy, breathless, and in immense pain—he looked at his attacker in the dim light, feeling blood and saliva drooled from the corner of his mouth. Breathing heavily, he tried to sit up against the pillar. The screams started to die but were replaced by strange, hushed voices. Joash gestured with his hand for Callum to stay where he was. His eyes were fixed on the dense mass of dust pulsating in front of him, he knew he was being watched. Unsure about what to do, he closed his eyes. His mind started racing, and he thought of the vision: 'Respect all creation...'

Just then his attacker screamed again. Joash watched it fly towards him and put his head between his knees, holding the back of his head with his hands waiting to be hit again. But it did not happen. He looked up, the mass of dust had stopped just a few inches away from him. He could make out two angry faces in that mass, no clear features but strong expressions. Another draught of air came from the deep end of the alleyway and the torch flame which was still on the floor got fuller and brighter. An almost human shape came floating by. It was a translucent brown, almost like shimmering sand, with black slits for its eyes and mouth. It looked like it had a long flowing brown gown on. The mass of dust separated into two shapes as the third one approached, but these two were much darker.

The third one which now had a slight glow, spoke in English. "Who are you, human?"

Joash's eyes widened in surprise.

"Thieves, they are all thieves," screamed the other two in unison. "No one should go back alive from here."

Joash gathered up his courage and spoke loudly. "I am no thief."

"We know," spoke the third one coldly. "This is our home, and we don't like intruders. Anyone trying to take anything from here will be punished."

"What are you?" asked Joash.

"We do not have to answer any of your questions. Just leave."

"I cannot leave without the sacred soil," came Joash's resolute reply.

The brown shape was still while the other two seemed to be looking at him.

"I know the light that follows you, tell me the name of your teacher," said the brown shape after a long moment of pondering.

"Swami Yogeshwarananda!"

If sand could change expressions, it certainly would look like the shimmering being, going from harsh to mellow. "So, you have come, Dhanay. I am Rayth. You know me but do not remember me. You wouldn't, in this human form." A sense of disdain was detectable in Rayth's words.

And that was true, for Joash could not recall meeting a being made of sand ever. With great curiosity and alertness, he watched Rayth as the being uttered its next words.

"Welcome to the unseen realm," said Rayth as he swished past Joash then Callum, and finally acquired a position higher up and equidistant from both. "Your companion here, hm… I wonder what karma brings him with you."

Callum was looking at the spectacle with a sense of awe mixed with fear.

It was clear that Rayth liked a bit of theatre and was enjoying this moment. "There is much more at play here than you understand right now, Dhanay. You carry a burden of karma not just one but at least two previous lives. Who can rise up to deal with so much in one life form, that too, in human form? None other than, the great Dhanay." There was a pause, and then he said, "Now I must answer your first question. But listen you must every word that I say, for I will not repeat it. What are we? We are the beings of Maathi, we dwell in the dark, close to what you call the sacred soil. We come from a distant world. You once ruled the realm of light in our world."

"Wow, did you?" whispered Callum, looking at Joash.

"I just want some sacred soil then I will leave," said Joash.

"I know what you seek. It was your teacher who asked me to guide you when you arrive. It is not going to be easy." Rayth's tone turned sombre and sullen. "The part of this underground city where you need to go is taken by Jhenats, dark beings of the dust of this world. Once a few shapeshifters, they have now multiplied in numbers. What once were quiet beings, now are fiendish and threaten our peace. We believe they are drawing on a dark power."

"I don't understand. Is it possible for me to go there?" said Joash.

"You are the one who can do it, oh Dhanay. Your teacher could see this day will come and you will need direction. Whether you remember it or not, you took it upon yourself to defeat the dark force. If you keep your promise, balance can be restored. Take the sacred soil, the purest earth, untouched from the time this world came into being, and thwart the dark power. In doing so, you will weaken the Jhenats, in doing so, you will help us keep our home."

After watching Joash ponder in silence, Rayth spoke again. "Questions you will have many. But this is all I have for you, and I hope you succeed."

Then, there was a sudden draught of wind and a loud creaking of old doors. They looked around, the other doors were slightly open now, it felt like a thousand eyes were watching them.

But Joash was undeterred. *Guruji knew this day would come*, he thought and said unfalteringly, "Help me then! Show me my path. Tell me how I can do what I must."

Rayth was quiet. He had no eyes, but the black hollow slits were clearly focused on the burning flame now held by Callum. At last, he said, "The higher soul that guides you knows, I am obliged to help you. You must cross the city. The others here and I will let you go but your real test will be at the other end of this city, at the bridge. Jhenats are dreadful beings; some you can reason with but most you cannot. Do not look at them directly and if cornered, draw a circle around yourself. The sacred soil will protect you."

Joash's dark eyebrows curled up in a frown as he tried to comprehend all that was just said. Unable to do so, his gaze went from the ground back to the shimmering grains in front of him. And then he realised, all he felt was a sense of familiar friendliness oozing from this strange being.

"I would do anything! Anything that is right and within my ability, but I do not know what you mean when you call me Dhanay," he said.

Suddenly Rayth rose even higher in the air. And then came the words that echoed and flowed with a cool wind like leaves in the autumn breeze, rough and solid, fragile and sharp:

"Do not fret,

For what you do not know yet.

For when you need the knowledge will come,

For the path you take has been trodden by none,

Your enemy may look like many but is just one,

One moment at a time, one hurdle at a time,

Carry on, step in the dark, for guiding you is a special light."

"Now go!" The floating shape came down again. "Go through this door. Do not touch anything. Keep going till you cross five doors. The sixth one is not a real door; turn right along that wall. There will be a large hall to your left then. Cross the hall and go left on the path. You need to look for the bridge on the right. It won't be easily visible. Once on the bridge you and you alone must take a plunge into the darkness beneath. This will be the darkness that you must trust. If you do this without an ounce of fear, with a clear purpose in your mind, you will emerge with the sacred soil from its depths. It will break the spell of the Jhenats, but I cannot say what will happen after that. If you have any doubt, do not jump. Once on the other side of the bridge, it's a straight path to the staircase of Hummad that leads to the desert outside. Be careful, it is also called 'the fall of the human'. Your trek from the bridge to the staircase might be the toughest part of your trek. Now leave."

Chapter 17

Saqqara

Joash and Callum were following the path opened by Rayth. Deeper and deeper, they journeyed into the long-forgotten city of stone. The door to the alleyway had shut behind them long ago. They crossed large empty spaces and halls full of sparkling treasures.

"How long do you think the distance would be between the two ends of this place that you saw?" asked Joash.

Callum did some calculations in his head, came closer to Joash, and replied in a muted voice, "About half a mile in a straight line, I think."

Just then as Callum remembered something he spoke excitedly again, "Hey Joash, the kropter! The power from the bright sun helped, I guess. It was almost fully charged."

"That's good." Joash looked up and flexed his neck. "There is a lot to do before we find the way back to it."

"Did you know you were going to see all this? Does all this scare you? You are brave anyway."

Joash looked back towards Callum with half a smile. "I am as scared as you are. And it's okay to be scared. It is a bit like chasing storms. I know I can die if I am not careful, but… Bravery is not the absence of fear but a resolve to overcome it. I had learned about other realms as a child—I thought they were just stories. The point is to just carry on…"

"And now here you are." Callum's body shuddered, more with a burst of excitement mixed with a little fear that was creeping into his mind.

Joash's tattered clothes unswathed the sore florid skin of his legs, his muscles and joints ached with every step from the thrashing he had received earlier, and a new nausea was setting in, but he gave no heed to it. He was glad that Callum had only received a few scratches.

Presently, their breathing started to grow deeper and louder. The torch became dim, but they had enough light to see a few feet around them. The stillness was stifling in the all-engulfing blackness beyond their small circle of wan orange. The deep ominous silence was disturbed only by their soft steps and heavy breathing.

They slowed down to avoid touching the jewels scattered in their path. They had been going on for nearly an hour by the time they reached the sixth door. It was decorated with a painting. This one was a rather large door—the red paint depicted a few men around a bridge and a staircase going up to blue skies and sun.

"Look!" said Callum examining the painting. "What is that?"

Close to the bridge, there was a large snake shown in the painting.

Joash leaned forward and with narrowed eyes looked at the creature painted red and black. "Let us just carry on," he said. At the right corner of the room, there was an open archway. "That should be our way."

Joash was the first one to bend and enter the small archway. As he did so, his torch light went off. Slowly, they moved on the slanting, slippery floor.

The floor dipped suddenly and as if on a slide, the two of them glided forward one after the other.

And then, there was a sudden chill in the air.

"It's freezing." Callum was shivering. They switched on the torch to find themselves in front of a high-arched entrance to the next dark space.

"Huh, this place is creepy, or should I say creepier…" Callum scrunched up his face.

Looking around themselves, with careful steps, they moved slowly on the stone floor. Soon they were facing a tall statue of a Pharaoh sitting on a throne. Over ten feet tall, the polished sandstone looked pallid in the dim light. Its clear black eyes stared straight ahead as did the three snakes carved on its head.

Suddenly, they heard a howl, short but sharp. Their hearts beat fast, and the flame they held flickered, piercing the gloom as Joash moved the torch around. Quickly Joash took his chisel out and moved it in a large circle enclosing them and the statue—the scraping of metal on stone sent their ears ringing. And then they waited, sitting together back-to-back in silence. The air in the hall felt heavy with a living presence like it had a pulse of its own.

Then, Joash saw some shadows leap from one side to the other at a distance. They were many, at least five, dark shapes of large cats or panthers slowly moving around them. The black faces with the golden rhomboids for eyes were watching them, measuring them.

Something told Joash that it was okay to speak. "We have taken permission to cross. We did not mean to disturb. Please, let us pass." He was breathing heavily but his words were steady. He just hoped he would be listened to because he knew he could neither fight these beings nor run from them. He could sense Callum's nervous tremble as the dark shadows continued to circle them. After a few minutes, there was a low growl and then, one by one, the shapes disappeared into the dark corner they had come from. The reek disappeared with them.

Joash turned to look at Callum. Without a word, they leapt to their feet.

This time, they ran and soon they were under another archway. As they turned left, there was an alleyway but doors only along the left wall. To the right, there were large equidistant columns. There were decorated arches between the pillars but total darkness beyond.

"Look for a bridge to your right," said Joash.

"Let's slow down a bit. I don't think they are following us," Callum said, almost breathless.

They marched on in total silence. In their exhaustion, the path seemed never-ending. Joash dropped down onto the floor; the dismal gloom had started to weigh on him.

"Have we missed it?" he asked slowly, feeling weak and weary.

"No, we haven't, Joash, and we can't give up!" Callum passed on a food tube to Joash and kneeled down beside him. "We will find the bridge. We need to be on the right edge, maybe even walk out a bit to see what's in the dark."

Joash glanced at Callum through his sweaty eyelashes. Looking at his face, he felt the same relief that he had felt several times before. At last, he was thankful Callum was with him. A tired smile crossed his lips.

Presently, they started again. It was not long before Joash spotted a dirt path running out into the dark. Down that path, came into view a dilapidated mouldering structure going over what seemed to be a deep gorge, just ten feet away from them.

They looked at each other.

"The staircase shouldn't be too far from here," said Joash.

As they stepped on the bridge, a cool draught of air met them, and a loud creak announced their arrival. On the precarious pieces of wood that were thin and cracking, cautiously they stepped forward into the desolation.

Standing in the middle part of the bridge, looking around, they realised there were giant columns along the gorge on either side of the bridge just like the ones they had seen earlier. Underneath them was the same unearthly gloom that ran through this buried city.

"Go to the other end and wait for me," said Joash.

"Are you sure about this?" Callum was never the cautious one but today he had tasted fear.

Joash did not want to leave his friend alone but looking doughty he handed over the burning torch to Callum, held his arms and replied, "There is no other way for me. If I don't join you in a few minutes, just go, as fast and as quietly as you can."

Now alone on the bridge, Joash peered at the bottomless gorge under the bridge. The only light was the pale glow of Callum's torch from the far end of the bridge. He closed his eyes and tried to clear his mind. He thought of everything that had gone by and how he had ended up here. He tried not to think of the consequences of him failing. His legs quivered with an uncertainty he did not want to acknowledge. He thought of Krupa, of Miria, of Guruji and his forgotten lessons.

Bitterly, he thought again—*Guruji could have been here, he could have shown me the way.* Then, as if in response to this thought a memory came to mind. *Just do your karma and detach yourself from anything else in this moment. Darkness is not all evil, it is the unknown yet holding a promise, it is what gives birth to light. Trust this darkness, trust yourself.* The words were spoken years ago on the terrace when Joash used to observe the night sky with Guruji, but today they made sense to him. He held the vial that hung around his neck with one hand and leapt into the unknown below.

He was falling free with his eyes closed. He felt the air rush past him as his body straightened and his head led the way. Soon, the air seemed like it was getting thicker, and he started to fall at a slower pace. He opened his eyes. The darkness had gone; a pale light of luminescent red soil was all around him. He was going down so slowly that he could control his movements and so he gently landed on his feet in a deep narrow valley of fragrant, glowing red soil.

He collected some soil in his glass vial. Closing it, he wondered, how was he going to go back up. He tried to climb along the slopes of the valley, but the soil was so crumbly that he tumbled right back each time. Before long came a whirling mass of sand, moving swiftly towards him. Joash had no way of finding a shelter and so it engulfed him like a hurricane, swirling him around and moving him up and up.

The mass of sand disappeared after laying him along the edge of the gorge. He coughed and spat out all the sand in his mouth. With his head still spinning he was flat on the ground when Callum found him and splashed water on his face. But the struggle was not over yet—a low hissing noise could be heard coming from the depths of the gorge. It seemed far away but it still sent waves of dread straight through them.

"We need to go. The staircase of Hummad—" said Joash urgently.

And they began to run once more. The ground was not hard anymore, it was only sand which made it difficult to run fast.

Whoosh! Something flew over them, stirring the air around them. Looking up it was just all engulfing blackness.

"Don't stop!" urged Joash.

There was a queer feeling of being watched from all sides. As they trudged on, suddenly what had seemed like a vast expanse condensed into an alleyway again. There were walls with pillars on either side. On the stony ridges on each pillar were perched black birds with hook-like brown beaks, two horn-like projections above their red eyes, looking menacingly towards the strangers.

Then came a sound, like a whimper, a muffled cry. Joash stopped and turned around. It was Callum, he had fallen behind. His head was hanging low, and his steps were laboured. A black bird was circling above his head. Joash started to wave the flame, frantically trying to drive the bird away. With a pang of anger, he flung the torch to one side and took the long chisel out of his bag. Turning around in a circle, he hurled the chisel at the bird with all his might. It barely touched its wing, but the bird burst into grey smoke, then fell to the ground in the shape of a small rodent and pelted away into the darkness. Immediately the other birds disappeared too.

Joash held Callum—his eyes were drooping, and his body felt as cold as ice. He pleaded desperately, "Stay with me, Callum."

As warmth started to come back to his body, Callum muttered, "I... I will try."

At the same time, the hissing noise was getting closer to them. There was no time to spare. A mud wall was just fifteen or twenty feet away from them and projecting from it were irregular pieces of stones going up in a staircase-like fashion. Through an opening near the top part of the staircase, a faint ray of light was filtering.

And then it happened—before they could turn around to see what was right behind them, a large serpent leapt above them and blocked their path. It looked straight at them with fiery eyes, a large open mouth, and yellow fangs. Its body was black and shiny, three times wider and much longer than a snake. It hissed loudly as if challenging the humans for a battle.

Joash was ready with a hammer in one hand and knife in the other, while Callum held the flaming torch. Joash closed his eyes; his face was covered with droplets of sweat and his forehead furrowed with a tense energy that was ready to burst out. As he opened his eyes, he drew the hammer back and flung it towards the Jhenat. The angry serpent lifted its head higher and reared back. As it charged forward, the flying knife grazed its tail. There was a burst of grey smoke and it seemed to slow down.

Joash and Callum were moving back and pelting stones towards the creature, but most of them were caught by the cawing birds that were now flocking around the snake.

As the squawking of the black birds grew louder, a sudden sandstorm filled the place. The wind bellowed hard and flying sand blocked all vision. The serpent was thrown to one side and then the wind spoke to Joash. 'Go now! Run!'

Through the blinding sand, Joash and Callum, bolted towards the wall, swaying, falling and getting back up.

Callum and Joash were now on the staircase as the serpent sprang towards them, only to hit the wall on their side, the sand still blinding it. They ascended on the treacherous stones and the storm started to ease.

The topmost step was a wide platform with three walls and an uneven roof. A small crack in one wall showed that there was still some light outside. Joash crashed on the floor next to Callum catching his breath but when he took a good look at him, he couldn't rest. His friend looked as white as paper and his breathing was uneven.

Just then, something stirred in the alleyway below and moved toward them. It stopped right next to the platform, slowly wavering in the air. Joash recognised Rayth.

"Did you just help us escape?" asked Joash as he sat up.

"Yes, I had to. No human could possibly cross this part alive. You did your bit and I had to do mine."

"I am so grateful to you."

"And I am to you. By carrying the scared soil through this part of the city you have subdued the evil here. That is why I could come here and that is why I know you are still the Dhanay you once were."

Joash's eyes travelled to Callum, who seemed to be drifting in and out of sleep, and then back to Rayth.

"He is getting a fever. Keep him warm. He needs the healing water as you do—the water touched by Asters, the beings of light. Follow the silver rain. Farewell."

With those words, Rayth diffused back into the darkness of the hidden city.

Chapter 18

Saqqara

Joash tried to climb up a shallow crater in the sand. Breaking out of the mud wall had been easy but covering the last few steps had been arduous as Callum's condition was deteriorating rapidly. Joash was conscious of the waning sunlight as he tried to pull him along with him.

"Come on Callum, a little more and we will reach the kropter." Joash knew that the flying machine was nowhere nearby. Endless rolling dunes were all he could see in every direction.

Callum had no energy to reply. As Joash supported him, he was barely dragging his feet, his head hanging limp.

Then, something came moving up and down the dunes at

a distance. Joash blinked and narrowed his eyes to make sure it was not an illusion. It was a sand truck.

***

"Not many people have come out alive from that place," said Hamza seriously as he and Joash made Callum lay down in the backseat of the truck. "He is ice-cold. What happened to him?"

"I need your help." Joash took out his shirt and more clothes from his bag pack and covered Callum. Sitting down in the front seat next to Hamza he continued, "I need water. Water touched by the silver rain. Urgently."

Hamza's eyes widened as he turned towards him. "You have changed. What did you find in there?"

"Creatures from a different realm," replied Joash loudly. "Do you believe me now?"

"Of course, I do. But I thought you would never believe me, so I never tried to tell you. You saved a man's life today. After the storm settled, I picked up on some human activity in the area. I was hoping to find you, but I found him."

"What made you come looking for me?"

Hamza sighed in disbelief, "In the many years that you have known me, have I ever abandoned you? Whatever the weather, I have stood next to you."

Feeling embarrassed about his tone, Joash looked down and

shook his head.

"I warned you the best I could about this new venture of yours. But I have to think of my little girl. I did not want to make her an orphan." Hamza spoke again after a pause, "I have seen all sorts of things—some people went mad, some went blind, and some died trying to get to the treasures down there. But I knew you didn't care about treasures. I think I was too spooked to ask you what was going on. I have never prayed so much as I have today for you to come out alive."

"Thank you, Hamza." Joash placed his hand on Hamza. They traversed the desert smoothly and soon the city lights were visible on the horizon. "I need this water—Callum needs this water—to get better. It has been called the silver rain in the media. There have been several sightings, but I need a reliable one, close to a water body." Joash looked at Callum. He seemed to be shivering now. "And we need to get there as soon as possible."

"Yes," Hamza nodded. "I have heard about it. My sister has seen one, near Sur."

"Can you take me there?"

Hamza raised an eyebrow and glanced sideways towards Joash. "Are you asking nicely?"

"This boy's life depends on it. I have been told that is the cure."

"Hmm. It's a river, near my hometown. At first, there was

an earthquake in the area. A few days later my sister went there to check the damage and saw the rain. She says it was the most beautiful sight she had ever seen. People have stopped going there, but nothing can stop her. She does not fear anything."

"Sounds like my sister." Joash sat back, wondering where Krupa would be.

Chapter 19

The Base

Far away from the dunes of Egypt, all was calm on Moksha Parvat. The sun was heading back to the horizon and there was a pleasant chill in the air. Swamiji and Professor Rollings were sitting in the balcony looking upon the clearing in front of the settlement and just below the ashram. Young men, women and children were getting ready to start a bonfire while older people were starting to gather in a large circle. Patrick Zuma had chosen a perfect spot close to the tower of wood. Sitting on a wooden log, he looked gleeful talking to some youngsters.

"It is unbelievably peaceful here. I might not feel like going back," said Professor Rollings to Swamiji.

He quietly smiled back at her.

"So, tell me your secret, Swami, why is this place so different?" She looked at him with eager eyes.

"Different? Do you feel it or is that from your tests?"

The professor chuckled lightly. She looked snug with a thick brown scarf wrapped around her neck and a fur coat. Bending over her legs, she leaned forward. Her gaze travelled to the small wooden hutch at the far end of the plain where people were gathering—her makeshift laboratory.

"This place is a mystery," she said. "There is no trace of the new element we have detected in almost all other parts of the world. And as you had told me, the weather is calmer here. I am wondering if there is something here that can diffuse the element."

"Let me tell you the story of this place—right here, where we are sitting now was the abode of a special soul. He lived a few hundred years ago. No one knows the exact period. I first heard about him from my guru's guru."

She nodded and urged Swamiji to carry on.

"We call him the Mahayogi. He lived here alone for several years, meditating. I have heard that he acquired so much energy once that he was glowing like a sun. Everything around him for about a kilometre was shining with his aura. People in a distant village could see the pinnacle of this mountain glowing. Some thought it was fire. Some curious people came here to check on him but found only a heap of ash right here. The strangest thing was a Primula, a white flower at the top of the heap with roots just inside the surface layer. Ash was spread all around this area, some people took a bit back with them and the flower was planted again at the same place." Swamiji's eyes pointed to a small bush with flowers quite close to the hutch. "My guru said this place will always keep that energy till the end of days. It is the same energy that has protected this place."

"So, what happened to the Mahayogi?" she asked.

"My understanding is that he attained nirvana that day." Swamiji smiled and continued, "I have seen him. Just a glimpse, on the day of my initiation with my guru. I was only sixteen. I woke up in the morning to find an unusually radiant person right next to my guru. I remember the room felt hot like a furnace, and he glowed amber. My guru bowed to him, and he disappeared. I have never doubted my path since that day."

"Interesting," said the professor. She went quiet, retreating into her thoughts for a few moments, and then spoke again. "I do believe that this story could be true. But then, how can such an energy field be generated to cover the whole world? This is just one small place, and the new element is everywhere."

"The new element, yes." Swamiji slowly nodded. "You

cannot be sure that there are no other places like this in the world. There is hope."

She looked at Swamiji with a keen interest again, a soft smile flicked her lips. "I think you are the best fortune teller, a positive one certainly. May I ask, is there any science or method to the spiritual ways—is there anything you think I will be able to understand?"

Just then, a sudden draught of wind blew Swamiji's shawl away. A silvery fluff filled the air - soft and shiny, floating gently in one direction. Shaking slightly with her astonishment, Professor Rollings got up from her seat and extended her arms out beyond the shade of the balcony, but the glittering shapes vanished into nothingness. The chitter-chatter stopped on the ground as the crowd stared at the passers-by with rapt attention.

Swamiji got up to his feet and looked all around him. Smiling with contentment, he closed his eyes. Others came out of their shelters, children started dancing in the unusual rain. It felt like a joyous hopeful moment, which was strange as no one really knew what it was. Soon, it disappeared just as it had appeared, leaving no trace.

She looked flummoxed. "What was that?"

"A sign," spoke Swamiji, "from the luminous beings passing this way. They are happy to show their presence."

Professor Rollings was speechless; she hadn't expected this

answer and certainly did not know how to believe it.

She cleared her throat and said, "Aliens?"

Swamiji smiled, "Aliens will come one day too. There are more forms of life on our planet than our waking eyes can perceive. Some are brighter than us, some are darker. They all have different energies. Again, I cannot prove any of this to you, unless you happen to witness things like this. The cloud of doubt on your mind will blow away eventually. You can understand much more than you believe you do."

Swamiji's expression was as kind as ever. He looked down as people started lighting small flames here and there. As the light of the sun started to fade, the faces of the people around the slowly kindling flames started to glow. Krupa and others were now sitting around the bonfire, a slow rhythmic clapping had begun, inviting the fire to warm their souls. Right next to Krupa, wrapped in his thick maroon scarf and hat, Captain Durgesh was beaming and swaying.

Professor Rollings sank back into her seat which was a pair of folded blankets. She folded her hands and crossed them in front of her face—her heart was dealing with polar emotions and her mind was befuddled with contradictory ideas. She wanted to accept everything her ears and eyes told her, but something was holding her back as if it would be cheating, it would be wrong. An undercurrent of exhilaration was getting stronger, and she just wanted to dive in.

Then, her eyes fell upon Krupa. A few minutes passed, and her gaze refused to shift. What she felt was inexplicable—a joy, a sorrow, a pull, or maybe something else. She felt Swamiji's eyes observing her.

"That girl, Krupa," she said, straightening up, "she is brilliant, isn't she? She manages this whole setup so efficiently. Everyone seems to go to her for answers. She should come and manage our country." She laughed and tried to change the subject saying, "Tell me more about these shining beings. Are they relevant to what is going on? Do you have a theory on the current climate crisis?"

Swamiji took his place next to her. "The world and the universe are not confined to what humans can experience and understand. There are several dimensions or planes of existence. Think of it like this, there is the perceptible existence and the imperceptible existence. And there are beings of all sorts—those who like the light or are light itself and those who like the dark. Some can perceive their existence way better than we do. The luminous beings belong to a higher dimension; showing their presence like this can only be an amiable gesture. Our world is entering a special phase—the Sangam—when different dimensions of existence meet. Some disturbance in nature is expected. Consciously or unconsciously, we have also created conditions to attract other beings who might not be as friendly or kind. By this I mean the collective karma of the entire human race. Maybe we have disturbed other realms—I don't know."

Through the wooden spindles of the balcony, Swamiji's eyes found the Primula again. He said, "I think one life form among us knows a lot more and can do a lot more." There was a twinkle of hope in his smiling eyes.

Tell me then! Professor Rollings thought with impatience.

"The plants!" Swamiji got to his feet again. "Answers will come. The riddle will be solved, Stella. For now, come and join us for some singing."

And soon the two had joined the singing crowd.

Chapter 20

Near Sur, Oman

The storm was trying to spin the kropter like a top in the hands of a giant. The siren started to blare as the flying machine rocked and rattled.

"Kropter seriously damaged. Evacuate!" came the voice from the control panel.

Joash winced. There were three of them in the kropter, but only two evacuation devices. "Hamza, lay Callum over me. I will tie myself to him and eject," he shouted. "Do it!"

Frantically, Hamza did as he was told.

Joash placed his arms around Callum and whispered, "I have got you." He looked at Hamza who was buckling up and pressed the eject button.

***

Joash opened his eyes and found two lenses focused on him. They were the eyes of a medical robot. He remembered staying stuck in the kropter seat for a while before he could hear the clamour of emergency services. A sharp scratch in his thigh and all had gone blank.

"Welcome back to the conscious state," the robot blinked. "A doctor will be with you shortly."

Joash looked around; he was in a bed with white curtains on four sides. Sitting up quickly he asked, "Where are my friends?"

"Oh! It does not look like the sedative was very effective." A doctor entered the enclosure. "Please rest, Mr. Pundit, you are safe. You are in a medical facility just outside Sur, close to your crash site. Our authority received a request for help from your country's authority. A certain Mr Bailey, he has already called a few times. His son Callum—what do you know about his illness? His fever is not coming down with any medication; he is unconscious."

"I just need to see him." Joash got up, pulling out the medical device attachments. As he pulled the curtain, he realised his friend was in the next bed.

"His breathing is good," the doctor said.

Joash placed his hand on Callum's clammy forehead. He

could feel the struggle of an innocent life underneath the languorous appearance. He could not help but feel responsible for Callum's suffering. He suppressed a sigh and suddenly thought aloud, "Where is Hamza?"

"In the next bed of course." The doctor hesitated. "Um, you should not see him just yet. He needs rest."

But Joash did not stop. He pulled open another curtain and was gripped by yet another shock.

Hamza lay unconscious, he had lost a leg. A woman sitting next to his bed had fallen asleep, her face buried in Hamza's blanket.

Joash gathered his composure and walked up to the woman. As he gently tapped her on her shoulder she woke up. Her eyes looked swollen, and her cheeks were covered with lines made by tears that had dried.

"I am sorry." There was a hesitation in Joash's tone. "I am Hamza's friend, Joash." Then, words refused to leave his mouth—how could he say that Hamza had lost a leg trying to help him? He swallowed and waited for the lady to say something.

"I am Hamza's wife, Fatima," she spoke sitting straighter and adopting a brave face. "He will live. He gets his new leg tomorrow."

The simplicity with which she uttered her words made Joash shudder inside, but he had no time. "I need your help, urgently," he said with an intense look.

***

Joash was pacing the empty hospital corridor. Slowly he moved his head towards one shoulder and then the other. His hand reached for the glass vial hanging by his neck, one-third full of the shimmering red soil but two-thirds empty. He wrapped his hand around it and sighed. Just then, a voice called from behind.

"Joash Pundit?" A girl was walking through the corridor, a questioning look on her face. She seemed to be in her early twenties; a brown scarf wrapped around her head and neck accentuated her sharp facial features and her big black eyes had been skilfully outlined with an even darker eyeliner. The most striking and perhaps the most beautiful thing about her was a prominent scar, a few centimetres long, running along the right cheek to the corner of her eye.

Her odd-looking, fluorescent-pink shoes made a rhythmic squeaky noise on the marble floor as she approached Joash. Her chin was up. 'I take no nonsense' was written all over her face.

"Yes?" said Joash as he turned around.

"You are coming with me," ordered the girl.

Joash quietly stared at her expecting more information.

"Okay, I am Yasmin, Hamza's sister. You want to go to the place where a strange silvery-white rain was sighted. Right?" Her eyes were now studying Joash very closely with her head leaning to one side, "I will take you. But those shoes will not do."

Joash looked at his rugged boots, slightly worn out but... Placing his hands in his pockets he shrugged his shoulders and said, "Okay!"

Yasmin rummaged in her bag and produced a pair of shoes that looked just like hers but green. Joash quietly changed his shoes. They felt too big at first, but then Yasmin bent down and pressed a button on them. The shoes folded and shrank around Joash's feet to fit snugly.

"Good," she said. "Can you swim and climb rocks?"

"Uh … yes!" Joash frowned but figured Yasmin was not one for long explanations.

She turned and walked away; he followed.

***

Outside, the afternoon sun was beating down. A small tram-like vehicle was waiting for them. They rode in silence; now and then Yasmin shot a glance towards Joash and quickly looked away.

The lone travellers went under a cloudless sky, on roads that were cracked and ditched. A dry kind of heat was building up, and a smell of burning wood lingered in the air. The sea to their right was too close to the road at times and it was clear that it must even cover the roads during high tide. Joash stared at the occasional stumps of barren trees.

"The soil here is parched. It has not rained for a while," said Yasmin looking at the road ahead. "Some afternoons are hot enough to burn the leaves."

After half an hour of the rough ride, they stopped in a clearing—there were high cliffs on one side and the remains of a decrepit concrete bridge on the other. Stepping out of his ride, Joash looked around. The sheer, sand-coloured cliffs were roasting in the sun, the air was still, and the sound of water trickling was coming from behind a heap of giant boulders that lay in front of him. He darted a glance towards Yasmin who was standing next to him and then to the broken, upturned boats lying nearby.

"We used to need boats to cross over to the other side of the stream but not anymore," said Yasmin as she looked towards the cliffs. "The water was already disappearing but then came the earthquakes. We have had a few just over the last five or six weeks, although I do not believe they were earthquakes. We need to go over these rocks to the other side." As she said that, she flung a harness and rope towards him.

They reached the top of the pile of rocks and the valley came into view. Rocks and boulders of all sizes were strewn along the path of the river. But there was no river, just a thin stream of water meandering around smooth stones, waxing and waning in perceptibility as it went. And yet this place was cooler with some green visible further down the path of the river.

"Where are we going?" asked Joash.

Yasmin frowned, though she seemed pleased that he had asked a question, "Along the river, deeper in the valley. The path ends at a cave, that is where I saw the rain. It will take an hour if your legs are strong and skilled. It is not easy." She looked at him as if assessing his fitness for the trek.

"I did not expect it to be." He started to follow her once again as she treaded the bumpy path with an uncanny ease. "How did you get to know about this place?"

"This is Wadi Shub, it used to be a popular, busy place, but now only crazy people come here." Her voice faded as she went further ahead at a swift pace.

"You seem quite familiar with these rocks."

"Who said that I am not crazy?" Yasmin's voice echoed in the valley.

Joash looked ahead and smiled. She was right, he was finding it hard to keep up with her. She was simply hopping from rock to rock, boulder to boulder.

"Are you sure that this is the place?" he asked.

She looked back at him out of the corner of her eye and made a show of slight annoyance. "I would not take someone out of a hospital and make him trek this place for my entertainment. It is all over the news, just like many other places all over the world."

Joash fell quiet. They continued to hike along the steep walls of the meandering valley. Some of the rocks that had broken away from the cliffs were razor sharp. Exhaustion was taking over Joash again. He looked ahead, shielding his eyes from the sharp sun, and in a dizzy moment, he slipped. As he fell, a sharp edge of a rock lacerated his right upper arm. Blood started to gush out of the wound. As he lay holding his arm, the rock scalded his back.

Yasmin came back quickly to his side. She took out a long scarf from her bag and tied it tight around Joash's arm. "It is quite deep. I should have thought this might happen."

Joash smiled fighting the pain, "Luckily I am staying at a medical facility." For a split second their eyes met.

Yasmin hesitated, then stood up. "Can you carry on?" she asked.

Joash rolled over and dipped his hands into the small pool of water by the side of the rock. He splashed water all over himself and then rose to his feet. "Yes, I can," he said.

Finally, they were standing next to a pool of turquoise water. At the other end of the pool was a wall, formed by large rocks and boulders that would have tumbled from the cliffs and somehow fit into each other like bricks. On either side, the sandstone cliffs still loomed high. It looked like a dead end.

"This is the spot. The white fluff was floating in the air

going that way." She pointed her finger towards the rocky wall.

Joash gave her a puzzled look.

"Beyond these rocks, there is a cave," she continued. "What is it you're looking for exactly?"

"Water touched by the silver rain."

"It is not a solid thing to touch anything. It was here, but much above the water. I think it's a visual phenomenon, that's all."

He looked ahead. How could he go beyond the wall and how would he know if the water there was what he was looking for? "If the silver rain was moving in that direction, I think I should go further," he said. "Is there another way?"

"There is only one way—an opening, a V-shaped space under these rocks." Yasmin kneeled and pointed towards the water pool in front of them. "These rocks look like a solid wall from here but if you dive inside you can see a tunnel-like space. You will have to be good at underwater swimming; the water level is high here today. You'll need to go underwater and swim to the other side. Once there, you will spot the cave easily. I can't promise if that is what you are looking for."

Joash nodded. He quickly slid down the side of the rock he was on. Yasmin attached a thin rope to his harness and held the other end.

The pool was shallow. He stood up in the water and turned to look back at her. "If you wish, you can go back now."

She sat down and shook her head, looking exasperated. "And how do you think you would get back? There is no public transport here. It's not like London." Her face was used to the sun, there wasn't a single wrinkle or fold of struggle with the sheer brightness and yet it displayed a tension as she spoke. "Look, the fact is that I was not allowed to come here and no one else I know wanted to help you. Just yesterday there was some rumble from the cliffs and some of my friends who were around thought another earthquake was going to hit. It didn't, then, but who knows if it might happen now? So, if you let me see this thing through, whatever you are trying to do here, it will be worth the argument I have had with my father. And Hamza might benefit too, right? It must be called healing water for a reason."

Yasmin was not as callous as she had pretended to be, and she certainly was stronger than he had thought. He quietly turned back to disappear into the cool water.

She shouted after him, "I will hold this rope and wait here for you. Don't take too long. If you feel anything unusual just come back."

But Joash knew that nothing around him was usual anymore, not Callum's illness, not his journey, and not this place. Near the rocky wall, the pool was deeper. He held his breath and went down looking for a space along the joints and he found it. He came back up to take a deep breath, took his final plunge, and then went sideways into the tunnel. A sharp pain seared through his right arm, but slowly he moved forward in the murky water, with rocks on three sides and his head barely fitting in the space. He thought he saw a shadow moving in the water further up his path. The sight sent a shiver through him. He braced himself and carried on. After a few breathless minutes it grew brighter, and he was through to the other side.

Emerging slowly from the water, he took in the place. The cave was a concave limestone structure with undulating lines on its walls. A small waterfall, almost in the centre of the cave wall, was burbling down into the pool. A smell of fresh water and wet mud lingered secretly in this hidden cool space. The holes in its roof sent shafts of daylight on the gently waving water.

Suddenly, it felt like a dark veil had covered the cave, but there were no clouds in the sky. Joash's face tensed up with alertness as he tried to feel, look and listen for the unusual. Just then, he felt tremors under his feet. It grew darker and a feeling of deep gloom started to grip him. He moved back, trying to keep his balance, his hands resting on the cave walls. The water around him started to swirl. He watched it rise above him only to fall back on him with force. Joash was thrown away.

As he stood back up, everything went strangely quiet. The next moment there was a wave, a movement in the cave wall itself as if it was not rock but a brown fabric. It felt like the whole cave was about to explode.

Abruptly, a piercing wail went through him. Then, he heard himself sob and, in a flash, saw his own face, full of rage. His head felt a strange force trying to pull it apart in different directions.

Instinctively he closed his eyes and, trying to fight the invisible enemy uttered the sound, "Hmm…"

Then… *poof!* A dark vapour escaped the roof of the cave and the atmosphere of the place changed.

Joash felt his mind going still amidst the tribulation. Time slowed down to an infinitesimally slow speed. The water became a play of millions of droplets, each touching him separately. He felt the most subtle vibration of the earth under his feet as he touched the bottom of the pool. A part of the cave rock fell away and turned into fine dust shimmering in the air and then sprinkling on the water. Joash blinked in what felt like a minute. When his eyelashes parted, a white shape floated into the cave, and with it came a light, milky white but gentle, like a star that was far away. Soon, it condensed to form a human-like shape.

He was looking at the white being who was just a few

feet away, but it felt like there were light years of distance between them. There was no sound, yet he could perceive a communication between them. It was subtle, yet so deep that Joash found himself concentrating with every ounce of energy he had. His mind became a blank slate on which the first words appeared. "I know what you seek." There was a certain mischief in the way the words were spoken.

"Who is that?" asked Joash in his mind.

"Oh, I am Sinuay, an ester. I just saved you from the Roga," came back the reply.

"Roga?"

"This place is a Sangam. Three realms are crossing here—yours, mine—the astral realm, and the dark realm. Your world has several such places right now."

"What happened just now?"

"You came face to face with a dark force, the Roga. It seems to have a fondness for your world. It tried to peak inside your mind, but you called upon *Dhi* and tuned into my realm. I had to protect you because you are a mere human. You could not have faced the Roga."

"I appreciate your help. I am here for the healing water."

"I know! I cannot help but wonder, what are you going to achieve by healing your nature if the Roga is going to destroy it anyway?"

"I will do my karma and face things as they come. Right now, I need the healing water, for my world and my friend."

"Friend!" The words came sharply. "You claim to understand your karma. Why do you interfere with another's? He is suffering his karma. Let him be. You will get just enough for your prime purpose. How would you rather use it?"

Yet another perplexing question for Joash. The ester's blunt words held an incredulous tone. "Why won't you let me have more? What harm is there in helping another life? He is suffering because of me, and it is my duty to help him."

"You are the same Dhanay you were in the astral realm. No wonder you suffer your decisions like you do. Take it if you must. But know this much that, he came after you to suffer his own karma. You did not invite him. Countless others suffer, who will give them the healing water? Your friend has a dark curse on him. There is no knowing if it will come to you if it will entangle you in another lifetime of suffering or push your soul into oblivion."

Joash's expression hardened and he closed his hands into fists. What truth could there be in this being's warnings? How could he not help Callum? "Give me the healing water and I will leave. It is not the time for me to know of my wrongdoings as Dhanay. Neither do I wish to know about the Roga."

"So be it. Go, Dhanay, the high seas await you."

An ache started in Joash's body and his concentration started to break. It had been a tremendous effort, nothing that could be described in words—trying to reach something that was light years away in one breath, in one leap.

Joash opened his eyes again to find himself bathing in the silver rain—silvery white fluff was falling from the roof of the cave and was all around him. He held out his arms into the fast-disappearing wisps of starlight and noticed his right arm; the scarf was gone, and the gash was already closing. The shower stopped and when Joash looked at the water he was standing in, it was milky white. He collected the water in his vial—it did not seep into the soil below but stayed above it. He closed it and put it around his neck again. At that moment, there was a tug on the rope attached to his waist.

It was time to go.

Chapter 21

The Base

It was dark and quiet at the base as everyone had gone to sleep, except Krupa. She tossed and turned in her blanket. The small candle by her side had almost run out as she closed her eyes and tried to quiet her mind yet again. But the thought of the book, Prakruti Saram, refused to leave her. She wanted to get her hands on it as soon as possible. The fact that it was with her family made her feel that it was her responsibility to get it back.

She had never doubted Swamiji since the first day. He had come to her school to speak about 'the great energy and the young souls'. He had invited Krupa to visit his Jispa ashram after finishing her studies. That summer when she told the headteacher on her last day at school that she was not going to the UK this time but to Jispa, he did not look surprised at all.

"Why don't you come here and try for a job, Krupa?" Aunt Sue had asked. "Spiritual studies are equally popular here and many schools are looking for good teachers."

Krupa had just told her that she would think about it after her trip, but the trip never ended.

When Krupa and Joash were young children a wave of keen interest in spiritual education had swept the world. The face of the earth had changed a lot in just twenty years. More and more people wanted to look inwards for hope when the speculation of the end of the world was rife.

Krupa's father and grandfather were academics in the field of yoga philosophy. She loved listening to her mother's stories about her father's trip to London and how he met her mother for the first time.

"I was a yoga teacher. I thought it was going to be a boring lecture, but quite the opposite came true. I was head over heels in love with him." Those were her mother Erin's words that made Krupa giggle with excitement and Joash feel awkward.

Their ancestral home was a special building in Jaipur. Made by their grandfather, it was exactly how a traditional royal mansion would have been; there were beautiful gardens with mature trees on two sides of the building and a central courtyard with a Tulsi plant in the middle. The second floor had the library with actual paper books of all sorts and a special section where kids were not allowed. Right next to the library was the vast terrace where Joash used to fly kites in winter. The first floor was their main home, and the ground floor had several rooms for guests and meetings. Their family had lots of other properties in Jaipur and three large eco-agricultural farms just outside Jaipur. They were privileged or 'just comfortable enough' as their father would say.

"Don't you miss London, Ma?" Joash had once asked their mother sitting on the kitchen counter.

"Umm, just a bit sometimes," she replied putting some flour on Joash's nose-tip with her finger. "You two don't give me time to think about anything." Her laughter filled the air.

"Oh, Ma." Krupa was missing her mother a lot that night. It wasn't like her to be emotional. From a young age, she was highly independent and an avid reader, a bit like her father. She could have long intelligent discussions almost about anything. Her mother loved to watch her speak like a grown-up woman. It used to fill her with pride, the knowledge, and understanding of the world Krupa had aged eight.

They had a regular guest each year in winter. Everyone called him 'Guruji'. Joash was supposed to learn some stuff from him.

He would disappear for hours sometimes. Krupa would often fall asleep waiting for her brother to come and play with her. She thought of Guruji as a nice old man who could be scary at times.

Once her father had asked her, "Would you like to join your brother and listen to some things from Guruji?"

"No thank you, Papa. I think I already know most things he might be teaching or maybe I can wait a bit," she had replied.

"Are you sure, Krupa? He is a very special person."

"I am sure, Papa."

But she was not really sure. She had wanted to know why he was so special. She did not realise how annoyed she was with him for taking away her time with Joash.

She did not know when, but she had stopped expecting anything from her brother. She busied herself with learning as much as possible about spirituality, religions of the world, and life philosophies—old and new. When she went to Jispa, the strong community of like-minded people from all over the world living a simple life in and around the ashram touched her deeply. They were self-sufficient in almost everything. On Swamiji's request, she started to teach older children in the local school and soon forgot all about going back to Jaipur or the UK.

She had seen miracles—Swamiji's ability to stay in meditation for days together and to heal people. The stories of the Mahayogi were mesmerising, and she secretly hoped that one day she would see him. She had been trying to meditate for years but could never sit beyond five minutes. When she expressed her frustration to Swamiji he simply said, "It does not matter how long you sit for as long as you try. Your soul might be waiting for some answers before it can let your mind rest."

Her thoughts then moved on to Joash. *I wonder, where is he? Will he do this?* she thought. *If I go back towards Jispa, I might be able to get in touch with him.*

It was a strange night for Krupa. After staying up for most of the night she fell asleep only to wake up in two hours. It was just before sunrise. She got up and decided to go for a stroll. The sky was dark with a faint red light behind the mountains in the east, getting ready for the day to break. There was another light quite close to the ashram. Krupa walked up to the place where a small bonfire was lit.

"Hi!" smiled Durgesh. "Good morning! You are up quite early."

Krupa smiled back. "Good morning! Yes, I was not very sleepy. Thought I'd take a walk. What about you? Aren't you tired after the long journey?" Her face glowed in the dim light of the dying fire as she sat on the stone next to Durgesh.

"I have had a good rest. Couldn't sleep much. It is quite nice to just sit here and wait for the sun to rise. You are lucky; people on my side of the world haven't seen the sun for days."

"Hmm, I know. My brother lives in London. That makes me think I would like to see the sunrise today too. I should go to the landing area; the view is good from there." She rose up. "Sorry, I will catch you later."

"Could I join you?" said Durgesh turning towards Krupa who had taken a few steps away from him.

"Sure," Krupa replied looking back. She was surprised by the flutter of delight she felt.

They climbed up together, constantly talking and giggling. When they trekked down after about an hour, Bheema was waiting at the bottom.

"I have been looking for you, Krupa," he said sounding concerned.

"I was just here, Bheema. What's the matter?"

"Just now, Swamiji was talking about you wanting to go to Jaipur. Won't it be dangerous?"

"Yes, I know, but it needs to be done."

"Can I come with you?"

Krupa was bemused. "Why?"

"I can look after you. Uboyo is not even here."

"No, Bheema!" said Krupa sternly. "Can I please talk about this later? We need to get breakfast organised for our guests."

"Okay. Swamiji is waiting for you."

Bheema stared at the two of them as they walked away.

***

Outside the ashram, a group of people were standing in a closed circle looking at something and whispering.

Krupa squeezed through the small crowd. In the middle, Swamiji was sitting up on a rock on the ground, a man and a woman were sitting close to him. They did not look well; their faces were white, lips quivering, fingers blue, bitten by the cold. Meera was trying to get the fire started right next to them. Alok pushed through the crowd with some blankets and covered the two. Krupa recognized the couple—they used to come for Jispa ashram's monthly public gatherings regularly.

"You will be fine Aarav. But why did you and your wife take this treacherous journey?" asked Swamiji.

"When we left Gemur, we did not realise how bad it was going to get, but I do not regret it one bit. The highway was already clearing fast. The authority has finally sent some robots to help us. Most people left for Manali from Gemur fearing the next storm. But when we heard all of you had made a settlement at the base, we decided to join you. It was okay to drive through Jispa and further. But we had to leave the car behind and trek through the forest to get here. Last evening's storm made us realise how unprepared we were."

"Did you not see anyone at Jispa? Uboyo and a few others are still there," asked Swamiji.

"No, Swamiji. It felt empty. They must have left or were probably inside a building. It was heartbreaking to see the remains of the big ashram."

"Hmm. I hope they were inside. But Aarav, why did you carry that big bag? The trek was hard enough."

"It is not much, just some dry food and seeds that should grow well here. I wanted to be useful."

Swamiji smiled and shook his head. "Even you did not stop him, Pallavi?"

"How could I? If this is the end. We would rather be around you in our last days."

Swamiji looked up and saw Krupa looking thoughtful.

As the crowd dispersed Swamiji got up. "Come, Krupa," he said softly, placing one hand on her shoulder. "Let us go for a walk. How are you this morning?"

"Very good, thank you."

"You are looking good indeed for someone who has not slept much."

A half-smile crossed Krupa's face looking at the familiar glint in his eyes.

"So, you have been asking me about going to Jaipur," he said.

"I cannot stop you if you want to go. But Uboyo is not here yet. You know, he is our expert when it comes to finding ways through unknown territory. We are waiting for him to arrive with some more people. Do you think you can wait a few more days?"

"If you want me to. But I wish to go sooner, Swamiji. And Aarav said the roads are clear."

"What about your brother?"

"I don't know. I can try and contact him as soon as I reach Manali. If he is already in Jaipur, I won't go. Also, I can go to Jispa first, and check on Uboyo and Kisna."

"Hmm, you have thought of everything."

"Swamiji!" someone called from behind them. It was Alok, "Professor Rollings is looking for you."

***

Swamiji climbed up the slope to the landing area steadily and swiftly, while Krupa took her time. Professor Rollings and Patrick Zuma were busy with some equipment they had set up at the far end.

"We are not able to connect to the global satellite system," said Professor Rollings, looking confused. "We cannot contact other parts of the world from here. But there is something strange. Let me show you. Look," she said pointing to a line marked in the ground. "There is some vague connectivity to the web on the outside but nothing on the inside of this line. It is not a gradual thing, a sudden shutdown. The electrical properties of the two are different too. You wouldn't think so because air is not confined right? More importantly, there is no Elusium here, on our side."

"I think this could be what you said about this place having a special environment." Professor Rollings looked at Swamiji who simply nodded.

"If you make the rest of the world like the base you might lose web connectivity." He laughed softly.

Just then a speaker that was kept beyond the line on the ground started making a noise.

"Let me see…" said Patrick Zuma as he changed several switches. "Yup, this is better."

Soon the indecipherable noise turned into a rhythmic beep and words started to appear on Patrick's computer screen. "I have sent a message to the team in Japan," he said looking excited. He read it aloud. "*We are investigating Elusium levels. Some encouraging reports of low levels from the Japanese Alps. Access has been a problem due to bad weather. We will be in touch.*"

Professor Rollings, who was listening intently, shrugged her shoulders. "What about the team from Italy? Lorenzo was hellbent upon following me here."

"Stella, can I intervene for a minute?" asked Swamiji. "Could Krupa try to contact her brother through this? I believe he too has left the UK to get here."

"Sure, just enter his name and device number here." Patrick helped Krupa to do this.

"It says his device cannot be reached; the last clear signal was from Egypt, somewhere near Cairo," Patrick looked at Krupa who stepped back to stand next to Swamiji.

Krupa's eyes were moving quickly, her mind trying to work out what this could mean. Before the sombreness of disappointment could settle on her, Swamiji said, "So we know he has started his journey. He will be fine, Krupa."

"I wish I knew. I could have got him with me," said Professor Rollings rubbing Krupa's back gently. "You must be so worried. Do you wish to contact anyone else?"

"Sorry, we have completely lost all connectivity now," said Patrick shaking his round head.

Professor Rollings pursed her lips and looked at Krupa. "So why was your brother travelling at all? Is he a scientist like me or a yogi like you?"

"He is a climate journalist, Joash Pundit." Krupa looked at the professor with a certain curiosity—something was strange.

As Krupa spoke, Professor Rollings' expression visibly changed from concerned to blank. "I think I have heard this name," she said. The name piqued a vexation in her as Joash's face crossed her mind.

"Yes, it's possible," said Krupa.

Professor Rollings sighed and said, "You would not want to lose such a bright mind to a terrible storm or freak lightning. How about the rest of your family? Where are they?"

Without a word, Krupa turned to leave and saw Durgesh who had been standing behind her. She blinked to hide a teardrop that had just surfaced without her permission, then, putting her head down, she hurried back to her tent.

Meera, whom Krupa shared the tent with, was quietly enjoying her steaming porridge. "Hey Krupa, try the Scottish porridge, it's yum. The professor has got tonnes of it for us. I think I am going to finish it all." She looked at Krupa who had hurriedly packed a bag and was putting on trekking gear. "Where are you going in such a hurry? Are you okay?" She gently placed her hand on Krupa's shoulder.

Krupa took a deep breath. "Yes. I think I am going to Jaipur."

Meera was staring at Krupa with eyes wide open.

Krupa held Meera's arms and said, "Don't you worry about me. I know how to get to Jispa. Roads are clear now, so I can easily reach Manali and fly from there."

"But Krupa—"

"No, no, please don't say anything more. Look after everyone here and don't argue with Alok much. I will be back before you know it."

Meera went out of the tent and came back in a minute. She put a few small paper pouches in Krupa's bag.

"What are those?" asked Krupa.

"Scottish porridge," said Meera innocently. Krupa squeezed her in a warm embrace.

***

Swamiji looked at Krupa and smiled. She looked as ready as she could—a nice thick bodysuit, a white balaclava showing only her eyes and mouth, snow boots, gloves and a light metal bag on her shoulders.

"So, you want to leave right now?"

Krupa nodded.

"Have you had something to eat?"

"Yes." She winked at Meera.

Swamiji's gaze was fixed on her, and a few moments passed in silence. Then, as if he had seen something new and he wanted to be sure, he looked at her again. It was hard to say if Swamiji was disconcerted by her decision.

At length, he spoke. "I am not going to hold you back, Krupa, my child. Go as your soul commands you but be careful. May *Dhi* guide you and protect you."

With that, Krupa bowed to Swamiji and left.

Chapter 22

Moksha Parvat, Himalayas

Walking in solitude had been nourishing for Krupa—the restlessness from last night had vanished and she was feeling one with the forest. Her body felt light as she skipped her way downhill. The birds and the squirrels had been good companions so far. It was unusually cold for the time of the year, but she was prepared. The balaclava—no, that was better inside her bag. The white carpet of snow was getting thinner with the sunrays exposing bits of green. The tall coniferous trees were still watching over her like guards. The woody sweet scent that hung around in the air reminded her of incense.

She had been on this path before a few times but never

alone. A fresh breeze caressed her cold red cheeks and ran through her long dark hair—she wondered if the forest had ever felt so magical.

A deer dashed crossing her path as if in a great hurry. *Musk deer again!* she thought, but this time the deer had given her no heed. Just then she heard some bushes move in the distance towards her left. Slowly, she moved a few steps back and hid behind a large tree trunk. Peeping out slowly she saw a snow leopard emerge from the bush. Her heart started to race as she turned back and ran to her right, going deeper into the forest. After running for a few minutes, she stopped and realised she was not being chased. Breathing heavily, she looked around. This side of the mountain was steeper; the trees looked taller too. Somewhere nearby, streams were trickling down these slopes as the sun thawed the snow.

"Was it clever to run in the same direction as the deer?" came a voice, crystal clear above the noises of the forest.

Krupa gasped. She looked all around her, slowly rotating on the spot.

"Who is this?" Her eyes were frantically searching for the source of this voice. The very nature of the sound had shocked her—it did not seem to arise from one direction but felt like it was in the air itself. *Who would play a prank in the middle of a forest*? she thought.

Then, a giggle followed. "Why do you look so worried? I am the one you disturbed but see I don't mind."

Krupa was rattled. "I don't understand. Come in front of me and speak."

"You can't find what you are looking for because you are looking in the wrong place," said the voice. "Look up."

"What?" Right above her head, on a tree branch sat a person, or maybe a monkey. It was difficult to tell. It was sitting with its legs folded close to its chest just like a monkey on a sturdy tree branch. *Monkeys don't talk*! Krupa told herself.

The next moment he was swinging upside down with his legs gripping the bough. He gave Krupa an inverted smile and then with one somersault he was standing straight in front of her. As Krupa looked upon him with great amazement, she could not believe her eyes. He was over seven feet tall, strongly built, and had long silver hair that moved gently in the breeze. He had soft-looking white hair all over his body except his neck and part of his face. On his broad forehead shone a brilliant diamond-like stone right between two thick eyebrows. He had a wide nose and a slightly protruding mouth—almost resembling an ape, his lustrous skin was orange-brown, and his big eyes were of no specific colour because they were so bright that Krupa could not look directly into them. As he stood there strong, a soft aura around him made Krupa feel warm deep inside. She dropped to her knees, folding her hands together and looking to the ground said in a shaky voice, "Oh lord, am I dreaming?"

"Even if you were dreaming it would be an important dream." The Mahayogi smiled as Krupa looked up at the monumental figure. "Oh, come now Krupa, get up! Let us walk together for a bit, shall we?" There was child-like fun in his ways.

A wave of happiness ran through Krupa's heart. She nodded and began walking next to the Mahayogi—her eyes not leaving his face, her feet not feeling the crunch of snow or the slush of mud, her lips quivering with excitement but fixed in a smile.

"Umm, are you—?" stammered Krupa, not knowing if she should ask the obvious.

"Yes, yes, there is no need to verbally confirm what your mind already knows. I just decided to grant you your long-desired wish, to meet the Mahayogi. I quite like that term you know." He winked at Krupa.

"But you look a lot like—"

"Like someone famous? Yes, I quite like this look, don't you? Ideal for this weather keeps me warm," he chuckled.

Krupa's mind went blank for a few moments as she fell silent.

"Wait a second," said the Mahayogi and sprang up to a

branch of a tree. The next moment he was back on the ground with a bright red apple in his hand.

"Here, have this; you need it, I think."

"But…" She hesitated to finish her sentence again.

"There are no apple trees here? Yes, it does not matter." He looked at her with his enormous eyes.

Krupa ate her apple and felt her nerves calm down immediately. "Mahayogi, could you tell me where my brother is?"

"Ch, ch, Krupa, don't you know yet? Yogis cannot answer specific questions like this. I could not even tell the exact time by your watch right now. I don't even know how old I am—one hundred and fifty, or two hundred or more." He shrugged his shoulders. "Yogis like abstract questions and may give you some abstruse answers. But anyway, he is fine—that is all I can tell you."

Krupa nodded again. "Should I go to Jaipur?"

"That is again a very specific question." The Mahayogi waved a finger at Krupa and said with a gentle smile, "Listen to your inner self. It has all the answers you seek. Oh yes, a cliché but true anyway. You have the freedom to choose your path. Once you start on it, don't worry about what you find because all the tests of this life will find you regardless. When you hold on to painful feelings, the mirror of your soul turns hazy, and you can't look inside. Let go, clear your mind. And you will see there is no limit to what you can do ... what you can know."

Krupa was in total awe of what she was seeing, what she was hearing. She did not want the Mahayogi to stop speaking.

"Are you the God my Lord?" she spoke with utter reverence.

"God is in me and I am in God." He looked up to the sky and then leaned towards Krupa. "The same is true for you, Krupa, and everybody else, everything else. You will feel it; it's only a matter of time."

"Please tell me more, Lord."

The Mahayogi stood still facing Krupa and spoke, "The *Dhi* flows everywhere, into everything. Do not dismiss anything as just a thing. When called upon to guard a specific life, do not sway. You are a Tirtha-Rakshak, a lot is resting on your tiny shoulders. And yes, be careful. The forest is awake." He stopped and smiled, "The energy from the esters is doing all sorts of funny things here."

The words resounded in Krupa's head. In a blink, the half-man, half-ape figure had hopped several feet away from her.

"Oops, it's time for me to go." He pretended to look at his wrist but there was no watch. He looked back at Krupa again with a mischievous grin. "Follow that rabbit—you will find your path."

With that, the Mahayogi jumped back up to the tall trees and moved swiftly from branch to branch soon disappearing out of sight. When she could no longer see him, Krupa looked down and saw that a small white rabbit with long black ears, and a black nose was nibbling at her suit, close to her ankle.

"Let's go!" she exclaimed, and the rabbit set off.

Almost flying, Krupa's feet touched the ground gently now and again. As soon as she reached the dirt path where she had seen the snow leopard, the rabbit stopped, looked at her and then vanished into the bushes.

From there she continued her trek. Several minutes later, she heard someone shout her name from higher up in the mountain. Two men were coming her way. As they came closer, she knew they were Bheema and Durgesh.

"What are you two doing here?" she asked.

"I told Swamiji that I would go after you. Captain joined me later," replied Bheema, catching his breath.

"Bheema, I don't need looking after," Krupa said, though she was beaming.

"You seem very happy to see us after all," said Durgesh.

She simply shrugged her shoulders and rolled her eyes.

"Can't believe how settled the weather is here; it feels unusually calm," Durgesh wondered.

Krupa knew exactly why that was. And with a bit of chit-chat, they carried on.

Chapter 23

Mountains near Jispa

Walking for several hours, they had braved it all—the spate of snow, gusts of wind, torrents of rain—and now the quiet of the forest welcomed them. Although the storms had wiped out the forest paths, Krupa knew her way well.

"Let us get some rest here," she said, "before the last leg of the trek, hopefully."

It was a small glade on the slope of the mountain where some tree trunks lay flat lending themselves as seats. The travellers made a small fire and had something to eat. Krupa had been smiling a lot, but Durgesh could not help noticing Bheema's unease.

"Are you okay, Bheema?" he asked.

"Oh yes, I am," stuttered Bheema. "I just hope we get there soon. Look, there are dark clouds towards Jispa."

"Relax, Bheema, it is all going to be okay. The worst is behind us," said Krupa.

It was late afternoon, but Krupa was certain they could reach Jispa before sunset.

"So, tell me more about your brother in London. Does he like it there?" asked Durgesh as they stretched their legs near the fire.

"I think so. My aunt is there. She is sweet and caring."

"That's it. It is the people that matter, right? My family has been there for four generations now. I have only ever come to India once as a baby. Even though I have been curious to…" Suddenly, Durgesh stopped talking and looked around. "What is that?" he took a long sniff. "It smells amazing. Is it the animal you were talking about, a musk deer?" He was staring at a dense bush, its leaves rustling with some movement behind it.

"It must be. I saw one this morning—"

"I think I will try to catch a glimpse." Before anyone could say anything more Durgesh got up and scampered off into the forest to his left. "Be back soon," he shouted, his voice trailing off.

Bheema seemed to be busy in his thoughts. Krupa walked towards the open view of the valley to her right. Standing at the cliff edge she realised they were still quite high up in the mountains. A waterfall far away looked like a thin white line wavering amongst the dark, dense conifers. Several tall mountains stood crisscrossing the valley like V-shaped hats with white tips. At the bottom of the valley, a river was snaking through with its white foam, splashing and polishing the stones in its way. As Krupa closed her eyes, she could just about hear its roar in her head. She thought of her meeting with the Mahayogi and a smile stretched across her lips.

"Krupa! Step back!" It was a loud cry which shocked Krupa as she hastily took a step back and bumped into something. Bheema had been pushed to the ground by her sudden movement. She noticed he was holding a thick log of wood.

"What?" A stunned Krupa looked at Bheema and then at Durgesh who was leaping like a leopard towards them.

Bheema looked enraged as he went charging towards Durgesh like a bull. He caught hold of Durgesh's hood, took him to the ground and started hitting his face.

The next moment Durgesh took control and was sitting on Bheema's chest. He yelled, "Why would you do that? Why?"

Krupa was watching in horror, screaming, "What is going on? Stop it! Stop it!"

Bheema was a burly man; he pushed Durgesh away and

picked up a heavy round stone. He was going to hit Durgesh on his head, but Krupa hung to his arm with all her strength and the big stone fell onto Durgesh's arm. He cried out in agony.

Krupa pulled Bheema to face him and shouted, "What are you doing? Why?" Her eyes were full of hatred and anger.

"You think too much of yourself!" An uncontrollable fury had taken over Bheema. "You think you are important! You reject me, treat me like a dog. But you like this man!" He pointed to Durgesh who was rolling on the ground holding his arm. "You are an outsider; you both can die. I will lead this ashram—me." His face looked grotesque as he bared his teeth and pressed his finger to his chest. "And I will have the whole country follow me."

Suddenly, as if he had woken up from sleep, Bheema's face went blank. He looked at himself and then at Durgesh.

"Bheema?" Krupa stared at him in disbelief.

Above them, thunder cracked. Dark clouds and a bellowing wind followed.

Bheema's expression turned from blank to frightened. He looked at the ground, the swaying trees and all around, stepping back as if something or someone was coming for him. Then he turned and ran towards the cliff edge. Without stopping or turning back he jumped off the cliff.

Krupa was dumbstruck, tears rolled down her shocked

face. She stood where she was, motionless, for several minutes. Durgesh's sigh as he tried to sit up brought her back to her senses. She leaned down to find he was bleeding from several places. He had fallen on a thick root; the back of his head had a bump, and his arm was not moving.

"Can you walk, Durgesh?" she asked. Her voice choked with tears as she helped him to his feet. "I am here with you. You will be fine."

He looked straight into her eyes, "I am glad you are with me, Krupa." He wiped her tears and said softly, "You will be fine too. I am with you, always."

She understood what was not spoken in words, she understood how Durgesh felt about her, she understood what had been missing from her life and what she had finally found. She held his hand to her face and wept. The brave face of a lonely little girl—a girl who had forced herself to grow up, forced herself never to ask for anything—was gone. And Krupa felt relieved.

Durgesh moved forward and gently wrapped an arm around her. "Don't worry, Krupa. There was nothing we could have done to change his fate."

***

Krupa made Durgesh sit against a wide tree trunk and cleaned his wounds.

"Do you want to go and check the spot he jumped from?" he asked.

"No. It is a sheer drop," she said ruefully as she dressed a wound on his leg.

"I had noticed him staring at you a few times today. When I saw him creeping up from behind like that, I had an awfully bad feeling."

"I understand." Krupa looked away, not wanting to talk anymore. She started another fire next to Durgesh. "Rest for a bit and tell me when you think you can walk again."

"Shortly, I think. It is going to be sunset soon. I don't want you to be here in the dark."

She shot him a sharp glance and suppressed a smile. "I can look after myself. You are the one who is hurt." She could see how easily he had masked the pain.

"I saw something very strange today, Krupa. You might be able to explain it," said Durgesh.

"Go ahead, I am listening."

"I saw that deer. It stopped and looked at me, we were just about fifteen feet apart. Then strong wind blew, and a big piece of rock flew in the air, it literally flew. But my feet were still on the ground. It went back in the direction I had come from and just fell back to the ground. I followed it back and where I stopped, I could clearly see Bheema was up to something. It was rock-solid, how did it fly like that? It might sound funny, but for a moment it felt like everything around me was alive and aware. Does it make sense?"

Krupa shook her head, "I don't—" She broke off. The words of Mahayogi came back to her: *the forest is awake.*

"Wait, can you hear something?" said Durgesh turning his head in the direction of the sound.

Krupa rose up. "People are talking! I will be back."

And within minutes she was back with a few more people.

"This is Uboyo." She introduced the sinewy teenager. "He does not understand English, only Hindi and Hausa." The boy smiled shyly. "This is Kisna." She put her hand on the young boy's head and ruffled his hair.

"Hello, my English is pretty good. I am eleven years old. I am Uboyo's best friend and Krupa madam's favourite student." Kisna went and sat next to Durgesh as everyone laughed.

"They are from the ashram, heading towards the base. And…" Krupa looked at the other two.

"Uh, I am Lorenzo." The man extended his arm towards Durgesh, shook his hand and moved back. The man was in his fifties, had an average build and seemed a bit nervous about his surroundings. His dry, flaky skin showed that he had spent a lot of time in extreme cold. "I am a scientist from Italy, a physicist.

And that is my colleague Phillipa. She has joined us from the US."

Durgesh looked at them amazed and confused.

"We were supposed to join Professor Rollings, but our plane crashed close to Jispa. These two boys very kindly helped us and are taking us to her now. In fact, it seems we have been a bit lost for the past few hours."

Phillipa, a young woman with bright eyes, came over to Durgesh. "Do you mind if I check this?" She pointed to his arm.

"It would be best if we all go to Jispa and start afresh in the morning," announced Krupa.

"Yes," said Phillipa. "Dr Lorenzo, that plane had a fantastic medical cupboard. The boys have salvaged things from there. He can be stitched up and his fracture can be stabilised."

***

The window in the basement room was left open for the fumes from the small fire under it to escape, next to which sat Krupa lost in deep contemplation. Durgesh was sitting opposite her with his arm resting in a metal casing. Two oil lamps were burning mellow in the far corner of the room. Others were sitting with their backs to the walls, wrapped in blankets and simply observing Lorenzo. He, on the other hand, was flummoxed and could not stop pacing the length of the room.

"He does that when he cannot understand something,"

muttered Phillipa.

"Will someone explain to me what that was all about?" Lorenzo looked helpless as he glanced at everyone hoping for an answer. He walked up to Uboyo and said, "We were supposed to leave in the morning, weren't we? Then we waited for the weather to improve, but we got lost in the forest. You said that trees have moved, and paths have changed. Storms can do that, right? You did not mean that trees have actually moved." Lorenzo's round eyes were wild with restlessness and his words were heavy with disbelief. "But then at times, we all felt like the branches were tapping us or someone was following us. Then we met these people, then we got to know a man jumped off the cliff." He kept moving his arms animatedly while Kisna tried to hide his smile by covering his face with his blanket. Lorenzo straightened up and looked at Phillipa, "And then, my good lord, I have never seen anything like this, never even imagined anything like this—the ground moved, mudslides trying to push us off that place, trees leaning over. It was like … like everything in that place was alive."

"Do not dismiss anything as just a thing. The forest is awake." Krupa realised she'd spoken aloud.

"What?" Lorenzo turned to her.

"The forest is alive, isn't it?" she said. "Everything in the universe is energy, right?" She was used to teaching children, but she thought she would try explaining anyway.

"Right."

"The same electrons, neutrons, protons vibrate in living beings as those in inanimate objects. Right?"

"Right."

"What then is the difference between the two?"

Lorenzo was too exasperated to answer.

"Life! Isn't it obvious? The universal energy pervades all. Do not dismiss anything as just a thing." Krupa's eyes had a glint of confidence as she spoke.

Dr Lorenzo looked at her puzzled while Kisna was in total awe.

"You might need to start thinking like a yogi. Swamiji has been telling all of us the higher age is coming, the next level of consciousness among all beings. Science and spirituality are not two different things, simply different ways to view the same thing. I am afraid I have no other explanation for what you witnessed today."

"Tell me again what happened to your other friend." Phillipa leaned forward getting her knees closer to her chest.

"Bheema? He wanted to push Krupa off the cliff. I intervened and we had a physical fight. He suddenly looked very scared of something and before we knew he ran and jumped off the cliff himself," explained Durgesh. "Bad intentions?"

Phillipa sat back and looked up towards the ceiling, her eyes far away, "It seems like the forest did not like us too. Or maybe just one of us. Imagine, just imagine if all of nature, forests, rivers, animals, everything decided to take revenge on humans for centuries of mindlessness—for the state we are in."

Krupa smiled, "Maybe not revenge! But the forest was expressing some intention today for sure."

"Anyway, what are we doing tomorrow morning?" Phillipa looked at Lorenzo and Krupa.

"I am setting off to go to Jaipur in the morning. I will be able to find some help further down the highway," said Krupa.

"Is there another way to go to the base avoiding that mountain?" asked Lorenzo sitting down.

Uboyo nudged Kisna. Kisna said, "Yes, but it will take twice the time. We will have to camp out one night."

"Can't we just send a message to the professor?" asked Phillipa.

"The base does not have reliable connectivity," said Krupa.

"It was a very bad decision to come here. I cannot stand this ghost village for another day." Lorenzo looked at Uboyo and Kisna. "We leave tomorrow morning, too."

Uboyo nodded.

Krupa knew Uboyo loved the longer route and often went

wandering in the mountains on his own. He was a bright young boy who could already meditate for hours. She was not going to ask him to come with her. The others needed his help more than her. She looked at Durgesh, who was already watching her. "I think you can go back to the base too, Durgesh," she said.

"There is absolutely no chance. I am with you. If you prefer, I can stay ten feet behind you."

She smiled and shook her head.

***

It had been seven hours since Swamiji had retreated to his room. Everyone knew he could meditate for days at a stretch, but never when he was living amongst people. Meera was restless, feeling she needed to check on him.

She opened the door softly; the last of the daylight was retreating from the window. After placing a small oil lamp on the floor, she looked up. Sweat was dripping down Swamiji's face—he was glowing amber as if something was burning inside him and yet his expression was calm.

Worried that she should not have gone in, she came out quickly and joined the others who were sitting around the bonfire singing together.

Within minutes Swamiji came down looking unruffled and sat next to her.

"Meera!" he said in his slow voice. "Everything okay?"

"Yes, Swamiji," she stuttered.

"Would you be so kind as to get me a hot drink with jaggery, Meera?"

"Yes, Swamiji," replied Meera, puzzled by this unusual request, and scampered off.

Her place was quickly taken by Professor Rollings. "You have been missing all day today," she said.

"I had to make sure children reached their destination safely," Swamiji replied as he waved to the people joining the group.

"And did they?" In her mind, all she wanted to know was that Krupa was safe.

"Let us say, everything is okay."

Professor Rollings looked at Swamiji. His head was shaking slightly, and his eyes were dim. "You look tired. What is the matter?" she asked.

Swamiji lifted his gaze to meet her eyes. "I have witnessed something today that demanded a lot from me."

The singing and laughter reduced to hum in the background as Professor Rollings leaned towards him; she knew there was more she needed to hear.

"The forest," Swamiji continued, "a part of it…" He paused again, his expression a mixture of awe and dread. "I have seen consciousness materialize in a whole new way. In this new age, we do not yet fully understand the forces at work here, but I fear nature may not be as forgiving."

Professor Rollings handled her perplexed mind with perfect composure as Swamiji described the events in the forest. With a solemn face, she asked, "Can you show me? Teach me a bit about Sheersha yoga?" The only way to understand the events around her now seemed to be a lesson on the ways of this man.

Swamiji gently smiled. He nodded and the brightness of his eyes returned with a twinkle. "Let us begin in the morning."

Chapter 24

Sur

All was calm the next morning. The gentle waves of the ocean rolled in to kiss the feet of the three men and retreated with a faint murmur. Together the men stood and gazed towards the orange-lilac horizon. The new day had filled each one's heart with a new hope.

Joash's mind was far beyond the horizon, readying itself for whatever was next. He looked at the glass vial in his hand—a thin layer of misty water still moved above the shining soil. He thought of the ester's words; he had hesitated to place the drop of healing water on Callum's lips. But in the end, the decision to help Callum did not feel wrong to him. What more trouble was in store for him, only time would tell.

Hamza had accepted his metal leg. He closed his eyes in gratitude. Turning towards Callum, who was standing right next to him, he noticed how just in one day the boy had become skinnier and pale. Yet he stood smiling, looking at his curled toes, trying to hold on to the sand that the waves wanted to wash away.

"You saved him, Joash," said Hamza.

Joash nodded pursing his lips, gave half a smile and put one arm around Hamza. "And you saved both of us."

"What next?" asked Hamza.

Joash sighed. "I need to carry on," he said, curling his fingers tightly around the vial. "Can you help me get the kropter back?"

Before Hamza could reply, his wrist-pad beeped and an image of his wife, Fatima, appeared. "People from the authority are here," she said. "They need to speak to all three of you."

***

A short ride away from the beach was a row of sand-coloured houses. One of them belonged to Hamza's family.

"These houses were built in just three days after the last tsunami," said Hamza as they approached the house in a small car. "The sea has moved in even more since then."

Joash looked at Hamza and then looked away; he understood his worry.

Soon, the men entered the room where Hamza's father and

wife were sitting opposite a couple of officials.

"Hope all of you are recovering well. We are here to give you some important information," said the man. "First of all, your landing in Oman was illegal. However, fortunately we have good relations with the country of your origin and we were alerted by your country's authority just minutes before your crash to expect you."

Joash and Callum looked at each other.

"Your authority manager has personally requested that Callum Bailey should not travel until further notice from them, as he did not declare his intentions when leaving the country. He can stay comfortably at the British authority office in Muscat for as long as needed."

Callum's jaw dropped. He looked at Joash, who shook his head in disapproval.

"Joash Pundit, if you wish to travel you can, but only by sea or land."

"Why not air?" asked Joash.

"Just in the last week, we have had eighteen deaths in hopling-related accidents. The Sultan has banned all flying till things get better."

Joash quietly thought of the aster's words: *The high seas await you.*

The woman continued, "Your aircraft has been sending repair requests to its service department in Glasgow, but the damage is serious and they are unable to remote-repair it. We have been asked to keep it safe till it can be transported back. We do not have any hoplings that would take you so far. Also, the risk is not only to you but to our people and property too. At least we are letting you go by sea; our people are not allowed to travel at all. We have lost numerous lives, fishing robots and vessels. You haven't chosen the best time to travel, Mr Pundit."

Joash looked at Hamza who was trying to work out a solution too.

"Thank you for coming here and explaining everything," said Hamza politely.

"And what about me? I don't want to go to Muscat. I am going with Joash." Callum was full of despair.

"Callum," said Joash thoughtfully, "your father has decided the safest route for you. I cannot take you with me."

The two men got up. "You can stay with your friends till tomorrow morning. We will arrange your transportation to Muscat."

"Well, thank you very much!" Callum did not want to hide his annoyance.

Hamza gestured for Callum to calm down as he went out to see the officials leave.

Callum tapped his wrist-pad and brought his air-screen up. He tapped a few times and the screen read—*Dad in a meeting.*

Do not disturb. Leave message. But Callum was restless and started researching sea routes from Oman. Fancy boats and large merchant ships were all flashing one by one in front of his eyes.

Just then, the curtain to the next room lifted and Yasmin came out holding a little boy in her arms, who was giggling loudly.

"This is Sophia, Hamza's daughter," said Yasmin. "She wanted to sneak up on you."

Callum found himself gaping at possibly the most attractive girl he had ever seen. Yasmin's eyes fell upon Callum, who gulped and turned back to his screen. "Staying here can't be that bad," he said.

***

While Callum clapped and cheered for Sophia's dance performances, Joash waited restlessly for Hamza to return. Sitting down felt like a crime to him.

"I do not know what to do," said Hamza as he walked into the house. "No one would give me a boat or vessel! No one!" He raised his voice in exasperation. "They are either scared of the authority or of losing their vessel. What was the point of allowing you to travel by sea?"

Joash was sitting with his elbows on his legs, staring hard at the floor, his temples pulsating visibly. Yasmin's eyes were fixed on Joash.

Suddenly Callum moved forward and spoke, "What is this?"

An image of a wooden boat had appeared on his air-screen.

Yasmin's eyes lit up. "A dhow boat! I know where to find one."

Minutes later, they were in a huge yard full of wood. They were walking amongst boats at various stages of manufacturing, but there were no people there.

"This is a lot of wood," said Callum.

"Yes, it is local cedar, also timber and teak. Boat-making tradition in Sur is centuries old. I worked in this yard for a bit after Hamza left, but now it lies abandoned," said Yasmin.

She overtook others and quickly got on top of a vessel.

"This is the one then?" said Hamza.

Yasmin nodded, "Possibly the only one that is seaworthy."

Joash was curious as all of them stepped on the deck. He had only ever seen a boat like this in children's books. It was dark brown and fully wooden, with a sharp bow, a raised hull, a tall mast, a small cabin with a few windows and a ten-foot wide deck. It looked nearly finished. Even if it wasn't, Joash wouldn't know.

"Does it have an engine or an operating system?" he asked.

"Neither!" replied Yasmin. "It is an ancient style of boat called 'Dhow'. No technology, so no risk of anything failing."

Hamza was deep in thought again. "I am not sure if it will be able to stand storms though."

"Do you have to go, no matter what?" A certain melancholy crept into Yasmin's voice.

Joash was struck by the way Yasmin was looking at him. Before he could say anything, Hamza spoke again, "Do you think you can navigate the sea?"

"I have done a lot of things recently that I have never done before," replied Joash.

"Sure, he can take on anything," said Callum with a smile.

Joash could see a mischief in Callum's eyes. "You are staying here, right?" he said.

Callum jumped in front of Yasmin and said, "May I stay here for a bit longer?"

She chuckled. "Of course!" she said and strolled away.

"The speed," said Hamza again, "it will take a few days to reach, maybe two or three. I don't know, Joash, if this is the best idea. I can go to other towns and try…"

But Joash had no doubts. Standing on the deck of that dhow, he knew that this was the boat he was supposed to take. He put his hand on Hamza's shoulder, "It is okay Hamza! I know that this is what I need to do. Trust me." He looked up to the clear sky and flexed his neck; he was ready for the storms.

***

Everybody had gathered to bid farewell to Joash at the port. The sail was set, and the cabin was packed with everything he thought he'd need. As the cream-coloured sail ballooned, Joash knew the wind was ready too.

Hamza was not pleased with Joash's choice of departure time, but the setting sun did not daunt Joash.

"This is the compass," said Yasmin pointing to a large dial mounted on a wooden stand close to the bow. "You might not need it if your personal device keeps working but then you never know. And this is the kamal that Father told you about." She pressed a small wooden card with a string in Joash's hand. She held his gaze for a long second. Unable to find any reflection of her feelings in his eyes, she painfully looked away.

Callum was unusually quiet and glum. Joash held him by his shoulders "It's okay, Callum! I hope to see you back in London."

"You better do," replied Callum loudly as Joash climbed up the dhow.

The dhow started to move, and Joash waved at the small crowd behind him.

"Remember all that you have learnt about sailboats today," shouted Hamza.

"I will!" Joash saw Yasmin's eyes fill up and he knew there was nothing he could have said.

He looked ahead now and took a deep breath in. He touched his wrist-pad, and it was working again. A map of his route appeared on the air-screen. He was heading east.

Chapter 25

At Sea

As his personal device was working, Joash decided to spend time learning more about sailboats and taking live help from Hamza's family. Hamza's father had already given him the first few simulation lessons. When the connection started to break, he just sat on the deck with his eyes closed, trying to control the sickness that had started.

However, the first thing Joash checked was the cabin to make sure Callum was not hiding among the boxes. He could not deny that he missed his friend.

The next morning, he woke from a dreamless sleep. It seemed like his nausea had been cured; his body had learnt to ride with the waves. His eyes explored the horizon in all directions—blue merging with blue. He was a tiny speck in the limitless expanse around him.

The voyage felt strangely smooth, so much so that when more than twenty-four hours had passed uneventfully, Joash thought that something was not right. The clouds were sailing away slowly in the sky, the imperceptible wind pushed the boat gently and the occasional clicks and whistles of dolphins were mixed with the slur of waves. Night came and he lay on the deck looking at the stars interspersed between the now fast-moving clouds. A strange feeling took his mind back to the day he had lost his parents. He saw his mother's face; he saw his father's smile; he never got to say goodbye. *Where are they now? Are they watching over me? Will I see them again?*

A big drop of water fell on his forehead. With his heart still feeling heavy, he came to his senses—the stars were gone, and it felt like it was going to rain. The ocean seemed unusually still. Joash checked the navigator on his device, the mast and the sail. There was no forecast of a storm. He was still going towards Gujarat, his destination, beyond the sunken port—Porbandar.

Suddenly, he felt the wind direction change in the most subtle way and with it came a chill. As Joash began to adjust the sail, a thin mist surrounded his dhow. The next moment he heard a sound coming from far away, a deep breathy singing that sent a current running through his flesh. It was no whale or dolphin but humans vocalising a wordless song—which felt like a forgotten memory, a calling, a longing, a heartrending tune of deep meaning—the groaning ocean providing the music. Tears surfaced in Joash's eyes as he looked for the source of this sound.

Through the mist, he saw the most unusual scene. A few feet away from the dhow there were shapes of people—translucent, luminous and moving. And there were other shapes he did not recognise. He rubbed his eyes to make sure he was not hallucinating. People were appearing out of thin air, walking on the waves and climbing up something that looked like a staircase made of clouds. He could not see any faces, but these shapes were emerging from the dark and merging back into the night sky. *Is this another Sangam?* he thought.

Far away, there was another bright area which looked like the silver rain. As he looked at these souls drifting into the oblivion, he felt a sense of deep sadness. He needed to get away from there. A tension started to build up in his body as he went from one end of the dhow to the other.

Then, the singing stopped. The fog grew thicker. He could not see the people anymore but known faces appeared in the fog. Wherever he looked, he saw his mother calling him just like she did when he was a toddler, his father's frown as he said, "Come on! Come here."

He felt a desperate urge to go towards them. He held the gunwale and looked down to the waves that were slapping the sides of the dhow. He got ready to jump but a sudden flash of light from the cabin stopped him.

No! What is this? he thought as he took a step back.

At the same moment, a loud chinking sound seemed to be calling him. A metal lantern, that Joash had failed to notice all this time, was swinging on a hook just outside the cabin. Inside it, a flame was dancing. It was the flame he had seen in Edinburgh, a white sparkling centre with a red periphery. But this time, no face was visible in the flame.

He held the lantern with his hands and rested his head on it. *What kind of test is this?*

Finally, the rain arrived. Joash checked the sail again. His device had stopped working now. He walked back to the cabin and lifted the lantern out of the hook. Then placing it on the cabin floor, he wrapped his wet body in blankets. Things were knocking around in the cabin and out on the deck. The noise did not bother him. If a storm wanted to take him, it could and maybe then he would meet his Ma and Papa again. If he had taken his steps carefully that day, he would have been able to help his Ma. He too should have died that day; he should not have come back.

Despite everything, sleep came to him and calmed his troubled heart.

In the morning, it was overcast still but quieter. He heard some noise and stepped out of the cabin; a dolphin jumped high up and dived back into the water, followed by several others. A pod of dolphins was swimming along the dhow, they were squeaking loudly.

The peace lasted only a few hours and nature's drama began to unfold. The waves started to swell up again in the buffeting wind. The dhow was tossing and tilting madly. Clouds grew darker obscuring the sun completely, frequent lightning emblazoned the sky. Joash held on to the mast tightly with his bare fingers. The water rose higher, falling back to hit his boat and slash his face. He took a deep breath and told himself that all his weaknesses had been washed off and he was strong enough to face anything. He looked at the flame in the lantern, back on its hook, still burning bright.

Just then, the wind bellowed loudly, pushing him against the mast, where he stood still trying to keep his feet on the dhow. But as another giant wave lifted the dhow high up, Joash was thrown towards the cabin. The rain started to hit the dhow with its full fury. The sky lit up as several zigzag white lines collided.

With a crackling noise, another lightning bolt travelled from the sky towards the boat like an axe on a tree trunk.

Joash watched aghast as the boat split. At the same time, another wave rose mountain-high ready to engulf him like a monster. He held onto the cabin door as his half of the boat was thrown high up in the air. The pieces of the boat and he came plummeting down going to the depths of the sea. A still blackness engulfed him, and his plight was over.

Chapter 26
The Base

The plight was also over for Uboyo, Kisna and Lorenzo when they finally reached the base after a difficult trek. Phillipa, who had found the story of Krupa's journey deeply interesting had decided to join her on her way to Jaipur.

Kisna and Uboyo found themselves sitting opposite Swamiji while Lorenzo wandered off.

Uboyo could see Swamiji looking at his bleeding feet. To him, walking in the mountains bare feet was no matter of tribulation, it was pure joy. He refused to wear shoes because he could not find the path without feeling the earth, so he used to say.

"Swamiji Bheema, I have something terrible to tell you,"

said Uboyo solemnly.

Swamiji's expression did not change. His gaze shifted to Kisna who looked distressed. Patting Kisna on his shoulder, he said, "Don't worry, I know about Bheema. No one could have done anything about it. His jealousy and deceit led to his downfall. 'The higher age' demands us to have a fair heart and fair purpose. Let us pray that Bheema finds his peace." He sat straight and closed his eyes.

Uboyo folded his hands together and bent his head down.

When Swamiji opened his eyes again, he smiled down at Uboyo. "You have done well, my child. Now go and get this looked at," he said, pointing to the cuts on Uboyo's feet. "Meera can do something about this."

As soon as Uboyo and Kisna left, Professor Rollings arrived.

"Did you venture further today, Stella?" asked Swamiji.

"I did," she said, raising her eyebrows as she took a seat opposite Swamiji. "I walked through to the other side of this mountain. I got quite curious about this old bridge I saw. Does it have a story?"

"Hmm, it is strange that you ask. I do not know when was it made and why. The next mountain, it is a difficult one. It is not inhabited, has a very rough terrain and the forest is quite dense. Some even say there is a complex tunnel network running through it. There are man-made paths but people don't venture there much. Sheersha yoga lore talks about a mountain called Tirtha and its significance as a preserver of life. But until now we did not know that Tirtha was right next to us. It was Krupa who discovered it, quite recently actually."

Professor Rollings' eyes narrowed. "And how does it preserve life? Do you believe in what you know?"

"I believe in *Dhi*. It was like the mountain had been hiding from me all this while. But since Krupa came back, I can feel its magnificence all the time. As if she has somehow woken up the sleeping energy of that place. Krupa and her brother have a role to play in all of this."

Not a shred of her resentment appeared on Professor Rollings' face as Joash's name was mentioned. She could not recall disliking anyone so strongly. "And what role that might be?" she asked plainly.

As he explained the role of Prakruti Saram in the present crisis and the urgent need to find it, Swamiji could see the glint in Professor Rollings' eyes but nothing beyond. He had never met a soul that guarded itself so tightly—perhaps wary of pain, perhaps something different altogether.

Noticing Swamiji's cogitative expression, Professor Rollings quickly said, "A very important quest then. Let us hope they make it. I am willing to help in any way I can."

Shielding his eyes from the bright sun, Lorenzo climbed up the wooden steps.

Swamiji and Professor Rollings greeted him. Lorenzo moved forwards to shake hands with Swamiji but suddenly his smile vanished as he looked at the man closely. Hesitantly, he nodded and stepped back. He tried to engage in a conversation with Professor Rollings but could not shake off the unease. He just did not want to be there.

The professor's eyes followed Swamiji as he suddenly got up and retreated to his room.

"So, Professor," Lorenzo paused, gulped and asked, "What have you found?"

"Hmm, it is a curious place, Lorenzo. It has less carbon as you would imagine. Also, it does not have the new element, Elusium. This place seems to be in an invisible bubble. Storms seem to touch and go at the borders. What would be interesting to find out is whether there are any more places like this one. Imagine, if we could put the whole planet in this bubble."

She smiled and looked down, amused by the impossibility of her idea. Shaking her head, she continued, "Swami here believes that some external forces have entered our environment and they are causing a further release of Elusium. He says the flashes of lightning, tsunamis, disturbances in the earth's crust or the so-called earthquakes are all linked. Perhaps the most curious thing for me is the way he assures me that we are moving closer to a solution each day. I am yet to learn how. Believe me, Dr Lorenzo, there is lots more that you will learn and that will amaze you. Welcome to Moksha Parvat."

***

Patrick Zuma reached the ashram balcony feeling out of breath. He sat down on a pair of folded blankets and said, "Oh how I wish the internet was working here instead of all the way up there."

"Patrick, remember Dr Lorenzo?" said Professor Rollings.

"Oh yes, of course! You look in fantastic shape, Dr Lorenzo."

Lorenzo gave a sardonic smile. He knew he had not had a bath in days and his cuts and bruises were covered in mud, but that was the least of his problems. He wanted to see what she had been up to. He sure could find something in the environment here that could trump her findings.

Patrick Zuma turned to Professor Rollings and said, "I have some news! On the other side of the bubble, I was finally able to get a decent connection and get in touch with the London team. The new element has been now identified in all parts of the world as you expected, Professor, and sadly also in water. The places possibly least affected are Bhutan and parts of Finland.

I have asked them to try and get data from various mountain ranges. We could assign robots but again technology is becoming unpredictable. And"—Professor Rollings leaned closer as Patrick Zuma continued slowly— "the silver rain! More and more reports relate them to being something positive. Some people have also mentioned it cures aches and so on. I think people are starting to get quite excited about this phenomenon."

"Hmm." She thought for a moment. "We would love to understand that better, won't we? For now, we study the ecosystem of this place in detail and in time maybe the next mountain too."

Chapter 27

Murdeshwar, India

Like a mountain, the statue of Shiva stood high above the wavering sea. It was a sight Ananya loved—the enormous sculpture of the God who wears a snake in his hair, sitting with his eyes closed, away from the shore with most of his body submerged in the sea.

For eight-year-old Ananya sneaking past her grandfather had been too easy this morning. Of course, she knew she was not allowed to go close to the water on her own. And she would not have, had she not spotted something unusual. Never before had she seen dolphins so close to the shore. She jumped and clapped in excitement as the dolphins continued to sing above the wind noise.

Slowly and curiously, she moved closer to the gently splashing waves. The pod of dolphins was moving towards the right. Not wanting to miss the spectacle, Ananya started walking along the beach counting the dolphins going up and down. With her eyes fixed on the dolphins, she carried on for several minutes. Suddenly, she stumbled. She looked down then jumped back with a shock. A man lay unconscious, tightly holding onto a plank of wood. He had several wounds on his face and his skin looked shrivelled up as if he had been in the water for too long. Ananya ran straight back home.

Within minutes her grandfather and a group of men came back and found Joash.

Murdeshwar was a small town and when something happened everyone knew. A small crowd had gathered around Gopalan's house to find out about the new arrival from the sea.

"It is okay. You all go home now. The man is still not conscious," said the old lady in her quivering voice. She was Gopalan's mother Leela, known as Amma by the whole town. She was also the oldest person alive in the town. She despised modern robots and technology, which is why she sat outside on the veranda when a doctor and two robots arrived.

***

"His identity has been confirmed by the UK authority. He is a low or no-risk individual. A storm-chasing journalist, I believe. No wonder he has ended up here like this" said the doctor going through some data on the air-screen. "Here, do you want to know his history and stuff? That is the access." He looked at Gopalan who was also the mayor of the town.

"No, leave all that. How is he doing? Is he going to wake up soon?" Gopalan was sitting in a cane chair next to the bed where Joash lay.

"Doctor! Patient moving. All vital signs near normal" announced a medic robot.

"There, you got your answer," said the doctor. He checked a few things on the machines attached to Joash's body. "Four fractured ribs, several deep wounds, torn ligaments... Uh, in short everything is fixable. Except for the mental trauma of being in a sea-storm. I am sure you and Amma can help with that." He smiled at Gopalan. "I have done all I can. He should be fine soon. I cannot say about mobility though. A long rest will help him heal. I will leave him with this one attachment to take care of his aches and pains." He looked at Joash thoughtfully and said, "He is either very lucky or very strong."

By the time, the doctor left with his paraphernalia, it was late afternoon. The crowd had dwindled now too.

"Shiva, Shiva," said Leela looking at Joash as she hobbled

into the room. "Take that wire off the poor thing!"

"Amma, he needs it," said Gopalan from the far end of the room.

"What is his name?" Leela settled in the cane chair.

"Joash Pundit."

"Oh! He is from around here," said Leela widening her sunken eyes with bright curiosity.

"No Amma, he is from the UK."

"Matters not. He has Indian blood in him."

Gopalan laughed lightly as he continued to work on his screen, "Yes, guess you can look at the dry blood and say that. He could be a tenth generation. Who knows!"

Leela was looking at Joash's face, transfixed. Then as if she knew him, she touched his forehead with her wrinkly hand and called out, "Joash! Wake up now!"

Joash moaned in pain, moved his fingers and slowly opened his eyes.

Leela was thrilled. "Hey, hey!" she exclaimed. "Look who is awake."

Gopalan quickly came over to the bed. "Hello! How are you feeling?"

Joash did not reply but tried to sit up in his bed. He first needed to comprehend that he was still alive.

"You are going to be fine. You have been checked and treated by medics," said Gopalan.

A sharp pain in his back made Joash realise he was not fit to move yet. His eyes fell upon a small figure of Lord Shiva on the table by the wall.

"India! Yes, you are in India," spoke Leela excitedly as if reading his mind.

Just then Ananya came running into the room, holding the lantern from the dhow. "Can I keep this? Please," she begged, looking at Joash.

"Anu, I told you not to come here," said Gopalan to his granddaughter. "How did you even know he was awake?"

"Even the neighbours would have heard Amma say 'Look, who is awake'," replied Ananya. She pouted and stared at Gopalan with narrow eyes.

Joash saw the lantern she was holding; it was from the dhow. "Where did you find—" he asked softly.

"Outside." She hid behind Gopalan as she spoke.

"It was lying next to you on the beach," answered Gopalan.

"Beach?" enquired Joash.

"Yes, Ananya found you this morning and alerted us. There were some pieces of wood nearby too."

Joash looked at Ananya and managed to say, "Yes!" hoping she would understand this concise reply.

He spent the rest of the day confined to his bed, partly because his body needed rest to heal and partly because Leela did not allow him to get up.

Leela was a highly intelligent lady. At one-hundred-and-two years of age, she had no dearth of energy and enthusiasm. She told Joash several stories from her younger years—how the majestic statue of Shiva, which was surrounded by water now, was once on dry land on the top of a hill. She believed the statue was magical and would survive anything. Joash did not mind her at all as she did not ask any questions. Gopalan came in a few times and requested his mother to let Joash rest.

"The area has only one medical facility which is a bit far," Gopalan explained. "Our doctors on call are rather good, I think you will be just fine here. I understand that your travel documents are fine and your destination is Jaipur. When you feel better, we can see what to do about it. What I don't understand is why you chose to travel in a dhow when the weather all over the world is going crazy."

Joash wanted to thank Gopalan, but his tongue was not taking instructions from his brain today. He just stared blankly at him.

Leela interrupted, "Don't ask him any questions yet! Let him be!"

To his relief night finally came and he could shut his eyes. He thought of Jaipur, thought of the things he wanted to do tomorrow. *Not far now, I am almost here,* he thought.

Joash would have stayed awake if he'd known where his dreams were going to take him. At first, he saw himself as a translucent being floating in a bright space. The next instant, he was Fingal. He hated himself. There was Miria again, just in front of him. He called her but she looked away. She was climbing up a great hill. It was quite dark. Suddenly, a large fire erupted at the top of the hill. It spewed lava and sent red-orange rivers of fire down the slopes. But Miria did not stop. He called her again. Then he understood that he was to reach the top of the hill too, but he could not move. The fire was growing bigger and engulfing all things while Joash looked at it helplessly. Overcome with fear, sadness and desperation he let out a gasp and opened his eyes.

He seemed unable to control the flood of tears. Leela was by the bedside, staring at him looking shocked and worried.

"Calm down, dear! Calm down," she said holding his hand.

Suddenly aware of what was going on, Joash sat up. His physical pain had become dull, but his mind felt full and heavy. He held the vial hanging from his neck and looked at it. *Fire, I need fire. But where to find it?* he thought.

"It … it was just a dream." As Joash uttered those words Leela sat back in her chair giving him a knowing look.

"Tell me about it, your dream, will you, Son?" she asked like a doctor asking his patient to describe his symptoms.

There was something about Leela that made Joash feel that he had to tell this lady everything. And so, as the first of morning light entered the room, he began the story of his life—this one and part of a previous one.

When he stopped, Leela leaned forward and said slowly, "I can take you to someone who can help."

Joash nodded. All he wished for, at that moment, was to be able to speak to Guruji again.

"Do you believe in karma?" asked Leela.

"Yes!"

She smiled. "Even if you did not, it wouldn't change a thing. Nothing is a coincidence; you might have heard this in your life sometime. You may have come here to find out about that dream." Her eyes twinkled as she rose from the chair. "It is morning! If you feel good enough to walk, we can go and see a friend after breakfast."

***

The waves were rising high and lashing at the shore loudly as Leela and Joash went along the beach. Palm trees swayed wildly in the wind as if in conversation with the grumbling dark clouds.

Joash could not help but notice how unruffled Leela looked with the weather.

"It is like this here all the time now. It does not matter." She had read his mind again. After a pause, she said, "The man we are going to meet ... he is a bit..." She pouted her mouth looking thoughtful and the skin of her forehead convoluted into several curves. He understood that she did not know how to describe this man.

***

It was a long walk, and not many people were out. Leela kept talking all the way. She told Joash that her son was a kind and capable man, the best this town could have. His wife and their son had died a few years ago and she loved looking after her great-granddaughter.

They reached a clearing about half a mile from the seashore. A man was fixing a thatch roof of a small shack. As he saw the two approaching, he jumped from the six-foot-high roof, landing smoothly on the ground. Coming closer, Joash could see the man was probably in his late seventies. Dressed in all white, he looked thin but agile. He had a white turban on his head and he wore a pair of large white circular earrings, but the most peculiar thing about him was his ears. The earrings were held by the middle part of the ears and just below them were the holes in his earlobes which were bigger than his ears. The lower part of his earlobes was hanging halfway down his neck. He had tanned skin and small beady eyes with bright thin, white eyebrows that matched his turban.

Leela walked up to the man. He bowed down to greet her; she placed her hand on his turban and waited for him to stand up again. They had a quiet conversation while Joash waited a few metres away.

She trudged back to Joash and said, "Go and speak to him, Son. He is a yogi and very knowledgeable. If at any point, you feel like you don't want to, just come outside and we will go back home."

"Where will you be?"

"Just outside here. I will look at my Shiva and pray."

She touched Joash's cheek gently with her hand and he could feel the reassurance she wanted to give.

"Be careful," she whispered.

Joash frowned, confounded by this comment.

As Joash approached, the man gave him a hearty smile that filled up his small face; he had no teeth. An inexplicably strange sensation ran through Joash's body.

Soon they were inside the tiny hut. There was minimal stuff there, probably no electricity too, just a jute cot and a few other things. It was easy to say it was a recluse's abode.

Joash sat down in the cot. The man quietly studied him with a keen interest.

"Hmm, where do you come from?" He spoke with a lisp and a keen interest; his voice had a grating tone yet it was as child-like as his face. He smiled, exposing his gums once again. Several creases lifted his cheeks pulling the corners of his mouth almost to his eyes. He was sitting down with his legs curled up close to his body with just his feet touching the ground.

"The UK," said Joash as politely as he could.

"Who brought you to this world?"

Joash looked at the man; he did not know how he felt about him yet, but he had nothing to hide. "I was born in Jaipur. My father was Kartik Pundit and my mother was Erin Pundit. My father was a yoga scholar and a philosopher. He was well known among the Sheersha yogis of the north."

"There! I thought I could see something in you," said the man.

"I lost them in the floods eleven years ago," said Joash.

"No, you have not, not really." Those words came out with an ease that stunned Joash.

"I am Jagannath. You can call me Jaggu Baba like everybody else in the town." The man spoke at a strange pace, quickly at first and then very slowly. "What's that around your neck?"

Instinctively, Joash's hand reached for the vial.

"Can I look at it?" Jaggu Baba brought his hand forth, a hint of expectation in his eyes.

Joash hesitated but gave the vial to him anyway.

Holding it in his hand, Jaggu Baba moved his chapped fingers slowly over it; his eyes opened wide and glinted with wonder.

"Blessed healing water on pious soil, together but not yet merged into each other." There was an edge of envy in his voice. "The bottle has seen some bad times, but just like you it is not broken." He gave the vial back to Joash. His face relaxed and suddenly, the innocence was gone. He held Joash's eyes in his gaze, scrutinizing what lay in their depths.

Again, a strange cold sensation ran through Joash, starting in his toes and settling on his forehead. He blinked and asked, "Who are you?"

The big child-like smile instantly reappeared on the man's face, "I just told you! Jaggu Baba!" He looked down and then darted a sharp glance towards Joash. "I used to live among the Sheersha yogis of Mount Kailash, a long time ago. I had some gifts. But drunk with the powers of those gifts, I did something I should not have. This life is my penance. I have been waiting for you to move forward."

"Waiting for me?" Joash was flummoxed.

"Yes," said Jaggu Baba quietly. Then he rose to stand, his eyes far away; a gush of wind found its way inside the hut. His voice rose to a higher place. "A message from the masters: 'A karma yogi will come to you, with blessings from the bright realm and this one. Help him on his path and your debt shall be clear.'" He paused and his body relaxed as he spoke softly once again, "Prakruti Saram—those who aim to go deep into Sheersha yoga must know this name. I have not read it, but what you carry around your neck is what the sacred text talks about. This means the time has come for a new age, a higher one." A certain excitement rose in his voice, his eyes had a new shine and his hands spread wide as if trying to catch the moment. "I can see all the signs. Yes! It is happening, powers are going to collide in this realm and we—you and me, child—are going to witness it all."

Jaggu Baba closed his eyes revelling in the revelation and Joash watched him. The man did know a lot about Sheersha yoga but Joash was waiting for something more.

With a curiosity in his gaze, Jaggu Baba bent his head slightly, looked at Joash and spoke again, "You are looking for something." His smile acquired a sly touch. "Maybe I can help you."

Joash remained quiet.

"I know who has tamed the fiercest fire. I know how to get it, but it won't be easy." Jaggu Baba threw a look at Joash from the corner of his eyes, he seemed like a different person from the one

Joash had seen when he had entered the hut.

"Why should I trust you?"

Jaggu Baba moved swiftly and brought his face close to Joash's. "There are a select few in this world who could know what you are carrying, boy." His voice grew louder with anger. "Do not question me."

The next moment, his wide eyes softened and the child-like innocence returned. Looking displeased with himself, he moved his gaze down.

"I will take you to the fire element if you give me something in return." The words come out softer this time.

"And what would that be?"

"Your mind." His smile showed that Jaggu Baba was relishing this conversation. "You have had visions of the past, but you do not know what to do with that knowledge. I can help you … help you understand the twists of your past lives. I can make it easy for you to navigate through this one."

"What do you get by helping me navigate this life?"

"I meditate upon the mind—I am the master of the mind. I can send your mind to the Stairwell of Infinity, a place where every level would show you the whole story of a different past life you have had. And there is also a window to the depth of other realms." Jaggu Baba's eyes narrowed and his voice dropped. "I can tell you have been close to a dark being—you have a connection. Let me come to your stairwell and have a glimpse of this dark power. Just a glimpse…"

Joash's ears twitched as he tried to process the demand, of which he understood very little. Jaggu Baba's head slowly moved, his mouth unable to close waiting for an answer, his eyes not leaving Joash's.

"You mean to let you enter my mind. And if you are right, let you see all my previous lives?" asked Joash finally. His palms had started to feel sweaty, but he kept his calm. He needed to weigh what was unfolding here.

"No. That is not what I said. Just open the door for me when you see the window to the universe. I cannot see anything you don't want me to—no one can."

"If you are the master of the mind, why do you need my mind to glimpse the dark power?"

"Because I cannot do it by myself. I have no connection with it … yet."

"But why, why do it at all?"

The silence between the two men, made the sound of wind whooshing seem very loud. After a few moments, Jaggu Baba said, "You did not finish your Sheersha yoga education with your guru, did you?"

Joash's face looked crestfallen with shock at the sudden mention of his guru. Unable to respond he looked down towards the uneven mud floor.

"Yogeshwarananda. He was your guru, wasn't he?"

Joash threw a sharp look towards Jaggu Baba.

"Do not be surprised and do not be disappointed. Do not dwell on matters you don't yet understand. Not every yogi you meet along the way will embrace you and bless you." Jaggu Baba raised his eyebrows. "A lot was written about this quest long before you were born. No one knows everything but a few know a lot. You, my boy, seem ill-prepared to carry on. Time is not on your side. For the sake of this world, if you want to succeed accept my help."

Joash brought his hands together, interlacing his fingers he squeezed them hard and shut his eyes. Various thoughts were flicking through his mind. *What are the implications of what Jaggu Baba wants to do? He knows everything, yes, he does. What else can I do?*

"What do I need to do?" he said, opening his eyes.

***

Joash lay flat on his back in the cot.

Jaggu Baba spoke into his ear. "Listen to my voice and let go. I will take you on a journey within your soul. Just let go of the present moment for a bit. Get ready." He brought out a large seashell.

The seashell trumpeted and Joash closed his eyes. Minutes passed by as Jaggu Baba kept his hand gently on Joash's forehead. The sound of the ocean waves found a rhythm with Joash's heartbeat, but nothing happened.

"What are you holding onto? You have nothing to lose. Look at your third eye and fix your concentration there," said Jaggu Baba.

The conch sounded again. This time Joash felt his hair stand up and heard a faint ringing in his ears. The waves were getting louder and stronger too. He lay there with his eyes closed, seeing colours and patterns of all sorts changing in intensity and brightness.

"Deep inside this soul is the story of all its journeys." Jaggu Baba moved around the cot. "A record of all the sins and good deeds. May the *Dhi* help you find what you need to know to settle your account." There was silence for a moment, then Baba whispered into Joash's ear, "Fall."

***

At that very moment, Joash felt like he really was falling. He was falling through nothingness, it was neither dark nor light, he had no form, no body, just an awareness. Then, he felt his awareness slowly falling alongside a structure that was like a multi-storey building in space, there were countless floors with changing scenes. He could penetrate the scene like mist and witness what was going on in each room of the floor. He went to the topmost floor, and he saw himself as a newborn in his mother's arms, then a baby, then a toddler. It was the present life—he could watch himself being held by his mother forever. He could feel the presence of his father and also of Callum. Although it puzzled him, the scenes were hazy, and he knew it wasn't what he was looking for. His awareness found itself in space again, devoid of any shadows of souls or the universe. He understood that in front of him were his soul's various incarnations stacked together. When he entered a level, he could see the whole life story of that birth.

He descended to the next floor; it felt empty with just blinding light all around and he was unable to see anything. He perceived this was also not the place to be.

Then it was the level below. This time the world was made of light—serene and tranquil. He was a white translucent being, first, the size of a drop, then steadily growing bigger and eventually much larger than his human self. He was surrounded by similar beings.

But the world of light turned grey. Shapeless black and grey wisps spread to the sky, blocking the light of stars and to the ground making the white dust go coal-black.

"Dhanay! The Rogas are running down the plains. We have

waited too long," said another Aster.

"I am aware! I shall not destroy them and shall not taint the Asters. But now I will banish them, that is my duty." Dhanay was five times larger than the other Asters and twice as bright. He held the silver star on his helm, the first light of the first star of this galaxy. He knew he could use the energy of the star to destroy the Rogas forever but that would mean losing the star too.

But more than that, Dhanay was a just leader. He was conceived by the powerful thought of Samaya.

"Every being, of lightness or darkness, has an equal right to exist. Do your bit for your kind but never be unjust to the other kind." Those were the words of Samaya.

Joash was aware that Samaya was none other than Guruji, his creator, teacher and advisor in the astral realm and he knew Rogas had entered the astral world because that is what they do. They spread through all matter; they dwell in the dark and feed on fear. But there was no fear in the astral realm and hence they had gone rampant with rage.

Dhanay used his powers to banish them. They retreated, only to wreak havoc in the kingdom of Maathi who dwelled on the dark side of the astral realm. Dhanay went to war alongside the Maathi and finally, the Rogas were banished forever but the Maathi did not win.

"Look at this world. It is destroyed," said Rayth, the golden Maathi. "You came to help us, Dhanay, but we lost the darkness because of your presence. We cannot live here anymore. We have no healing powers like the Asters. Oh, Dhanay! What shall we do?"

Samaya came forward. "There is another realm where your kind flourish already Rayth. The realm of colours, where beings on the surface are made of matter and not of ether like us. They call it Earth. The light of their star does not penetrate the surface and hence it can be a new home for you."

"We shall go as we must, Samaya," said Rayth. "But Oh Dhanay, you could have destroyed the Rogas and saved both our worlds. You chose not to. Who is to say the Rogas will not find Earth?"

"I regret the plight of your kind," spoke Dhanay. "And I promise that if that happens, I will be there to vanquish the Rogas."

With that, the scene dissolved, and Joash's awareness was back into nothingness next to the layers of his several incarnations. He continued his downward journey, going further back in time and diffusing into the next level.

This time he saw some captivating earthly scenes. Beautiful mountains and valleys were inviting him to come and have a look. He could hear the cry of a baby from a tiny hut. Smoke was ensuing from other huts around this one.

He went in to find his newborn self right next to an exhausted woman. The woman turned to the baby and said warmly, "My Fingal." Joash realised that his mother in that life was his father in the present one.

He watched himself growing up in that little village. He looked nothing like Joash but certainly was good-looking and thought too much of himself. He had short, light-brown hair. His eyes were blue and his face was long with a sharp nose. He walked with the arrogance of a teenager who knew he was popular.

He had no care for others and believed he was going to rise far above these common villagers. He had no father, as he had died of illness shortly before he was born. Something told him that the soul of his father whom he had never met was the same as Callum's.

His mother was all right but did not understand how great he was. She wanted him to start working at a farm, but he was convinced there were easier ways to make money. One of his older friends, John, had moved to Edinburgh and now he looked like a lord himself. His mother never thought much of him and warned Fingal not to follow in his footsteps.

If Fingal was the most desirable boy in the village, the most desirable girl was Rhona. To Fingal, she looked like a fairy every time she smiled at him. They would often meet by the stream and Fingal would tell her all about his dreams of being a rich man.

"My mother is not happy about me meeting you, Fingal,"

she said one day.

"Why?"

"She says you don't work; you are lazy. You can't look after anyone."

"She is wrong. And you know that. I have asked John to help us. We can run away from this place. We can get married and live in the city."

Rhona was too much in love with Fingal to say anything else but yes. Their wedding was a small and quick affair. John agreed to loan some money to Fingal and help him find his feet in the city. The first thing he taught him was how to earn money without working—gambling.

It was unbelievable! With the little money he had, Fingal kept on winning. That day he went back to Rhona with his pockets full. They got a small room to live in Mary King's close. It was dark and stuffy but soon he would have enough money to move to a better place, thought Fingal. With her innocence and kind heart Rhona soon won over the neighbours. She would stay there all day, while Fingal would come back at night. Some days, he would win some money and some days nothing.

"Why don't you find a job, Fingal? It would mean regular income," said Rhona one day.

Fingal did not like that. "I am learning how to make money.

Once I know, I will stop losing and things will be better."

Rhona wanted to say something but stopped. She was worried. Her neighbour had told her horrible things about gambling. Months passed by. One day, they had nothing to eat at home. A small candle was burning in one corner of the room. Rhona asked Fingal, "Can you borrow some money from John?"

"No. I have not fully returned the money I took earlier. He has refused to give anymore."

"Olivia says her husband can help you find a nice job in a mill."

"How many times have I told you? There's no need for me to mix with these people."

"I am pregnant."

Fingal looked shocked. Tears started flowing down Rhona's face looking at Fingal's reaction. It suddenly dawned upon her: *What have I done? Does he love me? Did he care? Was my mother right all along?*

Fingal was not sure how to behave.

"I want to see my mother and father. Can you take me?" asked Rhona.

"Yes," he stuttered.

As it sank in, Fingal grew comfortable with the idea of being a father himself.

In the village, there was a lot of shouting and crying with a crowd watching their family drama. Somehow, he just sat quietly waiting to go back. It did not matter to him how heartbroken his mother and Rhona's parents had been.

Suddenly Rhona's father was holding him by his neck. "You stay here, in the village. Look what you have done to my flower. You are not going back, not with her."

Fingal would not have it. He needed Rhona, at least to cook for him.

It took a lot of promising and convincing, but he managed to come back to the city with Rhona. Olivia's husband sure was kind enough to take Fingal with him to the mill and get him a job. It was hard physical labour and Fingal did not like it at all.

The baby arrived. Fingal could not believe how thrilled he was to see that little face. To Rhona, he was a transformed man until one day John came looking for him. He did not look the same—he had dishevelled hair and dirty clothes.

"He has gone to work," Rhona told him.

"Tell him to meet me tonight. It is important."

Fingal walked through the cobbled streets of the city and soon reached the dark corner where a group of people always sat gambling. John was smoking a cigar sitting just behind the group.

"Hello, Fingal! You have forgotten old friends," he said slyly.

"No, I have just been busy."

"I see! Even if you forget me, I cannot let you forget the money you owe me."

"What money? I gave it all back last summer."

"No, you haven't paid the interest yet."

"You never said anything about interest, did you?"

John stood up. Two big men were standing just behind him with their arms crossed.

"Now I am telling you. You will give me all the money back in two weeks."

"Are you threatening me?"

The two men moved in. Knowing he couldn't do anything, Fingal said, "I have got nothing to give you. I have a wife and a little girl to take care of now."

"I know. I know. Why don't you try the quick way?" said John pointing to the small table with cards.

It was not a bad idea, Fingal thought. He missed it anyway. He thought of Rhona's father. *He will not know.*

❋❋❋

"You haven't gone to work for two days," said Rhona one morning.

"Who said?"

"You know who. It's not good for you, John's company."

"I know what is good for me. You look after Miria and

let me be."

Little Miria was playing in the corner, giving her father big smiles. He smiled back, but the only thought on his mind was getting back to the cards. The thrill of filling his pockets every time he won was like nothing else. He could play with Miria when he had made enough money.

And then, it was the same scene he had seen in Edinburgh. He remembered it too well. He was not there for his Rhona or little Miria. But this time witnessing her lying all alone next to her mother's dead body, looking at the door, waiting for her father to come back before she took her last breaths, was more painful than Joash could have imagined.

How could I? There could be no man more blind than me—blind with greed and delusion.

It was also what he thought as Fingal. Fingal lay there in the dark for days, praying for the plague to take him too, but his wish was not granted. He was instead saved by some kind people, who took his weak body out into the sun, cleaned him and fed him. He found shelter but had no desire to live.

"Look at you! If you don't want to live for yourself, at least live for others. If you can't get over your pain, at least help others get over theirs," said a man with long flowing grey robes in a firm voice. It was like an order from above.

Fingal spent day and night helping others, not wanting anything in return. He lived only for a few more years after which he became severely ill. He only thought of the Almighty in his last moments and prayed to be with him.

His remorse was deep, and his heart had become pure. As he took the last breath, a wisp of white smoke came out of the centre of his forehead, gently floating away.

Joash's mind followed it. He reached a place that was dark and empty. Maybe not. The white mist kept going deeper and deeper until a faint light appeared towards the end of this tunnel-like space. Finally, he reached that source of light. It was a large moon—the tunnel opened into infinite space with stars and galaxies and clusters of white mist here and there.

Suddenly, he remembered what he had to do. He whirled around to find a door that had appeared behind him. He opened the door and Jaggu Baba walked in.

***

Jaggu Baba stared with amazement towards the infinite space and started to mutter something under his breath, rhythmically moving his fingers at the same time.

The sight of this shrivelled, fading man opposite the large clear moon somehow unsettled Joash. But before he knew it, the space started to change. All the black space between the stars started to move like a fabric, rolling and taking a highly irregular shape. A loud noise accompanied the change, shrill and painful, like a million horns blowing at once. The shape was enlarging and getting close to the opening of the tunnel, raising a feeling of terror and doom in Joash.

Jaggu Baba was still rooted in his position, watching the phenomenon like a child watching a magic show.

But Joash just knew, this was not right, so he pushed Jaggu Baba with all his might and immediately felt awareness coming back to his physical body. Sitting up in the cot he saw Jaggu Baba lying on the ground next to him, his body straight and stiff. As Joash watched on, he opened his eyes.

"You need to leave now." Jaggu Baba spoke dryly getting up on his feet.

Outside, Joash found Leela where he had left him.

As soon as they reached home, Leela instructed Joash to get back in bed and reattach his medication tube to the inlet on his chest.

"How do you know Jaggu Baba?" asked Joash.

"Well, you are not the only one he has helped. He has this gift … he can help people see the past. But he needs to be in the mood you see. Sometimes he doesn't want to meet anyone. He says he used to live in the Himalayas in the company of great masters for more than twenty years and then came down here to live with ordinary people. I believe him."

Joash believed too that Jaggu Baba was an extraordinary yogi, but he was not sure of his ways, nor could he tell if he would be willing to help him now.

Just then, Gopalan walked in. "Amma, where did you go without telling me? Have you seen the weather?"

"Oh! Don't you worry now. No storm is going to take me away for another hundred years." She giggled and winked at Joash.

Chapter 28

Murdeshwar, India

Sitting at the kitchen table, Joash and Ananya looked out through the window as the storm receded. Ananya pointed to the leaning coconut tree beyond the garden and reckoned it would make a great slide. Joash smiled at her, slowly moving his fingers on the coffee cup. Gopalan was busy on his screen which kept flashing and disappearing. He gave up in frustration and came to sit at the table.

"I thought you wanted to go to Jaipur," said Gopalan.

"I do. But there is no way to travel without breaking the journey, so I accepted Subba's invitation to visit him."

"Do you know him well?" asked Gopalan.

"Yes, we work together. Although, I have never been to this place," replied Joash.

"I cannot figure out how will you get there. It seems to be in the middle of nowhere."

Joash spoke slowly, "As long as you can help me get anywhere near the submerged Mumbai, I will figure it out from there." *I am not going to go looking for Jaggu Baba*, he thought. *But what of the fire element? How and where will I find it? What did Jaggu Baba know?* The dread and terror he had felt at the sight of the dark force still seared his mind.

"Are you sure you want to leave immediately?" asked Gopalan.

Joash moved the tangled mess of his long hair behind his ears, revealing the injuries that still shone red. "Yes." Pursing his lips together, he adjusted his neck.

"I haven't ventured out of here in a long time," said Gopalan, "but I know air travel is out of the question. The train line to New Mumbai is still working. Beyond that, I don't know. Large sections of highways have suffered serious damage. I am afraid I cannot map out your full—"

"I will take him," said a raspy voice.

Gopalan's head quickly turned to the door that led to the garden. Joash saw the shape of Jaggu Baba's lean figure standing tall and dark against the bright background. As he stepped inside the kitchen, Ananya gaped at him with an open mouth—his feet were now adorned by sturdy-looking white boots, he was wearing a tight white jacket and a very loose white *dhoti* with a wide silver belt. His white turban looked new and had a silver lining. He was standing straight, holding a tall dark wooden staff. The only thing unchanged about him was his gummy smile.

"Where are you going?" asked Gopalan as he moved back in his chair with a frown of confusion.

Jaggu Baba smiled impishly at Ananya. "Do you like my travelling gear? I wish someone could paint my stick white, too."

She giggled.

"Who? Me?" Jaggu Baba turned towards Gopalan. "I am off to the Himalayas for some urgent work." He spoke raising his chin and expanding his chest, trying to look important. His attention then turned to Joash and his posture softened. "And I figured you might want to go north too."

Gopalan shook his head. "Baba, it is not a good idea."

Leela came in hurriedly, not wanting to miss the conversation.

"Now, you don't tell me Amma—" said Gopalan.

"Shush Gopal, you are not my mayor! I am not going anywhere. My Shiv is here," said Leela as she sat down next to Ananya.

"Right then. What do you say, boy? Are you up for some company?" Jaggu Baba was still looking at Joash, who was silently staring at him.

But there was no time to ponder, so Joash got to his feet. "Thank you for everything; it is time for me to go," he said to Gopalan. Glancing back at Leela, he caught the twinkle in her smiling eyes—she understood he was grateful.

***

They were just in time for the only train to New Mumbai. The platform was deserted, except for a robot. When they boarded the train, there were no more than six people on the whole train.

"You see! No one thinks travelling is a good idea," said Jaggu Baba as they walked from compartment to compartment in the moving train. Joash's eyes wandered to the sky outside; its colour was changing from orange to dark red. As he took his next step, he bumped into someone sitting in an aisle seat.

"Ouch!" the person said. It blinked its very natural-looking eyes and even frowned. "Maafi mango!" When there was no reply from Joash it said, "At least say sorry! Some robots do have feelings!"

Joash was baffled by this very human-like female robot who got up and walked away saying, "How rude!"

"Come and sit here." Jaggu Baba gestured to Joash to a seat opposite him. "Never mind her. You and I are the only humans on this train."

Joash was quietly studying Jaggu Baba. Presently, he spoke.

"Subba has sent me detailed walking instructions from a stop near New Mumbai."

Jaggu Baba had a mischievous smile on his face. "Hmm, what are you planning to find there?"

Joash adjusted his neck as he considered the answer to that question.

A long moment of silence followed. Jaggu Baba's deeply contemplative stare was fixed on Joash. "You can meet your friend and after that, I can help you get the fire element. Even though you did not keep your promise ... not fully."

Finally, Joash spoke. "What were you doing?"

"As I told you before, leave this matter alone." Looking irked, Jaggu Baba turned away. Within a moment his smile had returned. "Things happen for a reason. Do you see? I am the only person who can take you to the fire element. No Sheersha yogi would know how to get it."

"Are you not a Sheersha yogi?"

"I said I lived with them; I am not one of them." Jaggu Baba sighed. "My ways are a bit different, but you can trust me still. How else would I know so much?"

"So, what are you suggesting?"

Jaggu Baba leaned forward, and a fire ignited in his grey eyes as he whispered with fervour, "How keen are you to fulfil this quest? How far can you go? What price are you willing to pay to shed the load that you carry from your previous lives and to rise in this one?"

Joash's body became tense, and he shut his eyes hard. To fulfil this quest and reach Krupa was the only purpose of his life now. The vision of a helpless Miria came back to him. Before remorse or grief could overwhelm him, he opened his eyes and said, "I will face all the hurdles that I must."

With his gaze intently fixed on his fingers Jaggu Baba moved them slowly, crisscrossing them. "So many threads are intertwined to make the events of one life; do not expect to understand the reason for everything that goes on. Lighten up, I am not the enemy."

He sat up holding his staff with two hands, a childlike look once again on his face and a warmth that confused Joash further. "Your guru…" he began. "I did meet him once on Mount Kailash. Men like him can choose not to have a physical body. He was very dear to the Mahayogi too."

"Mahayogi?" Joash looked at Jaggu Baba enquiringly.

"Yes! Have you not heard of him?" A radiant smile spread over his wrinkly face and then he broke into a song—

"Listen to this tale from a time unknown,

from days of old when the seeds of faith were not yet sown.

There lived a man unlike any other.

He could move mountains; he could speak to the wind.

With an aura so bright,

if you stared for too long, you would go blind.

The fiercest beasts bowed to him; the gentlest flowers caressed him.

In search of truth, he wandered the thickest jungles, scaled the highest of heights.

One day, he found a spot on a serene mountain,

he sat down, closed his eyes and dived deep inside.

And just like that, all closed doors opened, all darkness turned to light,

for the answers to all questions were in his sight.

Still, he roams the blessed mountains.

Some say he is a myth; some say he is a legend,

if you get to see him, consider yourself fortunate."

Jaggu Baba's eyes were closed, and he was still smiling.

Joash thought to himself, *this man's an enigma but there's a lot I have not learnt, a lot I might still need to know before I reach Prakruti Saram.* His gaze went to the bottle hanging from his neck and he held it once more.

***

It was nearly midnight when the train started to slow down

as they approached New Mumbai. Joash was woken up by the change in speed. He looked out—the shapes of many high-rise buildings, a dense network of roads and bridges loomed in the dark sky. It seemed too cluttered and dull; the usual sparkle of a busy city was missing. There were hardly any moving vehicles. As the train announced its stop, Joash gently patted Jaggu Baba's shoulder. "Baba!"

Jaggu Baba did not move or open his eyes but said clearly, "Ours is the next stop."

Joash sat quietly looking out towards the empty platform. Opposite him, Jaggu Baba was sitting with his head leaning to one side and eyes closed. No one got in and it didn't seem as though anyone got out of the train. After a few minutes, the train started to move again and picked up speed in no time.

When it stopped, Joash could not see a platform sign, just a paved stone surface and a path leading away from it. The two robots in their compartment got up and exited the train.

"Let us go," said Jaggu Baba as though he was never asleep.

They took a mud path, right next to the train track.

"We are a few hundred miles north of New Mumbai." Although Joash was leading the way, Jaggu Baba seemed to know the place. "You see that building behind you?"

Joash glanced back to find a dimly lit semi-circular structure made of dark glass, a short distance away.

"All the robots you saw live there. They are going to rest and charge themselves up. They work for the authority and deliver the data they have collected from the southern states. The authority will know now that you bumped into a pretty girl." Jaggu Baba laughed, then looked up as large drops of water started to come down.

A wan moonlight was filtering through the scudding clouds showing the ghostly shapes of trees and hillocks. The place was not inhabited. As the rain picked up strength so did Jaggu Baba's staff, hitting the pebbles and boulders in their path.

"Come on, boy," he shouted over the rain.

***

After trekking for more than an hour, they reached a big clearing in the middle of a woodland. Two cabins stood right in the middle. Each of them had a lantern hanging outside. Joash knocked on the first door.

"Finally! Joash" said an amiable man who opened the door and hugged him. He was tall and brawny, had several rings on his fingers and metal chains hung around his neck. He had long black hair and wore black eyeliner.

"Hello, I am Subramanyam," he said, extending his arm towards Jaggu Baba.

They entered the cabin which was a deceptively large space. They were seated on chairs fashioned out of metal boxes and tins. In one corner there was a pile of broken random stuff and wires. On a wall hung some fancy-looking suits and gadgets.

Just then, another man who looked strikingly similar to Subba walked in. He was carrying a large bag, wore strange-looking rubbery boots and seemed to be troubled.

He looked at everyone and spoke to Subba. "Something is happening in the area of the big pile. The tremors are back. You must come and see."

"Take a deep breath and sit down, Chukka, they have just arrived." Subba turned to Joash and said, "This is my brother Chukka."

"Let us go with him," said Joash.

***

The four of them walked through the bushes and sparse trees with their hoods on. It was still drizzling, and the moon had gone under thicker clouds.

Subba was doing the talking. "As you know, old Mumbai is mostly under water. Many people died and lots of stuff was lost to water in the big floods. It was much worse here than in Jaipur. The authority did minimal clearing up and then people were banned from going that side. We knew something was going on underwater, something more than rot. I used to go at night and collect samples of water. I was sure something was reacting with the water. I thought and still think it is the plastics. Recently, we detected some serious changes in the water, almost toxic. The authority here won't pay any attention, so I passed on our findings to Professor Rollings in London. As of now, there has been no response from her, either. I read your report on her conference, but I need the details of her research. We have support from a robot company in New Mumbai to carry on the research, but this could be happening in so many places all over the world. Our efforts might have been too little and too late."

There was a strange reek in the air as they halted at an edge where the ground fell away to darker depths. Suddenly, loud thunder brought several flashes of lightning, that seemed to be striking the ground not too far from them. The lightning revealed the scene in front of them—a very deep and wide pit, almost like a mine filled with junk. The pit had a tower of rubbish rising way above the ground. At the very tip of this pile, the white streaks of lightning from the sky were meeting similar streaks running up the pile.

"Look, it's almost as though lightning is emerging from this pile of plastic," said Chukka.

"Is it all plastic?" asked Joash.

"Yes, it used to be the authority's waste plastic disposal site.

And we have dumped some more from the old Mumbai site. But now look at this place," spoke Subba.

"Look!" exclaimed Chukka.

Joash felt the tremors under his feet. The ground was lifting and falling in small waves as if something were moving beneath it. He felt a strange sense of familiarity accompanied by a sense of doom. He pictured the scenes in the cave in Oman. Soon the disturbance disappeared.

Jaggu Baba's face was grim. Observing the ground closely, he muttered indistinctly, "Dark energy…" His eyes met Joash's and he immediately looked away.

Joash could sense Jaggu Baba hiding something. "How many such sites are there in the world you think?" he asked Subba.

"Hard to say, hundreds. Definitely, big ones close to all submerged cities. But this is a new problem. These tremors… I wonder if this is what people are calling earthquakes," he shook his head. "So many lives and homes, destroyed."

Joash's mind was racing—*Does it mean that places like this attract the Roga? When they enter the earth's environment, things change—Elusium. Unstable air, more storms. When they travel through the ground—tremors.*

Joash understood if his deduction was correct, he must move fast. He must get the elements together and see what solution

Sheersha yoga has to this crisis.

"These are creatures from another dimension," said Jaggu Baba as the gaggle made its way back.

Subba and Chukka looked at each other.

Soon they reached the cabins. The sun had already sent forth its first orange hues along the horizon. The rain had stopped, and birds had started their morning song.

Jaggu Baba took a long sniff and said, "Ha, it smells fresh. Subba and Chukka, what wonderful human beings you two are." He placed one hand on Joash's shoulder and said seriously, "We still have a long way to go. Get some rest."

Chapter 29

Close to New Mumbai

Joash was woken up by a strong nudge.

"Hurry up now. Get ready to leave," said Jaggu Baba. "Subba here says that he has a wonderful means of transport to lend us for our journey forward."

Outside, it was overcast again with strong winds as the four men walked towards a thicket not far from the cabins. They emerged through a path in the overgrown grass and soon an unexpected scene opened up—brilliant colourful flowers were blossoming around a small wooden barn. The rough uneven wooden planks of the building were reinforced here and there with metal poles—surely it was the brothers' creation. Amongst the flowers were other shrubs and bushes of various kinds—a lot of them trampled, but ravishing, nonetheless. The play of colours, the wafting scent of herbs and the slur of bees made the place almost trance-inducing.

Then there was the unmistakable neighing of horses above all other sounds of nature. Subba smiled and looked at Joash. "This place is our hard work over the years. Our food comes from here and those horses are our friends."

"We don't like to call them animals," Chukka chortled as he led the way pushing the grass and bushes to the sides.

"Nah! They are more civilised than us," added Subba.

Inside the barn, there were three horses—one white, one black and one brown—calm and free, swishing their tales and flicking their ears.

"This is a tech-proof way of travelling but will need constant refuelling. Leave them with your friend in Vansda and we will arrange to get them back," said Chukka patting the black horse. "The white one is Vaayu; he is the fastest and is my favourite. This one here is Monty and the brown horse is George—it is distantly related to a royal horse in England." Chukka laughed. "What about Jaggu Baba? Can he manage?"

Jaggu Baba moved his mouth, scratching his head.

Joash was quietly observing the horses, gently moving his

hand on Monty. He was not sure how he was going to handle this. Every summer he visited Aunt Sue as a child, she would insist that Krupa and Joash took horse-riding lessons. He could not say he had learnt anything; he was never comfortable sitting on a horse and gave up just before he would have started trotting.

Jaggu Baba placed a saddle on George.

As Joash wondered if he could even ride a horse, he placed his forehead on George's flat head. He breathed deeply. *Let me be able to do what I have set out to do. Help me, Dhi. Please carry me.*

The next moment, George moved close to Joash and grunted next to his ear.

"To Vansda forest," announced Jaggu Baba as both men sat on the horses holding the reins. He knew his way with the horses. The horses neighed loudly in unison and started, first a steady trot and then galloping away into the open plains beyond the farm. Subba and Chukka waved at the disappearing figures as Joash shifted right and left, trying to keep his balance. Any doubt that he might not be able to ride a horse, vanished within seconds. George was as smooth as a horse could be and knew exactly which way to go as it soon overtook Vaayu.

Like they were one with the wind, the two horses rode miles and miles. They passed through sodden forests and dirt paths, they rode through desert lands that were once expansive fields, they witnessed piles of waste and ruined buildings, they went along the broken roads that now led to nowhere and finally they stopped. After resting and eating, the horses and the men started again. They rode all day and into the night.

Jaggu Baba slowed down on the top of a hill. Both the horses stood side by side as Joash and Baba looked at the highway below. Lights went bright and dim as the trucks and cars passed by.

"You have avoided inhabited places," said Joash. He wondered if Jaggu Baba meant for him to see all that he had.

"Yes, it is quicker this way. We can ride slowly for the next hour or so. The roads seem busy, and the horses are tired."

The horses slowly carried on in the dim light from the road. Soon, their path was lined with trees spangled with countless fireflies.

Baba exclaimed, "Look! I am seeing fireflies here after many years. The higher age … the esters have crossed this way. I can feel it."

The two men closely followed the road for a long time. Then they turned into a dust path which led to a grove of dense trees. Within minutes the atmosphere seemed to change. The air was still and moist, the crickets were loud and dark shapes of huge trees hung about like monsters. Joash knew they had entered a forest.

Soon he could hear the burbling and splashing of a waterfall. The hooves of their horses were still going rhythmically on the boggy ground—together and slow. The awareness of Joash's senses was heightened too. His face tensed up; his eyes scanned the dark as he had a feeling of being watched. "Jaggu Baba?" he asked.

"Shh, don't disturb the trees," he replied.

They rode on through the bushes and under the trees, listening to the sounds of the jungle. Soon, in sight was the small shape of a circular mud house and its conical thatched roof. Its window was glowing orange.

As they approached the hut, there was a sudden low growl behind them. The startled horses jumped, sending Jaggu Baba to the ground. Joash swiftly rode towards him.

Jaggu Baba spoke to a shape in the dark as if reassuring it. "Shanti! It is me."

Whatever it was, it did not growl again, and neither did it come out of the bushes. Joash patted George soothingly and held his reins as he carried on foot behind Jaggu Baba in the direction of the hut.

The door was open. The clattering of a screen made of shells announced their entry. Inside, the place was hot like a furnace, the flames of a fire were swaying wild in an earthen pot at the far end of the hut. In the centre of the hut was a tree trunk going up through the thatched roof. One branch of this tree was inside the hut and from it hung a long curious thing that looked like a cocoon of white cloth wrapped on itself, over and over again. Or maybe there was something else wrapped inside it...

As Jaggu Baba moved closer, a pair of big eyes opened at the base of the hanging shape—someone was hanging upside down from the tree branch, body and head wrapped in overlapping layers of cloth with just the face exposed, the eyelids and the skin of the face painted over with a chalky white substance. To add to the strangeness of the scene a leopard came and sat behind this person and started casually licking and grooming itself. Then, very gracefully, two slender arms came out to hold the sheets, then the legs and finally the person inverted to stand straight in front of them. It was a woman—difficult to say how old, but she looked strong and tall. A faint orange hue made her fair skin glow like something was burning inside her. She was dressed in white and her golden hair was tied in a very tight bun on the top of her head. She had several earrings on her ears—the largest one was exactly like Jaggu Baba's. White dust was covering her otherwise golden eyelashes that framed her cat-like eyes. She held her guests in a soft yet intense gaze, then silently she bowed to greet them.

"Tejas! Here is someone who seeks a gift from you," said Jaggu Baba.

"So, the higher age is really upon us. If you say so, Baba," said Tejas casually as she studied Joash with a pleasant sneer. "A Sheersha yogi?" Circling Joash with slow steps she continued,

"You are just a child. Have you enough grit to carry my gift?"

The next moment, she reached out to the burning fire and picked up part of a flame-like she was plucking a flower from a bush. She watched the small flame dance between her fingers and gently placed it back where it had come from.

Joash drew his breath in. "I carry the sacred soil and the healing water," he said holding the vial. "And I believe I have the grit to carry the fierce fire."

"Show me then," said Tejas raising her voice, "that you are not soft like the gurus of your Sheersha yoga. Show me you carry a fire of purpose, will and resolve to do your karma. Place your hand in this fire and do not remove."

Without another thought Joash took a long step, sat down next to the earthen pot and immersed his right hand in the fire. A burning pain seared through his arm and spread to his entire body, making him shake but he held on. His eyes turned the same colour as the fire and countless droplets of sweat covered his face. Pain was all he felt for the first few moments and then he let it become a part of his being.

As his eyes shut, his mind started winding, turning, stopping and restarting through memories, losing itself in the cacophony of several voices, drowning in the swirl of several scenes. Suddenly, one voice rose higher above others and a scene started to play in front of his eyes.

**

"Look up, Joash. Look at me, child."

Young Joash looked at Guruji with tears welling up in his big eyes.

"It has died Guruji, I could not help it." Joash was holding a dead pigeon in his hands.

"Are you upset that it has died or are you upset at the failure of your effort to save it?"

Joash looked at his teacher innocently.

"Don't be upset. Both these things are not in your control. You tried to help an injured bird; that was a kind act. I am sure its soul is thankful to you. But it was time for it to be free from a pigeon's body and fly to eternity."

Guruji smiled and gestured to indicate the boy should sit next to him. They could hear lots of birds chirping in the garden.

"The pigeon is happier now so there is no need for you to be sad. This body and the pains that come with it are but momentary, a mere stop in the long journey of the soul. Death is not the end of the story, just the end of a chapter. And remember, your action is more important than the result."

Joash opened his eyes as he felt his hand being held gently by two other hands. He glanced down and found Tejas holding his hand. There was no sign of any burn on his hand, neither was there any pain.

"You do have it." Her smile carried a warmth this time.

***

The three of them sat next to the fire on the mud floor. The heat of the fire had turned mellow and the orange glow of Tejas's skin was gone. The leopard had fallen asleep too.

"He is Snel, my companion here in the jungle," said Tejas to Joash who could not take his eyes off the majestic cat. Her voice was breezy and Joash thought a wisp of vapour escaped her mouth as she spoke.

"I see you are not scared of him. Good!" Her accent sounded familiar too.

"Are you—" Joash was intrigued by this woman.

"Dutch?' she replied. "Yes, by birth. Now let us talk about what you need."

"Tejaswini does not only meditate upon fire," said Jaggu Baba. "She is also a master of the mind. The way I could help you see your past; she can help you see the present. She can read your mind only if you allow her to. Choose your questions wisely."

A frown had been sitting on Joash's forehead as Jaggu Baba spoke. *The present?*

"Tell me what I should know," said Joash.

Jaggu Baba was holding an earthen bowl with some burning leaves in it releasing strong-smelling fumes. He moved back, leaned against the wall and pulled out a small brown pipe from the bowl. Holding it close to his mouth with cupped hands he drew a long breath in and vented white smoke through his nose. With half-closed eyes he looked at Tejas, urging her to continue.

"You carry the burden of the world," said Tejas. "First, you want the fierce fire. Second a girl—uh, that's your sister—and third one is an object you must find. I think I can help you, but do you want me to?" She bent her head and looked at Joash. "You cannot trust Baba fully, yet you have come with him all the way. You are just starting to wonder about me."

Tejas chuckled and continued, "Weird as all this is for you, just feel the power around you. You do not feel intimidation but confusion. I do not have the serenity of Sheersha yogis, and neither do I seek it as it is not my *Dhi*. I live amongst animals, my *Dhi* is fierce and that is how I protect the beings around me." Her eyes opened wider and the words came loud and bold. "In you, I see a karma yogi, a ruler, a warrior, part-awake, part-asleep. Deep inside you, is all the knowledge your young mind has absorbed, the teacher of which still follows you like a guiding light. Blessed you are, but blessings will be of no avail if you do not stir your mind if you do not awaken fully."

Joash was humbled as every word rang true to him. Jaggu Baba too was sitting straight now and listening to Tejas intently and so was Snel.

"Where is my sister? Can you tell me?" asked Joash.

"No, I cannot," replied Tejas. "Whatever you want to know, you will have to find out yourself. For now, you will have to choose. What is more important for you? To find out where the object you search is or where your sister is?"

Joash took a long breath in and looked up. Then, closing his eyes he adjusted his head and neck. "The book! I need to know how to find it. Can you help me?"

Tejas smiled. "Well chosen! I can send your projection to your house in Jaipur. But you will not be able to touch anything, neither can you speak as your physical self will still be here. Meditate upon the thing you want to know about or the place you want to go to with a still mind. Shake off any turbulence and persevere. Dig into what you have been taught. I can guide you to the depths of your mind, but no one can go with you further. Are you ready?"

Joash nodded his head firmly.

Tejas picked up the bowl of burning leaves and took it closer to Joash's face. "Breathe in and calm yourself. Close your eyes and sit with your back straight. Blank yourself, until you feel a warmth running up your spine to your head."

Joash closed his eyes, but his mind was not blank. The scenes of desolation from his journey started to cloud his vision— storms, ruined buildings, people crying. The more he tried to get away from it, the more painful it got. He opened his eyes, breathing heavily.

Tejas moved closer to him and whispered in his ear, "Let nothing sway you. Draw on the best memories of this life to calm your mind." Then she looked at Jaggu Baba. "Baba…"

Jaggu Baba got up and brought a big bag of musical instruments from the corner.

"Joash," she continued, "cast all weariness aside. No one is ever given more than they can carry. If this is your karma you need to get through it now. Sit up straight again; do not disappoint your teacher. Let us do this together."

She moved right opposite Joash; both of them sat facing each other with their legs crossed. She placed the tip of her index finger on the space between Joash's eyebrows. As they closed their eyes, the music of the didgeridoo began. The air in the room started to vibrate. Soon Joash felt it in his fingertips and then his entire body as if everything was rhythmically humming with the deep drone of the didgeridoo. In the next moment, Joash's mind was tumbling through dark spaces. Then the scene changed.

He was young again and ran up to his mother who was

smiling. She hugged him and he felt so calm. Guruji was sitting in the same place under the tree, he too smiled at him and nodded. Then he looked up towards the sky—it was blue, then black and then all was blank. At the same time, something warm seemed to be travelling up his spine. It was the music of flute now that filled his ears, but he had no thoughts anymore.

"Try to think again now, the book or the house. Concentrate. If you can hear the flute, you can hear me. If you feel lost walk towards the sound of the flute," said Tejas.

Minutes passed; Joash was just blank as if he had forgotten to think. Then he felt her finger press on his forehead gently. And it began.

***

It was the house. He was outside the study on the top floor. The door was partly open, but he did not need the door to enter. Inside, everything looked the same except the wooden table which was rotting. There was an open book on the table— the pages had gone yellow and nothing was legible. A dated computer tablet with a broken screen lay on the floor. He went to his father's section of special books. He could see some of Aunt Sue's paintings there, rows of books and a large computer screen, but no sign of what he was looking for. But what was he looking for? He tried to think if he knew what Prakruti Saram would look like. A vague memory told him that it would be in a wooden box that was always kept locked. He looked around and checked the whole study but found no wooden box.

He headed downstairs. It was underwater but he had to check. The water was halfway up the stairs, looking dark and dirty it was moving slowly. He went through the water, into the bedrooms. Through the murky water, he saw the walls and other large objects. And then he conceded he could not find it like this. He followed the sound of the flute and went back up the stairs onto the open terrace. The sun had started to rise—he felt a sense of urgency.

He now wanted the box, if the book was with his family it had to be that box. This time the memory was clear. His father had told him while registering his fingerprints to lock and unlock that box. "Son, this box has some precious old books and things which we have preserved for centuries. Remember to keep it safe always. When you and Krupa grow up, it will be your duty."

Back in the hut, Joash sat pressing his eyelids together, trying to remember what the box exactly looked like. Snel was pacing the breadth of the hut close to the back door as a storm was gathering outside. Jaggu Baba played the flute making sure his notes were audible above the howling wind.

And then it happened—Joash could see the box, a big beautiful wooden box, dark-brown with copper-plated corners and an antique metal latch. The lock looked special, there was a smooth black ring in the latch. He could see mud, lots of it in all directions. The next second, he was looking down towards the ground—it was dry and dusty. He understood the box lay buried in the ground right at this spot. But where was he? He looked around—this place was in ruins, a broken building with no roof and incredibly old. Something was written on the outside wall in Hindi— '*Pundit ji ki haveli.*'

Somewhere far, dawn was breaking and turning the sky above a light grey. He moved on the dusty streets; all around him were ruins of ancient buildings.

This is not Jaipur.

"Joash, you need to return now," he heard Tejas say.

But he needed to find out where this place was. He seemed to be going round and round. There was a castle or an old fort on a hill on one side. He went up along the path and came back. Finally, he saw the 'Exit' sign. He went out and saw the place was enclosed within an outer wall.

'Archaeological Society of India-Bhangarh'—that was it. He had a name now. But where was the flute? He could not hear anything. He did not know how to come out of this. It was all silent, then he heard a faint voice that seemed to say, "Oash, oash." He went inside the walled village and then back to where he had started. "Come back, Joash." The call was clear now.

*****

Back again in the hut, Joash opened his eyes, but he could hardly open them with the wind hitting his face hard. Jaggu Baba was nowhere to be seen and Tejas was holding on to the tree trunk. "We need to go," she said. "Baba has gone with the animals."

They made their way through the dense forest. For every three steps they took, they were pushed back a step. The trees were swaying madly and broken branches were flying in the air. They crossed an old broken road, then a stream and reached the foot of a rocky hill. It was then that it started to pour down as Joash had never seen before. Tejas climbed up the slope with steady speed holding onto rocks and Joash followed her. Halfway up the hill on the other side was a cave.

Inside, the cave widened up into a large space. Jaggu Baba and the two horses were resting in one corner, a torch flame was lit on one wall. But there were also many other small animals and birds near the mouth of the cave, sitting quietly. The cave was full of stuff, possibly Tejas' other home.

Joash got out of his wet clothes and wrapped a dry sheet around his waist. His head was still dripping water, his body was covered in cuts and bruises. He went and sat next to Jaggu Baba.

Tejas started a fire and then sat amongst the birds with

a basket full of seeds. A rabbit hopped into her lap and two pigeons perched on her shoulders.

"She was a panther in this very forest," Jaggu Baba said slowly. "In a previous life." He glanced sideways at Joash.

The pungent smell of burning leaves was heavy around them.

"What is it that you are smoking?" asked Joash.

Jaggu Baba puffed out a whirl of white smoke and looked at him with dreamy eyes. "It's magic, it's peace, it's warmth. Helps me think." He shot a gummy smile at Joash. "Did you find out anything new?"

"Yes." Joash now knew where he needed to be. Not far from Jaipur was a five-hundred-year-old deserted village—Bhangarh, his next destination.

Jaggu Baba let out another big cloud of smoke from his mouth. "So, you know where Prakruti Saram is. Have you been to this place before?"

"Never inside. I remember crossing the place several times as a child. My father had said we have an ancestral building there. But the locals called it a ghost village. I think that is why I remember the place."

"All rumours stem from something." Jaggu Baba had that sly smile again.

Joash looked up at the stalactites hanging from the cave roof.

"I don't know if there is anything that can shock me anymore." He held the glass vial up in front of his eyes. "I should leave soon."

The next moment Jaggu Baba sat up on his haunches and pulled the bowl with fire burning inside, in front of him. "Tejaswini!" he called out and bade her to come.

The storm noises started to quieten and Tejas got to her feet. She sat down next to the wavering flames. Then, with the utmost attention and care, she picked up a small flame with two fingers. She looked at the flame with a certain reverence and slowly her entire body took on the faint orange glow of fire. The countless droplets of water on her skin and her clothes dried out in the blink of an eye. She placed the flame in her palm and curled her fingers over it. When she opened it, there was sparkling ash in its place.

"Give me the vial that you carry around your neck." She extended her other arm towards Joash. She sprinkled the ash on the milky water and it formed a third neat layer in the glass bottle. As she returned the bottle to Joash, she rose again. "Baba, I will go out and check on Snel; he will not come inside while these other animals are here."

Jaggu Baba nodded, then looked at Joash. "I will take you to the nearest train station. Going to Jaipur will not be hard from here."

"What will Tejas do now?" asked Joash thoughtfully.

"Oh, she is going to be busy. She will rebuild her hut."

"In the same place?"

"Yes. She has meditated at that spot for a long time. She will not leave it."

"Can she get help to build?"

"She doesn't need help. Also, no one lives in these forests anymore. This place has seen several storms over the years. Villages were destroyed but the forest grew denser and larger each time. It is a magical place if you are brave enough to live here. Now go to that corner, I need to shut my eyes for a bit."

**

And by the next afternoon, Joash did get on to a train. It was after another hour on horseback and an hour-long wait at an abandoned platform which had broken glass all over the floor and a half-hanging metal roof.

It was as though Joash had two minds now—one was actively thinking of what was next and the other partaking in everything he witnessed: the damage and the unseen agony behind it. But all was not lost—the sun still came out after the storm; the air was damp yet clean. On either side of the train track, amongst the flattened trees there were some that stood defiantly tall. Through the open window, he could hear bird songs and the trickle of several streams above the sound of the racing train. He thought to himself, *Nature will find a way, even if I do not.*

Chapter 30

Jaipur

Krupa, Phillipa and Durgesh stood together facing the vast water body in front of them. It was a dismal sight—several house-tops projecting above the dark, stagnant water. An inescapable acrid smell hung in the air. There was no other life-form for miles around them; not even a bird passed them by.

"Why has it been left like this?" asked Durgesh.

"There is nowhere for the water to go. Not far from here is the valley that was dug up for a new artificial river. It is full and stagnant now. After the floods, authorities were sure all the dead were accounted for and retrieved, but they had no resources left to clean up the place," replied Krupa, her voice dull and quiet.

As she stared out, a pain that was buried deep, started to surface in her eyes. Somewhere in the depths here were the streets she knew, the home she loved. She hardened her gaze and mustered up a cold indifference; she could not let the gloom melt her.

"You cannot just go in there, Krupa. You need underwater navigation; you need diving equipment," said Phillipa.

"Do you think you can help me, Durgesh?" asked Krupa.

"I can certainly try. We need to be in the area with the best possible connectivity. Let us go."

***

The three of them were sitting around a table. It was a café in New Jaipur. Durgesh was tapping his fingers on the wooden table waiting for a reply from his London office while Krupa was listening to the news update with a frown.

The small screen on the table blared, "The storm today in Gujarat has caused ten deaths and major loss of property. Authorities say it could have been worse, but most people heeded advice and stayed indoors. Major road networks are damaged. A few train lines have withstood the storm. Please check the active services before planning to travel."

"Is everything okay, Krupa?" asked Phillipa.

"The national news never seems to say much about the Himalayan region."

"Why don't you try and speak to your brother while we are here?" said Durgesh.

"Hmm." She pretended to consider the idea, but Durgesh knew her better.

He put his hand in front of her, offering his wrist-pad. "Come on," he said with a gentle nudge.

Joash was quick to answer. "Krupa!" His surprise was clear in his hazy image. He looked at Phillipa and Durgesh, who waved at him and quickly left the table.

"Where are you?" asked Krupa. "Is that a train?"

"Yes, I am about to reach Jaipur," replied Joash. "Where are you?"

"Oh! So, you made it. I am in Jaipur."

"What? Why are you in Jaipur?"

"I wasn't sure where you were," said Krupa sounding annoyed, "so I had to try and get the book. I made it anyway, though I haven't got the book yet."

"I know where the book is. It is in Papa's special box. I can open the lock. I don't think you will be able to."

Krupa sighed. Of course, she knew she would not be able to open any locks in the house—something that had always galled her. But she had to prove that she was no less capable than Joash. "So, you are going to get here soon. I can get the box out of the house for you. I just need to figure out how."

"No, you don't need to go to the house. It is buried underground in Bhangarh. Do not go to the house."

She looked baffled.

"Trust me, Krupa. Just wait for me." When she did not reply, Joash spoke again. "Are they your friends?"

"Yes." That was all she wanted to say.

***

The sun had set by the time Joash reached Jaipur. Outside the train station, not much was visible in the heavy rain, but he could feel the life in the city. The road lamps were lit and clangorous autotuks were splashing water on passers-by.

An autotuk came and stopped right in front of him. "Do you need help to get somewhere?" the robotic voice asked.

Half a smile crossed Joash's unexpecting face. This was the Jaipur of his childhood after all. He remembered squeezing in these tiny things with his mum and Krupa when they were still run by humans.

"Yes please," he said and jumped in.

Within minutes, he found himself outside a tired-looking building. Durgesh approached him as he got out of the autotuk. "Joash?"

"Yes."

"Hi, I am Durgesh. We are upstairs." They shook hands.

As Joash entered the apartment, Krupa noticed the scars on Joash's face, as if he had returned from a battle. Reluctantly, she hugged him and said, "This is Phillipa."

"Hi!" said Phillipa loudly. "You have had quite a journey by the looks of it."

Joash smiled.

***

The four of them sat down on the floor in the front room.

"Where is Bhangarh? How soon can we get there?" asked Krupa.

"It is not far. Do you have good connectivity here?" enquired Joash.

"It's decent," said Phillipa.

The next moment, they were looking at a map that Joash had projected in the air.

"It is due east and then north. Looks like there was a road in the past but not anymore," said Joash.

"Looks like no one lives there," said Phillipa.

"Yes, it is supposed to be a ghost town," answered Joash.

"Really?" Phillipa raised her eyebrows mockingly.

"Some old legend about that place. But I don't know for sure."

"Interesting. How far is the nearest town or city?" asked Durgesh.

"According to this, the other towns and villages near it were vacated recently and people were moved to Jaipur." Joash was reading the information about the area.

"Why?" Phillipa could feel some excitement building up about this place.

"Unexplained tremors in the ground," Joash continued.

Phillipa got up to get another mug of coffee for herself and said, "Lots of things are unexplained these days. Especially when authorities don't have the resources to investigate or to keep on repairing buildings."

"I guess, you are right, but at least they are trying to keep the population safe," said Durgesh.

"Ah, so shall we leave early morning?" interjected Krupa.

"No! You guys stay put here. I am going by myself," said Joash firmly.

"But why?" said Krupa. "So, you can be the hero?"

"No, it might not be safe."

"What do you mean by that?" asked Phillipa.

"Look, there is no way these girls are going to sit and wait here. Let us all go and get it. It's only one hour away, right?" said Durgesh.

"Glad we have you here, Captain!" shouted Phillipa from the pantry.

Before Joash could say anything, he felt a tickle in his wrist-pad. He touched it and the map in the air was replaced by Callum's puzzled face.

"Hi Joash," said Callum. "Uh I am glad"—his voice faded and then came back again—"to see you alive."

Two seconds of silence followed as Joash took in his friend's confused state. "Callum! All okay with you?" he asked.

Callum gulped and the prominent Adam's apple in his neck moved visibly. "I am in a bit of trouble…"

Joash raised his eyebrows. "And…"

Callum spoke as quickly as he could. "Please don't be annoyed with me. I am in Jaipur and the kropter has been confiscated by the authority. I cannot reach my dad and they won't listen to me. Is there any way you can help me?"

"What?" Joash was shocked.

"Wait!" said Krupa, "Is he your friend? Where is he?"

Joash was frowning, he could not believe Callum had done it again.

"I am, I am his friend from the UK," Callum pleaded. "I am in Maalia Nagar. It is the old commercial airport."

"Malviya Nagar, I know where that is," said Joash finally. "Wait there, I will be there soon."

As Joash got up to his feet, Krupa said, "I will take you."

***

If Joash was secretly pleased to see Callum, he hid his feelings well. The kropter was with the Jaipur authority now, but Callum was sure his father was capable of sorting any situation when it came to his machines or his son. Throughout their way back in an autotuk, he had been excitedly explaining to Joash how he had managed to repair the kropter and set off from Muscat, but Krupa was enjoying his story more than Joash. When they reached the apartment, he found an eager audience in Phillipa, Durgesh and Krupa. Taking centre stage, Callum stood up while others sat, and spoke animatedly—first the story of the development of kropter, then meeting Joash, then their journey together and of course, the adventures in Saqqara. While Joash had retreated to bed early, others could not get enough of Callum's stories.

Joash was up with the first of the daylight. The first thing he noticed was that Callum was missing from his bed. He came down to the driveway to find him sitting on the ground between the two large motorbikes that were parked there.

Spotting Joash, Callum got up and began explaining, "I have taken permission from Phillipa. She reckoned the lender won't mind."

Befuddled Joash looked at Callum and then at the bikes. One of them now had a third seat attached to it on one side, held up by three smaller tyres or wheels—Joash could not say. He looked back at Callum who pressed his lips and shrugged his shoulders.

"A sidecar? Why?" asked Joash.

"Because two motorbikes can take only four people. Hence, I decided to make a seat for myself. Isn't it clever?" Callum seemed thrilled with his handy work.

"Callum—" Joash started to speak but stopped. If his father could not change his mind, how could Joash?

Soon they set off on the bikes towards the east border of the city of Jaipur. The landscape changed as soon as they left the raucous streets of the city centre—many bushes and plants everywhere, the houses were more spread out and solar capture points were on every corner. But the pink city was pink no more. As they reached the outer part of the city the land looked barren, pools of water were everywhere after last night's rain and the road abruptly ended at a spot where a lonely robot stood guard. The bikers stopped.

"Remove your headgear," demanded the robot approaching them.

"Wait, wait, wait." Callum got off the bike. "Let me do this." He walked to the robot and said "Hello, uh—"

"Where are you going, Callum Bailey of Glasgow?" the robot said scanning his face.

"To Bhangarh."

"Your purpose?"

"To explore the place as tourists. We have a keen interest in archaeology." Callum tried to put on a sophisticated English accent.

The robot had scanned all the faces by then. "None of you have any such qualifications."

"We are amateurs. Novices." Callum spoke with his chin lifted as Phillipa suppressed her laughter.

"That is odd," blinked the robot. "Bhangarh is not connected by road anymore. There is no connectivity there and the place might not be safe."

"What do you mean by not safe?" enquired Phillipa.

"I have not been provided with that information. And I am the one who asks questions here," came the mechanical reply.

"This is an arrogant one," Phillipa could not decide if she was amused or annoyed.

"Yes, I was made that way," said the robot turning its head slowly. "So, all of you are from different countries indeed. Once you leave here, the authority is not going to look after you. Neither are we going to retrieve your bodies if you die. Our resources are stretched. Do you still wish to go?"

"Yes," said Joash.

"Whatever then." The robot moved to the side of the road.

Durgesh and Phillipa followed the remnants of the old road

and the landscape changed yet again. The ground was arid now; somehow rain had not wandered this way.

Soon they came across a battered road sign that read, 'The Archaeological Society of India-Bhangarh.' Joash looked at the place—the broken outer wall and the lonely banyan tree next to the entrance; this was exactly the place he had seen.

"This place has an eerie feel to it," said Phillipa.

They had left their bikes outside and were walking on the cobbled street. The sunshine was hazy and the light wind felt dry and dusty. Empty ruined old buildings were all they could see. Every few metres, there were big holes in the path, as if the ground had sunk in.

"What are we looking for?" asked Krupa.

"*Pundit ji ki haveli*—it's written in Hindi on the outer wall of a building," replied Joash. As his eyes studied the surroundings, suddenly he felt like he was back walking on the path in the underground city in Egypt. Before he could think of any relation between this place and Jhenats, he stopped and turned to his right—there it was, the ancestral building of the Pundit family.

"There it is!" exclaimed Krupa.

Hundreds of years ago, what would have been a mansion was now a decrepit structure in a forsaken village. It had no roof, like most of the other buildings there; mounds of stones lay next to the half-broken walls but still, the name of the building stayed untouched by the lashes of time and nature.

Joash located the exact corner he needed to dig. Krupa and Callum climbed up the open stairs which led to a small, raised platform while Phillipa decided to go on her own and explore the place. Durgesh and Joash started digging with the small metal tools they had.

The weather started to change as Phillipa reached a higher part of the ancient village that seemed to be better preserved. She saw a small well which was full of water. She went closer and suddenly jumped back in terror. Instead of her own reflection, she saw a pair of large eyes looking back at her from the water. Unsure if it was her imagination, she went closer again. The water was dark, not reflecting anything and there were silent ripples on the surface as if something were dropping down.

At the same moment, Joash encountered something hard in the ground. Durgesh quickly removed more mud with his hands and a wooden box came into sight. Suddenly, a loud scream reverberated in the air. Krupa looked up towards the old castle. "Phillipa!"

As Krupa and Callum ran down the stairs, there were tremors in the ground and the stone wall next to the steps started to collapse. Joash and Durgesh put their tools down. Standing on shaky ground, Joash tried to understand what he felt at that moment—a presence that he had felt before—the Jhenats. His eyes widened with the realisation as Krupa and Callum jumped off the final step.

He started digging around the box with great urgency while others raced towards the old castle. But the tremors were relentless and the wind started to send the dry soil back in the hole.

Racing back from the well, Phillipa had come halfway down the path. "Krupa!" she shouted looking shaken. "Let us get the box and leave this place as soon as we can."

"What happened?" asked Krupa.

"I saw something strange in the water up there. It was like the tail end of some kind of snake." She was breathless. "I don't know what it was, but it was huge, too big to be real. It disappeared in a large hole in the ground right next to a well. Trust me, it just felt like we should not be here."

As Phillipa was speaking more walls of the ancient ruins started to collapse.

Back at the digging spot, Joash's efforts to dig the box out of the four-foot-deep hole were proving futile.

"Let me widen this thing," shouted Durgesh as he pulled Joash out of the hole.

The wind was whipping and throwing dirt in their faces now. Durgesh and Krupa were frantically digging but more and more rubble was falling in. Callum and Phillipa were struggling to hold the side wall which was threatening to collapse on the hole.

Joash had walked away, slowly looking around trying to gauge the situation, his eyes fighting the dirt, his feet fighting the wind. Some distance away he saw the ground undulate. A scene flashed in front of his eyes—the sight of the dark energy. He had a sensation of being pulled into a black hole.

At that moment, the ground shook and the whole area of the haveli sank down. The wind and noise started to quieten. Joash surged from the rubble again, he could now see the other three getting to their feet at the far end of the wide space—the walls between them had flattened. They were now in a pit that was a few feet deep. On the mud walls of the pit, some openings were appearing. Joash bent down close to one and could hear the ominous hissing noise. He looked up in the direction of the sun and saw a small flame floating in the air, unperturbed by the storm. Suddenly he knew what he had to do.

He sat down crossing his legs on the reverberating ground, closed his eyes and began to chant loudly. "Humm…" He was inviting the *Dhi* to flow through him, to show him the way. It was all in the mind, the fight began there, and the fight would end there because all the power lay there. He had let *Dhi* flow through his mind, when he went to the stairwell of infinity, when he saw Bhangarh and now he could do it again. So, in the midst of turbulence, he sat like a rock and concentrated all his attention towards the box he wanted. Soon, he felt like his body had started to merge with the soil around him, he was one with the earth.

He opened his eyes and saw two serpents emerging from the holes in the walls. He lifted his arms with all his might and enormous mounds of mud lifted with them. He threw his arms forward and the mud was hurled on the serpents. He threw his fists in the air and the soil above the pit started to fall in like a waterfall from all directions. The Jhenats were retreating.

Joash brought his arms down and looked at his sister. A look of horror mixed with awe painted her face. She was holding the wooden box next to her chest.

Chapter 31

Near Bhangarh

Sitting right across him, Krupa quietly glanced towards Joash who was looking pale and weak. He had gained new abrasions and wounds today, but something seemed very different; an air of contentment lingered about him.

He was sitting on a raised platform made of local sandstone. The platform had four carved pillars and a roof that was shaped like an umbrella. The landscape was dotted with many of these structures, built by the kings of the old times. Around them, the ground was barren with a few brambly shrubs here and there. They were not too far from Bhangarh, but Joash needed to rest.

Callum and Phillipa were resting flat on the ground

looking at the dull grey sky above. Krupa's hand was resting on the wooden box.

"You must be used to this by now," said Durgesh sitting next to Joash. "But what were those things and how did you do it?"

Callum sat up, eager to listen to Joash's answer.

"They were Jhenats," said Joash seriously. "Beings of the dark. They live underground or in empty dark buildings. We could never see them before. But times are changing, they are drawing from the dark energy—"

Durgesh shook his head. "What you did today felt like something we saw in the mountains. The trees and the ground everything moved like they had life in them."

Joash glanced at him briefly.

Presently, Krupa placed the box in front of him and everyone surrounded it. It was square—about a foot and a half, had an intricately engraved floral design and was made of dark wood with metal corners. It must have been shiny once upon a time.

"Do you know how to open it?" Krupa looked at Joash.

Quietly, he held the box. He placed his right thumb in the centre of the dial which immediately turned blue and moved one-hundred-and-eighty degrees. Joash removed his thumb— the dial was now a screen that read, 'Say Your Name'.

"Joash Pundit," said Joash loud and clear. The dial moved

out a bit and moved another one-hundred-and-eighty degrees. There was a click and the lock opened.

Callum gasped.

"It's open," said Phillipa excitedly.

Joash opened the box and examined the contents. There was not a lot. A small round box with a clear lid had some seeds in it. Tied with a piece of red thread there was a bundle of old-looking yellowing paper, possibly part of a book. The text was in Sanskrit.

"It is not a book, just some loose pages," said Joash.

"Can you read Sanskrit?" asked Phillipa.

"Yes, both of us can. But how do we know this is the missing part of Prakruti Saram?" Krupa was looking closely.

"The text is about growing some plants and how to look after them," replied Joash.

"But why would that be so important?" said Durgesh.

"What is that at the bottom?" enquired Krupa.

Joash placed the papers carefully to one side. The base had a piece of cloth, neatly folded. He opened it.

The striking scene of a mesmerising waterfall unfolded.

"This is Aunt Sue's!" He was baffled. "One of her paintings."

"Wow!" said Callum.

"Is it a copy?" asked Krupa.

"Must be, because the original is in her gallery. *The Waterfall*."

"But there is nothing ancient about it." Krupa touched the cloth and turned over the corners for any more clues about the painting being kept in the box.

"There is something about it," said Phillipa. "The painting... I am no art critic, though. Everything here looks so real."

Durgesh put his hand on Joash's shoulder. "It is going to rain heavily soon. We need to leave if we want to avoid getting the bikes stuck."

Joash nodded quietly and looked at Krupa. "Is this what your Swamiji wanted?"

His sister's eyes were searching the painting for something, but before she could reply, big droplets of water started descending from the sky. They quickly put all the contents back in the box and closed it. As water splashed on the closed lid, the colour of the metalwork started to change.

They all leaned over the box as bright silvery Sanskrit words appeared on the metal plate in the left corner of the box. *Prakruti Saram.* Next to the words was the sign that Krupa and Joash were so familiar with.

"Yes! This is what we were looking for." Krupa was elated. "It is not just a book. It is the whole box. I am sure Swamiji will be able to make sense of it all." She turned to Joash. "You are free now. I will take this back. Can you register me to open it?"

"I don't know how to," replied Joash.

She looked displeased. Durgesh came over to her and said, "We can look into all that later. Let us go back now."

Krupa picked up the box and walked away as Joash looked on.

Chapter 32

Jaipur

Back in the apartment, all the contents of the box were out again as five of them sat analysing them.

Joash rose up and retreated to one of the rooms. He opened the balcony door and sat down on the floor. A certain restlessness was taking over him. Somehow, he knew he needed to sit alone.

"Hey Joash!" said Callum as he came looking for him. "Everything okay?"

Joash sighed and moved his head adjusting his neck. "I think so," he said. "Feels like something is not fitting together."

"Hey, you have done it. Now it is only a matter of time."

"Thank you, Callum!" Joash looked at Callum and felt light

in his heart. A smile crossed his weary face. He wondered what had made this boy follow him halfway across the world.

"You take your time. We can figure this out together." Joash blinked and nodded as Callum left the room.

He looked towards the falling rain that had obscured everything beyond. He realised his restlessness had turned into a serene calm. He closed his eyes. Guruji's face was the first thing he saw.

***

He was nine years old.

"Just sit still, Joash." Guruji's words resounded in his mind. "Focus on this moment. And then decide what you want to know."

The shade under the tree was cool under the afternoon sun. The birds were chirping loudly, maybe a bit too loudly. Then with his eyes closed, the young Joash saw a sparrow's nest—two birds with shades of brown and a dash of black on their wings and three eggs. The eggs were cracking. Joash knew he was not imagining it, but it was too much for him. He suddenly opened his eyes, breathing heavily.

Guruji asked, "So, what did you see?"

Unsure of what had just happened Joash said, "I saw a bird's nest. It is in this garden. I was floating up in the air, but I did not plan to know about the bird."

"It is okay, Joash," Guruji laughed. "You concentrated on

some aspect of the bird. And that was your moment. You were transported to the nest. Now try something else, what is it that you could know, that would be helpful to you?"

Once again, Joash was transported to another moment. It was winter. Wrapped up in his school jumper and woolly hat, he walked through the thick early morning fog on the terrace and knocked on the study door.

"Good morning, Joash," said Kartik brightly as he opened the door. "Ready for school, are we?"

Joash nodded and quickly entered. It was too cold to talk.

"Okay, it is not going to take long." Kartik pulled a shiny wooden box on the table as both of them sat down.

"So, as I have told you, there are some things you will need to take care of as you grow older." Joash nodded again as Kartik continued, "This is one of them. This box has something important—a message, knowledge—that we need to protect. And when the time is right, you or maybe your children or maybe your grandchildren will need to use this knowledge."

Joash giggled.

"So, we as a family must look after this. Now that you are thirteen years old, I am going to register you as one of the lock-openers. Fancy title, huh?"

"Why do we need to keep it a secret, Papa? Why protect it?"

"Because some actions need to be timely. Too soon or too late, they fail to serve a purpose."

Joash yawned. Half asleep, he put his head to one side as Kartik did something holding his thumb. His father was always doing some stuff which Joash did not understand. But today he was sleepy, too.

"Come on now, say your name loudly when I press this button. And next time when we open this box together, I will tell you all about the hidden codes in the most colourful thing in this box." With that, Kartik tapped the tip of Joash's nose with his finger and smiled.

***

Now, sitting on the balcony floor, Joash opened his eyes wide to the present. The rain was still pouring down. He could feel strange buzzing around himself.

Tying his hair back into a ponytail, he went to the front room. Callum and Phillipa were examining the painting. Krupa was translating the Sanskrit text while Durgesh was editing it on an air-screen.

"I remember something now," Joash announced. Everyone in the room turned to look at him. "My father had told me that there is an important coded message in this box ... in the painting."

Callum stood up with the cloth painting in his hand. "You

must be right Joash. Touch this, it is no ordinary cloth."

Phillipa said knowledgeably, "I think it is a super-fabric. It is what soldiers' clothes are made of. It is resistant to water, and fire and cannot be pierced."

"Oh and it is fluorescent," added Callum.

Joash looked directly at Krupa. "We need to ring up Aunt Sue."

***

"I will tell you the details later, Aunty, but please answer my questions first." When Joash spoke those words, Aunt Sue's mouth was half-open and ready to speak. She moved her head back a bit, looked at Joash, and then turned to Krupa.

"Okay! I shall do that," she said. "But let me just quickly say that I have never seen you both sitting next to each other like this, and my heart is utterly delighted today."

Krupa shook her head and looked away. Joash continued, "Do you remember when we celebrated my thirteenth birthday with you in London? You and Dad used to discuss making a copy of your *Waterfall* painting?"

"Yes, yes we did indeed," replied Aunt Sue.

"Please tell me how it all happened and who copied it?"

"Uh yes, of course. Your father wanted a copy on cloth. And he told me he could get it done digitally and that it would be indestructible. He had a friend ... I had never heard your father speak of him before. But anyway … it was a certain Dr Church or Churchill from Oxford University. He and your father took the painting away to his lab for a day. That is all I know. Could I see it?"

"Sure Aunty," Krupa held up the painting for Aunt Sue to see.

"It looks as fresh as it did then," said Aunt Sue.

"You look tired, Aunty. Is everything okay?" asked Krupa.

Joash suddenly looked at Aunt Sue and guiltily he realised that he had not noticed her sunken eyes and unkempt hair.

"Thank you, dear, for asking. I am not sleeping very well as I'm worrying about you two and I have been doing a lot of hiking in the Trossachs to keep my mind off things."

"Hiking in the Trossachs?" Joash was surprised.

"Yes, the floods in London were not getting any better. There haven't been any flying accidents yet, but some more buildings have been damaged. The authority has asked people to vacate. I have moved to a lovely cottage here in Scotland with my friend, Linda. At least the rain is not constant here. But I am glad I could see you two today; I am sure I will sleep better now."

"You should rest, Aunty," said Krupa.

"I will, darling." Suddenly, Aunt Sue's weary face lit up. "And you know what … I saw something amazing yesterday here—the silver rain, on the top of a hill. You must have heard about it in the news by now. It seems things have started to settle in London a bit."

Joash looked at Krupa, but his sister ignored him.

"How was that Aunt Sue?" asked Krupa.

"Oh, wonderful! It truly was, I cannot describe it, but I have already started a painting of it. We need to sit together dear, the three of us, and share all these things."

Joash could have listened to Aunt Sue for hours today. He felt something heavy in his chest, when he uttered his next words, "We have got to go now, Aunty."

By the time, the conversation was over, Callum was ready with an update.

"So Joash, it was Dr Churchill, the only Dr Churchill in Oxford University at that time. He was one of the important figures who promoted DNA as a storage medium. His work has led to many practical applications of non-cellular DNA including—" Callum looked at Joash, his eyes shining with excitement, "—DNA and paints."

"So that means—" Joash's eyes were moving quickly.

"That means the paint used for this painting could store a whole book, maybe even more." Callum was quite pleased with himself.

"We need to decode it somehow and then we will have the book," said Phillipa.

The next few hours were spent doing research and making calls to see who could decode the painting for them. An image of the painting had been sent to London, Toronto, New Delhi and Oxford. But Krupa had her doubts—who was going to believe this was urgent and take a real interest in decoding it? But it was clear that they could not leave Jaipur until they had the text with them. There would be no way of doing this in the mountains.

At night she quietly sat in the bed looking at the box of seeds—there were seven of them and one was at least six times larger than the rest. She picked up the loose papers from the box—they had seen better times, but now they were just ready to crumble. The images of plants, one on each page, that were fading now would have been brightly colourful once. With these thoughts, she gave in to sleep, the box of seeds lay close to her chest.

**

It was 3:45 in the morning. Joash woke up as Callum shook his shoulder gently.

"It is done, Joash," whispered Callum. "I have done it."

They sat in the front room. Callum had made the screen several feet wide.

"It is not just one text but there are several others here too. But the one that says *Prakruti Saram* is this one." As Callum tapped the screen, the others emerged from their bedrooms too. "Great! I don't have to whisper anymore," he said.

Together they started to read the text that was written in

both, Sanskrit and English:

When the burden of our karma rises,

So will the seas.

Ignorant deeds would have laden air, water and land with poison.

But, as the first ten thousand years come to a close,

It will be time for the Sangam again and a new cycle shall start.

Rejoice! For the higher age will be upon us.

But you cannot turn away from what else might enter our world,

When this realm crosses some others.

Centuries of filth, sloth and stagnation shall attract forms that dwell in them.

Roga may be many but the source is one. But a karma yogi with sacred blessing may yet face it, may defeat it or be defeated.

All will not be lost if those with courage find these seeds of hope.

When nurtured with sacred soil, healing water, fire and uncorrupted air in 'the abode of snow,'

The seedlings shall thrive under the care of Tirtha Rakshaks.

When taken to seven corners of this realm, the seedlings will consume all poison.

"The abode of snow—that means Himalaya," said Krupa thoughtfully.

"This first part," Phillipa looked at Krupa. "You know about this, don't you? What is the higher age? I have heard this before."

"Yes, I understand this part," Krupa walked around the room slowly, recalling things she had learnt from Swamiji. "The higher age is the next phase in human evolution. It means a time of increased awareness of the energy which we call *Dhi*, around us and within us."

"So, is this *Dhi* similar to what scientists call consciousness?" asked Phillipa.

"I think so. However, Sheersha yoga says even inanimate objects have *Dhi*," replied Krupa.

Callum changed the page on the screen.

Joash's hand reached for the vial around his neck as he read, "The five elements will nurture these seeds and as they grow these plants will consume all poison."

"What are the five elements?" asked Durgesh.

"Earth, water, fire, air and space," said Joash without taking his eyes off the screen. "I have the first three right here."

Callum walked closer and held the glass vial that hung around Joash's neck, in his hand. His eyes glinted with amazement as he stared at an unusual yet beautiful sight—three clear layers—a layer of glittering grey powder, under it a layer of milky white liquid and below it, the sacred soil, a reddish-brown in colour with highly coarse grains. "Wow, that is so cool!" he said.

"Look at this drawing—mountains, trees and this sign," said Phillipa, standing close to the screen.

Krupa tilted her head and observed the sign for a long moment. "This is about the remaining two elements—air and space. This is the location for the first seedling to be planted." A sudden exhilaration was noticeable in her voice. "I know where it is, the Tirtha." She looked at Durgesh, feeling the happiness of a lost sailor who had found land. "Let us go to Moksha Parvat. Swamiji is waiting."

Chapter 33

The Base

Swamiji opened his eyes after his morning meditation. Today Lorenzo was first in his thoughts.

"Where is Dr Lorenzo?" he asked.

"He has gone to the other side of the mountain, Swamiji," replied Alok. "Yesterday we were discussing about everyone contributing to the base in different ways. He insisted on starting some cultivation on a small patch. He had sown some seeds too and today he has taken some more. Meera has gone with him."

"I must go see him."

"It's very slippery outside the base, Swamiji."

"I know, Alok. Come along if you want to." He smiled at

him. "Let us check on Professor Rollings first."

The professor had set up a large tent—this time just outside the eastern side of the base. Inside, Patrick Zuma was asleep in his sleeping bag, but Professor Rollings was looking intently at the virtual image of the earth rotating on top of the worktable.

"Looks like you have been working all night, Stella," said Swamiji.

She got up from her chair looking cheerful. "Good to see you here. I have been thinking all night. Patrick has been working; I have some new findings to pore over."

"Let us hear them. Would you like to come for a morning walk?" asked Swamiji.

"Why not?" She picked up her jacket and the three of them started to trek the uneven path. The sky was removing the blanket of night, only to reveal another of dark clouds, but the air was fragrant, and birds were singing merrily.

"As you suggested we have been investigating the soil on different mountain ranges. Something quite extraordinary is happening. Anything new that we plant has been growing at exponential rates. The Elusium content of air on mountains is relatively low. But something more has been happening—storms are getting milder too, though only by a fraction." The professor stopped and looked at Swamiji. "I wonder if we—humans, I mean—need to inhabit mountains?"

"Look, Swamiji!" exclaimed Alok.

Lorenzo could be seen at a distance. He was amongst vibrant green plants that were reaching his knees. He looked happy as he walked around with his arms spread out and his fingers stroking the leaves.

"Those were planted just yesterday," Alok was amazed.

"This is what the touch of esters can do," said Swamiji.

The three of them observed Lorenzo from a distance and Meera joined them. The next moment, a shrill screech pierced through the air and Lorenzo disappeared. They quickly crossed the patch and saw a large leopard dragging the man down the slope of the mountain. Meera was horrified and Professor Rollings looked at Swamiji who had a calm yet intense look on his face.

Lorenzo's cries reverberated in the valley.

Swamiji gestured with his hand and said loudly, "Stop!" His outstretched arm was still for a few moments, his robe gently wavering, and his eyes locked with the leopard's.

As though the leopard understood him, it just stopped and released Lorenzo's bleeding leg.

"I request you to leave him," came Swamiji's earnest words.

The leopard left Lorenzo where he was and sprang away.

"Meera, please stay with him. Alok and the others can bring

him back to the base," said Swamiji.

Meera nodded.

Professor Rollings had been standing immobile and awestricken. She had felt something strange connecting the leopard and Swamiji. For a moment the imperceptible had become perceptible, the intangible had become tangible, and she had no words to describe that feeling.

"Come, Stella, we can walk back now." Swamiji placed his hand on the professor's shoulder, snapping her out of her trance. "A severe snowstorm is going to hit the area later today. Please get all your things and go back to the base with Patrick as soon as you can."

***

Professor Rollings stood in the ashram balcony looking out at the settlement, her mind full of questions.

Swamiji stepped out of his room. "I think I must tell you a story today, Stella," he said as they settled in their seats, his voice weary, his expression as equanimous as ever. "There was a nun, a long time ago in the Netherlands. Just before the second world war, she was captured by Nazis as she was a Jew. She was to be sent to Auschwitz, but a Nazi soldier took a particular interest in her and decided to batter her to death with his own hands."

Swamiji paused and she waited for the deeper meaning of this story to unravel.

"That nun was this Swami right in front of you and that soldier was Dr Lorenzo."

Professor Rollings closed her eyes and felt an agony she was not expecting to feel. A suppressed anger started to well up in her. *Where is the justice, then?* If it was her, she would have fed Lorenzo to the leopard. "Why did you save him?" she asked.

"I had to forgive him in a true sense and give him a chance to lift his soul. He is not the same as he was and neither am I. Souls progress and they change. His soul has repented his karma. Any hatred or vengeance will block both our souls. I have done my bit and my physical body is tired now."

Turning her head slowly towards Swamiji, she said in a low voice, "So is that why he came here? To settle his karma with you?"

Swamiji smiled quietly.

Professor Rollings had seen everything now. She believed in the theories of Sheersha yoga but some things still did not fit. *A wrong deed is a wrong deed. Who knows if a person is truly repenting? And what does repenting change? A wrongdoer must face punishment...*

"Why am I here then, Swamiji?" she wondered loudly.

"You are a soul who does not want to be read by any other. You have a pain running through you but you have shut yourself. You intrigue me: I hope you find your peace."

Chapter 34

The Mountains, Himachal Pradesh

Joash awoke to the whooshing sound of wind against his tent, reminding him where he was and what he must do. The same thoughts were flicking through his mind as the ones he had slept with. *Has Krupa forgiven me? What else is my karma? What is this unease I feel?*

He stepped outside into the dull morning in a picturesque valley to find a beaming Callum with a slice of warm toast.

"Are we keeping track of the weather?" Durgesh emerged from another tent rubbing his hands together.

"Nope," said Phillipa, "it is absolutely useless. No one understands what is going on with the weather anyway. If we just look out for extremely dark clouds moving in our direction, we will know a storm is not far away. We have been lucky so far."

"We are not far from the base now," said Krupa. "A few hours riding north and then maybe a couple of hours trekking will take us to the foot of Moksha Parvat."

"What about Swamiji? Were you able to send a message to Patrick?"

"I did, last night. I do not know if it was received."

Joash looked at the snow-capped mountains in the distance. He thought he saw a black fleck hiding behind the peak. He shut his eyes and took a deep breath in.

They packed up their tents and took to the road again on their bikes. After a few hours on the serpentine roads that wound around the mountains and dashed across the valleys, they stopped for a break. A tall lorry approaching them from the opposite side of the road slowed down as it came near. The man in the lorry gestured them to turn around and go back as he shouted towards the group, "Road blocked!" He stopped and continued, "Where are you going? Haven't you heard about the earthquakes? The villagers have all run away or died." When he only got silent stares in return, he shook his head and moved on.

And so did the group. Even if fear of what was ahead of them was building up, none of them displayed it.

By late afternoon, the scene started to change indeed—very dark clouds were moving in fast from the north. The wind had a terrible chill in it. The mountains and valleys felt mournful. There was no sign of any human. Soon, the bikes had to stop as they found themselves opposite large rocks and boulders that had blocked the highway. It looked like the mountain had split.

"Krupa, do you know any other way?" asked Phillipa.

"We need to stick to the road or go up along the river," said Krupa.

"We will have to leave the bikes and carry on," said Joash as he looked at the impassable road and the valley strewn with rocks and flattened trees.

They descended to the river and rain started. It was not water but hailstones that hit them hard as they trekked with their heads down. The five figures clad in white bodysuits trudged along the debris-ridden riverbank in a dismal valley. As the sun retreated behind a mountain, the wind roared, throwing the hailstones at them with full force. The need to find shelter grew urgent.

Joash caught Krupa quickly as she slipped on a boulder. Just then Durgesh shouted, "Over here!" It was a shallow cave, possibly recently formed, large enough for the five of them and with an entrance that was partly blocked by a large round rock.

"We cannot carry on today. This place should shield us better than the tents for now," Durgesh yelled over the howling wind.

"Joash rub your hands together a few times and the suit's heating system will kick in," said Phillipa as they sat side by side in the cave.

"Hah! What a relief!" said Callum making himself warm and comfortable.

"Careful, Callum! Don't keep the temperature too high or you will be dehydrated," said Phillipa.

Callum laughed. "Imagine that in this weather!" With that, the group settled to rest for the night in the cave.

***

The first light of day found its way straight to Joash's eyes through the gap between the rocky wall and the tent hanging on the cave mouth. Outside, the sky was orange-pink and strangely calm as if yesterday never happened. At a distance, someone sat perched up on a big round rock by the river. As Joash approached him, he recognized the familiar style of sitting with legs folded close to his chest and the strong smell of burning leaves. The sight of Jaggu Baba was somehow comforting.

"Jaggu Baba!" Joash was now facing the man whose eyes were half closed. The deep lines on his face were stretched in a smile as if he were in a trance.

"Do me a favour, boy." Jaggu Baba opened his eyes as he

spoke—his sudden reappearance was no matter of discussion at all. "Go up along the river a bit." He pointed to the meandering burbling river. "There should be some apple trees on the slope behind that hill. Can you get me some, please?"

He pressed his lips and frowned at this odd request, but Baba simply smiled at him, his eyes twinkling with a hint of mischief. Joash looked at his destination and said, "Yes Baba."

Remnants of the storm were still scattered all over but at least there was no wind and no rain. Joash had left his bodysuit in the cave, feeling light on his feet he leapt along in a direction opposite to that of the running water. As the river curved right behind a hill, the cave and Jaggu Baba went out of sight. There were some trees and shrubs there, and a lot of them were broken or uprooted. One tree looked particularly appealing, its apples were shining bright red and many lay on the ground around it.

He bent down to pick up some apples and someone said, "Be careful! Don't take the ones with holes."

Startled, Joash turned around and was even more surprised to see what was in front of him. A very tall person or maybe a monkey. Well, he had the face of a monkey, the body of a human and was covered with very soft-looking long white hair all over. He even had a tail. He looked mighty with his hands resting on his waist, standing some ten feet away, higher up on the slope of the hill.

Clearly, he was amused by Joash looking dumbfounded. "I only mean to say leave some for the poor insects."

Joash blinked but still could not find any words. As it came closer, he noticed the faint glow around him. Suddenly, the distant sound of birds seemed much louder, every drop of river water could be heard moving distinctly, and every movement of the leaves around him became perceptible; it was like he could feel every atom in the air against his skin, it was like becoming aware of the universe in a strange wholesome way, it was like time did not exist. It struck Joash that this was no ordinary being.

"Hmm, ordinary? Depends on what you class as ordinary," the Mahayogi spoke instantly. "For now, think of me as your Guruji's friend. Let us take a short stroll, Son, shall we?"

Joash wondered what was going on but only for a moment. Then it dawned upon him, the song that Jaggu Baba had sung to him.

The Mahayogi's crystal-like eyes emanated a mellow light of their own as he looked down at Joash. "I am here to help you. You need to understand what you must do and why." The next moment the Mahayogi was much further up the hill but could be heard just the same. "This … is the last leg of your journey. And it is going to be hard."

Joash tried to follow the Mahayogi on the steep slope. With

every step, his feet gently pushed the ground, and his body floated several feet up.

"Keep your mind still, your will strong and it will be easy. Your karma awaits you. And your guru awaits you on the other side."

Joash folded his hands together. "What is it that I have to do?"

The next moment, the Mahayogi appeared right next to Joash. "Fight a monster!" The Mahayogi laughed. "Almost like the games you played as a child." The two walked side by side as he continued, "The Roga goes from one universe to another looking for dark places, it leaves much destruction in its wake. In his desire to master the dark power, Jaggu Baba—the fickle one—led it straight to you. Remember, the Roga neither belongs to the physical nor the astral realm which means it does not have a shape. This also means that they can take any shape. When on earth, it can only be destroyed in its physical form. It hides like a thief from the beings of the realm it is in. It can penetrate the mind and peek into one's painful memories. Above all, it is only as strong as you allow it to be. "When you looked straight into the Roga at the staircase of infinity, you formed a link with it."

Suddenly Joash wondered why Jaggu Baba was here.

"He seeks just the fruit of power, but he fears it all the same. He has his own battles to fight. He knows the Roga goes the same way as you and ahead of you. You, Son, must stop the Roga before it destroys the Tirtha and the Moksha Parvat."

"Oh Mahayogi, I am an ordinary human. How could I possibly defeat a being from another world?"

"You can! Because when you decided to come back to this world, seeking forgiveness was not the only karma you wanted to clear. Look inside you, there is the power of your soul that you had mastered but it sits forgotten now. You are Dhanay and you are Joash. Know this much, if you annihilate the one Roga that is demolishing the Himalayas right now, you will destroy them all. You will give this earth a chance again. But if it pollutes the place that awaits the seed of hope, decimation will follow."

Joash got down to his knees, suddenly feeling weak. The enormity of his task had left him trembling. "I have no doubt that every word you speak has wisdom in it. But I am unable to understand which power you are referring to. Maybe it is someone else you seek for this big task."

The Mahayogi looked at Joash with pity. He then looked up to the sky with his big arms wide open and the dark clouds in the east suddenly moved away, the bright rays of the sun shone on Joash's troubled face.

"I know what I seek, it is you who does not. I am one with everything and thus I know whatever there is to be known and not to be known. I am your mother, father, guru, sister and also you.

Forget not the lessons from your past. Forget not that human is not the only form you have had. You can choose not to remember and turn back, but karma will bring you back right here."

"Tell me, then, Lord, how can I remember what I seem to have forgotten? Help me Lord," pleaded Joash.

"Sit under the very tree you were taking fruits from. Look inside your soul. You will find the answers." With these words, the Mahayogi disappeared.

***

Everything around Joash was very still, even the sun seemed to be fixed in the same spot. He sat cross-legged under the tree. For what felt like an eternity, he sat still with his eyes closed. Thoughts of all kinds started to crowd his mind—scenes from his life, his dreams and his imagination. Then it was nothing—just a blank stillness, a vacant space. A single drop of water fell on his forehead. He heard it land and felt the subtle softness of that moment. Then he was the drop itself falling in a moment going deeper and deeper. Finally, he was at the same place he had been when Jaggu Baba had sent him to his past—at a window to the universe.

This time he jumped right towards it, only to float like air through different worlds. He was an aster. He felt his own immensity in a bright white realm. There was no air, no land but an all-encompassing light. He felt strong and limitless.

Next, he saw Guruji looking down at him with an intense gaze. Joash was young again, shivering and standing waist-deep in a pond of water. Guruji's words pierced through the cold mist around him. "Concentrate! The extraordinary is in you. You can walk on water, you can fly without wings, you can shake the ground, you can turn the winds. Call upon the *Dhi*, feel it flowing through you and achieve the impossible." As he breathed heavily, the shiver turned into a blaze running through him. Drawing strength from every cell of his being he lifted himself out of the water onto the edge of the pond and then ran across the pond from one end to the other, his feet touching the water only to cause gentle ripples. With a thud, he landed on the other side.

Under the apple tree, Joash still sat motionless, but his eyes behind their closed lids were moving fast. The visions of Guruji and his younger self condensed into a small white dot in a colourless blank space. Suddenly, there was a burst of different colours and a white light appeared which engulfed everything. The light then turned yellow and started to shrink until it was the shape of a small flickering flame. He saw the flame enter his chest and opened his eyes with a gasp.

***

He found himself shivering slightly in his warm suit in the little cave. Others were fast asleep. Joash went out and found Jaggu

Baba sitting in the same place. It was a gloomy morning and Joash knew another storm was about to set in.

A wide smile was pasted on Jaggu Baba's face as he spoke. "Aha, I knew I would find you here. Didn't I tell you I am off to the Himalayas? So here I am. Which way are you going next?"

Joash looked at Jaggu Baba and then his eyes travelled to the north, where an array of mighty mountains waited for him.

Suddenly, the valley reverberated with a wail. Joash whirled towards the cave. He went inside to find Krupa looking distraught.

She dashed towards Joash and asked, wiping her tears, "Please tell me you have my bag?"

"Bag?" said Joash looking confused.

"The one with Prakruti Saram in it. I slept with it close to my head and now it is nowhere in the cave."

Joash's heart sank. He joined others in looking for it, but it was gone.

Jaggu Baba watched the commotion perched on a large rock.

"Let us go back to the road and look for it," suggested Durgesh.

"It has not just fallen anywhere. It was with me till I fell asleep," Krupa was agitated.

"What about your friend, Joash?" asked Phillipa looking suspiciously at Jaggu Baba.

"He has just arrived," replied Joash.

"He does not have anything on him other than that tall stick, I think," Callum observed Jaggu Baba curiously.

"You guys—don't let him leave while Callum and I go towards the road and come back," said Durgesh.

As soon as the two disappeared out of sight, a low rumble and a tremor ran through the valley.

Joash knew he could delay no longer. His fingertips and toes were buzzing. He unfastened the string around his neck and tied it around Krupa's. "This belongs with Prakruti Saram. I am going ahead."

"What? Where are you going?" cried Krupa. "And for what? What is the point of anything without the seeds? You … you are escaping again. This is what you do, run away when you are most needed."

One part of Joash wanted to embrace Krupa and comfort her. He did not know what could have happened to the box in this wilderness. But if he did not confront his enemy in time, all will be lost. He held Krupa's two hands in his and looked her in the eyes. "I can feel the call of Tirtha, Krupa. I must leave."

Joash glanced at Jaggu Baba. He winked at Joash and bit into a very shiny red apple.

Chapter 35

Near Tirtha

Joash looked north towards the tall mountains. Tremors in the ground under his feet and a distant rumble of crashing rocks told him the Roga was at work. Leaving his white suit behind he sprinted through the valley like a leaping stag. The icy air felt warm against his bare skin, the ground was soft under his feet and his injuries bothered him no more. Soon he reached the site of desolation; part of a mountainside had collapsed, and rocks were scattered all over the remains of the forsaken village that lay at the foot of the mountain.

He slowed down, walking through the village. The street still reeked of blood; the broken walls, the shattered glass, the upturned vessels and the abandoned toys told a story all too familiar to him. He picked up a muddy scarf from the road and the moment he looked at it, he perceived the pain and anguish that still lingered around that place.

He carried on, till in clear sight was the mouth of a cave from the depths of which arose deep growls of the destruction.

Standing in front of the mouth of the cave, he looked up to the sky and adjusted his neck. The tremors continued below and dark clouds scud along above as he took firm slow steps with his gaze intensely fixed on his path.

Joash entered the cave. Deeper and deeper, he went on the slowly descending cavernous path. It got bleaker and danker with every step. Suddenly, the tremors stopped, and all went still—no sound, no vision and no movement. He continued as his path started to ascend sharply and get narrower. He felt his way forward pressing his hands on the razor-sharp edges of the rocky surface. Finally, the path opened up into a vast space; the sound of water dripping was all around him. A strange stench made him hold his breath for a moment. As he looked on, a wave like movement arose in the cave wall at the far end. His eyes followed the ripple which moved towards him and overhead and boom—it burst sending a shower of sharp stones towards him. Crossing his hands over his head, Joash had already jumped into the pool of water made by a flowing stream. With droplets of blood shining all over his back and arms, he emerged from the water again, only to face another onslaught from the Roga. Enraged, he lifted up a large boulder and flung it towards the new wave forming on the cave wall. As it crashed and the pieces tumbled, he shouted, "Is this all you can do? I do not fear you."

The moment Joash's attention shifted from what had happened to what had caused it, something changed. There was a loud bang, the ground shook and light poured in from an opening in the cave wall away from Joash.

He understood that he needed to hold the Roga in his attention to stop it, to make it face him. Joash's heart and mind started racing. All he had was now, this was the moment to act. But how could he concentrate on something that had no form or shape? The answer came to him; he just knew he could. He thought of all that he had seen and fixed his mind on the force of destruction. With unwavering attention, he darted towards the new opening and came out of the other side of the mountain.

He was breathing heavily, his eyes hawk-like. The furious wind was screaming in his ears, he had reached much higher than the mouth of the cave. To one side, along the mountain was a clearing with a lone standing tree. He approached the area slowly. A flicker of delight touched him as he saw the engravings on the mountainside and the tree. Krupa had described the place well. He had reached the Tirtha.

Underneath him, the slope of the mountain fell away; the tall pine trees were kneeling to the angry weather. To his right was a wide couloir which started near the summit and ran straight down to unseen depths.

Directing his senses towards his enemy, Joash stood still. His ears perceived a swoosh, that was not the sound of the wind and his eyes found a grey smoky mist hovering close to a bush. His gaze hardened and his fists curled up tight. A fleck of the grey mist floated towards him, against the direction of the wind. He stood still and strong, rooted to the ground, ready to thrash any monster shape that was going to emerge out of it. But the small fleck disappeared, and a fuzzy feeling arose in his head. Disregarding anything that he felt in his physical self he maintained his focus on the remaining grey vapour. Before he knew it, that vanished too, but something else was behind the bush.

Joash stepped forward ready to charge and that very instant a little girl emerged from behind the bush. Her state was wretched, her forlorn eyes stared mournfully at the man in front of him.

"Miria!" he exclaimed his mind utterly bewildered. His fists uncurled.

But Miria's expression changed to fury, as if she did not

want to hear her name, and then her eyes filled up with tears.

That was enough to bring Joash down on his knees. "Who are you?" he asked, knowing somewhere in his mind that his questions could not have a real answer. "What are you doing in this storm? Where are your parents?"

She did not speak.

As his emotions started to waver his attention, he saw the colour of her skin turn ashen grey and her shape started to dissolve into a grey smoke.

Joash stood up and screamed with a ferocity that started to bring the Roga back to a physical form. Shaking with rage, he tore off a branch of a tree next to him and lifted it high to strike the form of Miria. But he stopped an inch before her face. Her innocent eyes stared pleadingly at him and then looked at something behind him.

He turned around and saw Krupa. She was standing just a few feet away her eyes open wide with disbelief.

"How could you?" said Krupa looking infuriated with what she had witnessed. Before Joash could react, she quickly went towards Miria. "It's okay!" she said softly. "I won't let him hurt you."

"Do you believe me now, Krupa?" Professor Rollings came out of the mountainside, her face a picture of disdain mixed with regret. "He is nothing like you. I am sorry you have a brother like him."

Joash's eyes widened as he tried to comprehend what was going on.

"She was coming down to help us when she saw you trying to destroy Prakruti Saram. When you could not break it, you threw it down a cliff, but she recovered it." Krupa's arms were wrapped tightly around the box.

"He would do anything to prove that all this is nonsense. Your family's legacy is nothing to him. I know him Krupa, I have seen his ways. But hurting a child…" Joash could see a burning hatred in Professor Rolling's eyes.

Before Joash or Krupa could speak again, the form of Miria disappeared, and a fleck of grey smoke entered Krupa's head. Befuddled Krupa stepped back shakily.

Joash held her. "You should not be here," he said.

"Where is she?" Krupa had no other concern right now but the poor girl.

The tremors started again with a loud pounding coming from inside the mountain. Thunder from above tore off more rocks which went flying down the couloir. And then began the blizzard.

Joash needed to concentrate on the Roga again, but his sister looked miserable. She sank to the ground covering her face and wept. "Who was that girl? I know her. I think she needs help. Please…"

Professor Rollings walked over and wrapped her arms around Krupa while glowering at Joash.

Joash glared back at the professor, bursting with anger over her lies. As he stared directly into her grey eyes, he had a sudden revelation—she was Rhona, the soul that was his unfortunate wife in another life.

"Krupa!" A lean, teenage emerged at the opening in the mountain. It was the younger self of Joash.

While Krupa's mind was confounded by what she saw, Joash braced himself and waited for what was next.

Through the thick snow falling between them, the younger Joash said with a sardonic smile, "I am much smarter than you. I am older and strong, and I have been chosen by a guru you cannot even dream of."

With her hands moving vaguely, Krupa started to move backwards unable to take the excruciating agony caused by the words that were being thrown at her. Joash sprang towards her and held her. "Let go of him, Krupa! Let go of this thought," he yelled above the storm.

But the words continued incessantly. "Krupa, you are worthless. You are better off living away from home, so go now. You should die alone, too."

Professor Rollings was watching the drama with a look of shock.

Krupa freed her arms from Professor Rollings' embrace with a jerk and ran towards the cave, but Joash stopped her.

"No, no, Krupa." He held her face in his hands, his whole body was shaking. A fire was running through him in the midst of snow. He said with unswerving intensity, "Look at me! That is not me! I never said all that. You know it. It is okay if you imagined all that, do not hold on to it. Let go and I will take care of the rest. Believe me, Krupa." She looked into Joash's eyes and felt their pain become one. Warm tears rolled down melting the snow on her face. Joash held her tight and said, "Whatever I have done, however I have been, I am sorry for your suffering. But I promise you I am here for you now. Forgive me and free yourself from this load. Forgive me…"

She gasped. As she closed her eyes with relief and held on to her brother forgetting all the chaos in her mind, another voice called, "Krupa!" It was Durgesh this time. "What? Both of you … look at your state!"

Before she could think it was only a mental construct she was seeing, Durgesh came to her side and started to put her arms in a snowsuit. "Just get in this, please. Why did you not listen to Phillipa? You are freezing." Krupa was feeling numb- was it the cold or the unexpected pain—she did not know. Quietly, she got into the snowsuit as Durgesh helped her. "And what about you Joash? Are you superhuman?" Durgesh looked up but Joash was nowhere to be seen. All was white around them, and the blizzard carried on unabated.

Inside the cave Joash stood with his fists held tight once again, his bare feet firmly on the rocky floor, his eyes closed, and his mind focused on Roga with an inexorable intensity. His breathing grew deeper drowning the sound of dripping water in the cave. He wanted to face it, he could not let it escape and he called it back with the full might of his mind.

And so, it did. This time it was a wail, shrill and heart-shattering, of a child in pain. It came from the outside. Joash emerged in the snowstorm once again, his eyes searching for Miria's image. While Krupa held Durgesh back, knowing very well that a drama beyond her understanding was unfolding here, Joash proceeded to the same bush again.

Joash saw Miria's back—her face was buried between her knees, and she was sobbing. He thought of pushing her down the cliff edge, but with a quirk of her head, she pierced him with an accusing stare.

He was pushed back once again.

"You are a bad Da." Miria got up and spoke innocently. "When will you come? I am hungry. You let Mama die. You want me to die too. I will not go anywhere without you." There was no evil in those words, just a forlorn cry for help. Joash's resolve wavered as his sense of guilt started to resurface. But his eyes stayed fixed on the wretched little girl. He was not able to lift his hand to hurt her; it felt far too heavy.

Trembling, Professor Rollings had moved back to lean on the mountainside. All her bitter rage for Joash was leaving her and remorse was setting in.

For several long moments, Joash and the girl held each other in their gaze, not moving, not speaking. In Joash's mind, he could hear Guruji say to him from far away, "What's in the moment? What's beneath the layers?"

The image of Miria started to go hazy again. Joash redirected his mind towards the Roga, but Guruji's voice had mellowed him. His hair was laden with snow and blowing across his face. His skin under the white flakes was still warm—he blinked his eyes and the answer to this riddle dawned upon him. When he opened his eyes fully with Roga once again held in his focus, Miria was standing next to the couloir.

Joash reached her and extended his arms gently towards her, it was indeed a real physical form. As he touched her, several scenes crossed before his eyes in quick succession—deep dark space, heaps of garbage on earth, wars, famines, floods, eyes full of lust, greed, hate and eyes full of pain. He had seen what was beneath the layers, he had seen what had brought the Roga to this world and he knew the world was ready for a new beginning.

So he picked up Miria and embraced her, accepting all that had gone wrong in his past life and in this world. His guilt vanished and all he felt was love. "No, you do not need to go anywhere without me," he said.

Miria did not want to be held. With a force unimaginable for a little girl, she started to push Joash, trying to free herself, but he held on. A sudden fury welled up in her eyes as she pushed him against the rocky mountainside.

Krupa ran towards Joash; the ground shook and large boulders came crashing in her way. As she watched horrified, in the scuffle that followed, Miria pushed Joash down the steep gully. Wrapped in his arms was Miria, the physical form of Roga, looking as scared as any other human of falling from a great height, waving her hands in futile attempt to catch something.

But Joash was immersed in the free fall. His hands sealed around whatever it was he was holding, his eyes moving all around him, and all he could see was a faint blue-white glow enveloping everything else. To him, he was simply moving towards the source of this light. His body hit the rock, halfway down the mountain side but he felt no pain. He floated above his physical self, watching the form of Miria turn into ash around his body, and continued to float towards the welcoming light.

Chapter 36

The Base

The flames of the bonfire performed a dance of shadow and light on Krupa's still face—her eyes were swollen, red and listless and her heart numb. With one hand she held the glass vial around her neck and the other rested on Prakruti Saram. Meera gently placed a shawl around her shoulders and sat next to her. Nearly everyone present at the base had gathered together this evening, sitting in three concentric circles around the bonfire.

"Today is a special day," Swamiji spoke in a loud voice, something that everyone had forgotten he could do. "Yet again we are in the debt of Pundit family and of course the brave souls who helped them." He looked towards Phillipa and Callum who were sitting behind Durgesh and smiled. "Joash Pundit will always be revered by Sheersha yogis and everyone else who knew him. And now it is our turn to do the work. The higher age is finally here." His gaze travelled to his right, towards a thicket of pine trees.

Luminous silvery figures were passing through air in front of the trees, floating up and disappearing into the vast unknown. That place on Moksha Parvat was a Sangam, like many other places on earth, where the astral realm crossed the earth. The spectacle had started early morning, with the esters appearing intermittently, going about their business, not interacting, not looking towards the awestruck earth dwellers. Children had made their den nearby, observing and waiting, but now everyone seemed used to them.

Swamiji relished the look of wonder on children's faces as his twinkling eyes smiled at each one of them. Then, his eyes fell on Krupa, and he spoke again. "The new cycle has started. We have the opportunity to rise, to recognize *Dhi* and we have help at our doorstep." He looked towards the thicket once again and then back to the crowd. "The job is hard, but we must do it now. And that is how we will honour Joash Pundit's life and his sacrifice."

Something stirred inside Krupa and her eyes that had been fixed on the fire moved towards Swamiji.

"The caretaker of the first seed is here with us." Swamiji

smiled at Krupa and continued, "Let us all pledge to spread the seeds of new life all over the earth. Durgesh, dear Son, will you be willing to stay on and help us here?"

Callum nudged Durgesh. "Come on, answer him," he whispered. "Do you really want to go back to your boring job?"

Durgesh glanced sideways towards Callum and shook his head. "Swamiji, I do believe you know my answer already. The moment I met Krupa I had a feeling she would do great things." Krupa frowned and stared at Durgesh with eyes full of wonder. Durgesh carried on with his smooth words, his eyes found the ground as he suppressed a smile. "And I think she could do with some great support, like me." Callum covered his gaping mouth and fell back while Durgesh looked straight at Krupa. "I am willing to offer my support and friendship for an entire lifetime with a promise to share all her adventures."

The small crowd burst into an applause. Swamiji smiled and nodded, he knew these words were just what Krupa needed to start her healing and when he looked at her, he was relieved to find her smiling again.

Swamiji raised one hand to quieten the crowd. "All the seeds will be sown here at the base in small pots at sunrise tomorrow. In one day, we will see the seedlings sprout. After that, the largest of them all will be planted on the Tirtha, a spot Krupa is very well aware of. We will have to help Krupa and Durgesh make an abode there. They will have to nurture the tree and guard it for seven years. In one week, when the tree will become taller than its sower, it will start purifying every element around it for several thousand miles. The tree will be laden with magenta flowers with yet more seeds. And we have to be ready to spread the seeds. But first, I will need some people who can carry the six seedlings to six different mountain ranges on the other continents, plant them with love and care and again appoint more people to look after the trees and spread their seeds."

Phillipa and Callum looked at each other and their hands went straight up. And along with them there were several others, ready to embark on a journey to free the world of all poisons.

Behind them, Jaggu Baba sat with his eyes half-closed. The pungent aroma of burning leaves hung about him.

Callum turned around and said, "What are your plans, Jaggu Baba?"

"Me?" Jaggu Baba was struggling to open his eyes. He said lazily, "All this is for you good people. I think I would like to deal with the Jhenats now. I have learnt a few things about the dark powers."

Callum frowned with surprise. For the first time he did not know what to say.

He looked ahead as Krupa and Durgesh bowed together to Swamiji.

Swamiji's eyes met Professor Rollings'. She was sitting away from the crowd. She had told Swamiji about all that she had done wrong, but she had found her peace and had decided to return to London.

"My dear children." All was quiet once again as Swamiji spoke. "Tomorrow I will retreat to solitary life in the mountains." There was a collective sound of shock and dismay from the crowd. Krupa had known this was coming, but sitting right next to Swamiji she still clutched on to his robe hoping she could stop him. He looked at her with warm affection and said, "It is time for me too—Mahayogi has called me." He looked up at them all. "My seat can stay empty till Krupa feels ready to lead the ashram."

The hum of discussions broke out in the gathering as people started to disperse. Swamiji walked up to Professor Rollings. Both stood facing each other with their hands folded.

"Now that Elusium will be taken care of, Stella, what will be your next project?" asked Swamiji.

"You are right, the storms have started to quieten down already. This morning the rain stopped in London too." Professor Rollings' words were thoughtful and slow. "But yet again more land has been lost to the seas. I think I will continue to work to improve our climate. Consult our new friends…" She pointed towards the esters.

"Are you okay, Stella?" asked Swamiji gently placing his hand on her shoulder.

A lone tear rolled down her cheek as she looked up at him. "It is strange. Of course, I cannot remember anything about my past life with Joash, but I think he knew it. The way he looked at me… Although I did not know him well in this life, I can feel the loss. At the same time, I have never felt so peaceful."

"Have you forgiven him?"

"Yes."

"Do you yearn to meet him again?"

Reluctantly, she replied, "Yes," and squeezed her eyes tightly.

"Then you will." With these words, Swamiji retreated to his room for one last time.

Chapter 37

It was all blue and glorious—a soothing light that was calling Joash. Floating in nothingness, as he approached the light, the glow slowly changed to white. Then, all of a sudden, the white glow condensed into a white dot, a moon amongst the countless stars in a space where he found himself. In front of him, appeared a man draped in all white. He too was floating effortlessly in the space. Finally, he came close, and Joash could see him clearly.

"What is this, Guruji? Where are we?" asked Joash.

Guruji smiled back—he looked just the same as he did when Joash was a child. "This is the transit." He spoke with his usual astuteness. "The place where you decide what's next."

Joash looked at himself; he had a form—a human form—and he too was dressed in all white.

"You are still attached to your human form and hence you see both of us in that form," said Guruji.

Joash realised he was filling up with questions, just like he used to when he was a child.

Guruji chuckled and said, "Carry on, speak. Worry not. Time does not exist here. Nothing is unknown here. It is the place of all revelations. You see me here because to you this form of Guruji is the source of all knowledge. But in truth, you are the enquirer, and you are the responder."

"What about my karma? Have I done what I should have?"

"You have mended all that had gone wrong in your last birth on Earth. Krupa's soul is free to progress and yours is free of guilt. Don't forget Stella; her journey has been very lonely, but she can move forward now. And you have achieved much more for the world you loved in the process."

"Will I see them again?"

"This question shows a desire and so it shall manifest at some point, in some life."

A shooting star went past Guruji as the quiet of the space grew deeper yet lighter. Joash let himself sink into his new reality; he looked at his human hands and moved them in the space around him. It felt like the space was alive with an invisible energy. It was strange yet believable. He was ready with his next set of questions.

"You can touch *Dhi* in this form," said Guruji. "That is what you have learnt to call the cosmic consciousness. But that is not what you want to ask. You are thinking about Callum."

"Yes, Guruji! What made him do so much for me?"

Guruji looked amused. "He was your grandfather when you were Joash and your father when you were Fingal. In a different life, long ago, he had caused immense suffering to a family. His soul chose to pay for it by cutting short his time with his family. Every life he lifts himself higher. He had been waiting to help you in your journey. You tried your best to get rid of him, but he showed you who was the real grandfather."

That was truly a revelation for Joash. Astonished, he listened to Guruji as he continued, "He will be around Krupa for as long as he can. You are all young souls who came from the same source."

"What about you, Guruji? Why did you choose me?"

"Because I have always chosen you. I found you on the street in Edinburgh. I picked up your wretched body and nurtured your soul. You shone so brightly that I found my salvation as a guru. I touched *Dhi* in that birth. I was born again in a village in Nepal, but a part of me moved on to the astral realm with you."

"And what about my mother and father?"

"Oh, that is a particularly good question! They are in a different physical universe, very much like the one you have been to. Your mother is a fierce warrior now, planning an epic war against the evil forces of her planet. And your father is by her side."

Joash considered Guruji for a long moment. He was excited but confused.

"Can I choose to be born again?"

Guruji laughed. "You have risen, but not yet escaped the cycle of birth and death. You might never want to. You are still a Karma yogi, a leader, a saviour. So, do you know which world you would like to go to?"

"Yes!" Joash spoke with certitude. "Would you be there with me?"

Guruji smiled and raised one eyebrow. "Wait and see!"

Author's Note

This book has been a journey of learning and revelations for me. Some special people deserve a mention for their contributions –

- Romesh Gunesekera – my Guru, my mentor. Thank you for your guidance and patience.
- Namita Purohit – the most talented person I know. Without your creative input, right from the conception of the cover page and the art on page 1 to the minor details, this would not have come together.
- Neeraj Purohit – my rock, my biggest supporter.
- Dr Anjali Rao – My first editor and Sanskrit expert.
- Dipti, Mamta and Vikram – thank you for having faith in me.
- Mary Torjussen – my editor.